THE
CORNERSTONE

By
Anne C. Petty

JournalStone
San Francisco

JOURNALSTONE
YOUR LINK TO ARTISTIC TALENT

JournalStone books may be ordered through booksellers or by contacting:

JournalStone
199 State Street
San Mateo, CA 94401
www.journalstone.com

The views expressed in this work are solely those of the authors and do not necessarily reflect the views of the publisher, and the publisher hereby disclaims any responsibility for them.

ISBN: 978-1-936564-67-5   (sc)
ISBN: 978-1-936564-68-2   (ebook)

Library of Congress Control Number: 2012953062

Printed in the United States of America
JournalStone rev. date: January 25, 2013

Cover Design: Denise Daniel
Cover Art: Vincent Chong

Edited By: Elizabeth Reuter

For Bill, Lynn (who will especially appreciate all the Marlowe lore), April, and Lissa

ACKNOWLEDGEMENTS

Several editions of Christopher Marlowe's play "The Tragical History of Doctor Faustus" were consulted for the history, quotations, and paraphrases from the play, including:

Christopher Marlowe: The Complete Plays, edited by J. B. Steane, New York: Penguin Books, 1969.

Doctor Faustus (Norton Critical Editions), edited by David Scott Kastan, New York: W. W. Norton & Company, 2004.

Doctor Faustus and Other Plays (Oxford World's Classics), edited by David Bevington and Eric Rasmussen, Oxford University Press, USA, 2008.

Thanks to: Lissa Griffin, LMHCA and Sex Therapist, for reviewing all the psychological material in the book.

Ugly hell, gape not, come not, Lucifer!
I'll burn my books. Ah, Mephistopheles!

—Christopher Marlowe, *The Tragical History of Doctor Faustus*

INCEPTION

Brú na Bóinne, Ireland 1581

Doctor John Dee—accomplished mathematician, alchemist, Hermetic magician, herbalist, astrologer, and advisor to Queen Elizabeth herself—pulled his fine wool cloak tightly across his shoulders. The late afternoon sun was disappearing behind a cloudbank massed low over the rolling hills, their deep green shaded to mossy black. A chill wind whipped at his beard and the mane of his mare.

An adequate horseman, he guided his skittish palfrey over the narrow footpath skirting the riverbank, a firm hand on the reins. He glanced behind him. Dee envied the easy grace with which his hooded companion sat the stallion he'd acquired from the stable back in Dublin. The horse had gone wide-eyed with nostrils flared and shivers rippling over its hide when Monsieur C had put his booted foot in the stirrup, but the moment he was seated it was as if horse and rider had become one.

On their left, the river meandered between shallow banks thick with fen sedge, marsh-horsetail, and bulrush. To the right, dense woodland. Stands of ash, hazel, alder, and oak, trees Dee knew from Mortlake in Surrey, near his riverside house, occasionally thinned enough to reveal distant hill country dotted by limestone outcroppings and wild, untended grasslands covered in gorse.

Dee watched the thunderheads piling up over the valley ridge. He supposed it mattered little if the rain caught up with them; the scheme in hand would go forward. He was glad to be in the lead as he searched for the landmark left by the witch, marking the turnoff into the trees. He preferred not to look at the drugged body of the girl draped lengthwise over Monsieur's lap, her thin arms hanging down and flopping with the horse's gait. She was a prostitute and cutpurse, which was why he'd taken her. They were likely saving her from a worse fate…imprisonment in Newgate amongst other thieves and worse criminals, and eventual death on the gallows platform. No reason to feel remorse for her soul, as she'd already damned it herself, but he *would* say a small prayer for her passing.

The river took a sharp bend where clumpings of silverweed and meadowsweet grew thicker along its bank. It flowed more swiftly over a rill and around low-arching willows trailing their long fingers in its gray waters.

"Not far now, my lord. The mark should be up ahead."

"Nay, my good doctor, as I've told you, I am no lord. Merely your devoted friend and mouthpiece for the One who is above us." The voice radiated intimate good humor, the kind of voice you'd expect from a close friend. Dee relaxed his shoulders.

He'd met Monsieur C on the continent more than a year ago, during a series of so-called "spiritual conferences" he'd conducted for the edification of kings and courtiers, from the Polish King Stephen and his court to Emperor Rudolf II, who'd not been moved by the notion of summonings and divinations. In Bohemia, however, the angel Uriel had spoken through C's mouth to an assemblage of nobles and scholars, and had given tangible proof that his presence was not mere imagination. A crippled child had been made whole, his mother collapsing at the sight of him tottering across the chamber toward her. Uriel had given his blessings to all who witnessed the miracle and assured Doctor Dee that he would continue to send guidance through his chosen interpreter.

They'd traveled far and wide together since then.

Encouraged by Monsieur C, he'd delved deeply into the angelic languages, convinced the key to creating a unity of all mankind lay in the books he'd laboriously penned through his companion's willing communion with the higher spheres. He felt no conflict in the crossing over of his mathematical and navigational studies with his magickal and spiritual explorations. In his mind the two were one great bridge to the Eternal, to the revelation of Mysteries beyond man's waking life. Mysteries that could describe and define the human *spiritus*. This evening's mission, while related, was somewhat darker. Dee felt his resolve slipping at the enormity of what they intended.

Apparently sensing his thoughts, Dee's companion remarked, "Be of good cheer, my friend. Think how our success in this experiment will affect the community of the learned, those *cognoscenti*, mages and masters who have failed to acknowledge the brilliance of your hypotheses regarding the nature of death and the human soul."

"True enough," Dee said, sitting straighter in the saddle. "'Tis not that I question your angelic guidance. But I do wonder..." He bit back what he'd been about to utter. That if the witch proved inadequate to the task or if the exchange went wrong, the consequences were unimaginable.

"I am here to support you," the honeyed voice replied. "You will not fail."

Dee flexed his fingers, stiff and chilled in his calfskin gloves. The cold was retreating from spring with petulance, keeping buds underground and dusting the higher elevations with lingering snow. His horse stumbled on the path as the ground became stonier, veering away from the river and curving slightly uphill. Near the treeline he spotted the cairn, an arranged pile of rough-cut limestone cradled among the roots of a mammoth oak.

"There," he said, pointing. They turned off the path and into the trees where the lemony scent of forest gum sweetened the air.

A few minutes into the canopy, Dee pulled up and dismounted. "A moment, if you will." His companion smiled indulgently in the gloom, or so it seemed to Dee as he removed a glove and rummaged through the leather bag affixed to his saddle. His thin fingers closed on the round brass casing and pulled the contraption out, an amazing invention given to him by Gerardus Mercator, his mentor at the University of Cambridge. The combination sundial and compass rested heavy in his palm. Underneath the arm of the sundial, a glass-covered rose compass with a spindled needle indicated the position for magnetic north at zero degrees. East lay at ninety degrees. The tomb where Radha Ó Braonáin, a sorceress of great depth and cunning, had agreed to meet them was a few degrees away from the eastward mark. Dee's previous dealings with her had convinced him she was not to be taken lightly or ordered about in this particular endeavor, regardless of his own paranormal prowess or that of his companion. They must tread carefully.

She likely would not have agreed to be party to this day's task at all if she did not have a personal interest in it (a fact C had discovered and revealed to Dee as the means for enticement). At his initial description of the plan, she'd laughed aloud and called him mad. It wasn't every day someone asked her to help catch a banshee.

Confirming their direction, Dee remounted and guided his horse into the underbrush thick with enchanters—nightshade and urbanum, woodland herbs he knew well. The heavy compass rested in his ungloved hand. His fingers were cold to the bone, but he would not take the risk of handling it clumsily, or *Jesu* forbid, dropping it. The girl across C's saddle moaned and Dee looked back. Monsieur rested a hand on her back and she stilled again.

Dee shivered and wished he'd brought a heavier cloak. Something fur-lined, perhaps. His sense of chill was not entirely due to the weather. He recalled how he'd finally persuaded the widow Ó Braonáin.

"The banshee is the gateway guardian between life and death, is it not?"

She'd nodded, her wrinkled mouth drawn into a purse, her eyes hooded under dark brows.

He'd continued. "Everyone knows that her wail precedes the passage of the departed's soul into the afterlife. It is she who calls Black Coach." The manifestation of Death on the physical plane. Dee shivered again. He'd never seen the apparition itself nor heard the blood-freezing cry of its herald, but if things went as planned, he would experience both those things before the night was done.

"Aye," the witch had said, frowning.

"What I propose," he'd stated with what now seemed arrogant confidence, "is to create a magickal object that can hold death at bay...nay, time itself." He'd waited for the impact of those words, but the witch held his gaze without a blink.

"If the gateway guardian could be trapped within an object of power, I have the means to bind it to the will of the object's owner—literally to stave off dying and age not a year beyond the instant of the talisman's creation."

"And how would ye do that, Master Dee? What spell d'ye have in yer black bag of tricks that could command such a spirit?"

"I was hoping you yourself might know," he'd said. He knew she would deny any such ability, but he held his trump hidden, waiting till the right moment.

She'd emitted a rude noise and made as if to walk away, leaving him standing at the gate of her croft-covered cottage in the foothills of the Boyne Valley. Its crumbling walls and much-patched roof suggested great age, its foundation possibly much older than the present pitiful dwelling. He knew her family line was ancient, leading back to the days of the great Brian Boru or even further. The weight of her family name was not lost on him either. Ó Braonáin—descendant of sorrow.

"Wait," he'd called. "Hear me out. You have a son, I think..." After a few heartbeats, she turned.

"Did have."

He knew this full well and carefully played his hand. "The banshee is an elemental, not something that can be controlled by modern alchemy. What's required is old magick, something that draws from the Earth itself. I know your lineage, Radha Ó

Braonáin. Your ancestors helped build the great mound further up the valley."

"What would ye know of any such thing?" Her voice was haughty, dismissive, yet she remained where she stood.

"I have studied the transmogrification of souls enough to believe that if an offering is made when the Black Coach is summoned, the herald may allow an exchange. One soul for another." He waited for the implication to take hold.

"Such a thing is not possible."

"No? My companion in the paranormal, Monsieur C, is a conduit for the Divine. Through him, I have witnessed loved ones returned from Death's doorstep to their grieving families, the wandering soul brought back from the land of Shades."

"Have a care, Professor Dee, e'er ye blaspheme." The witch had actually laughed into her threadbare muffler.

Dee's cheeks flushed, but he held his anger in check. "'Tis said, a witch will get her wish though her soul may not get mercy."

She cast him a baleful glance and held her silence.

Dee tried again. "Think on this. A life for a life, with the promise of control over Death itself. That is what I offer you…and your son."

He stood quietly as the silence between them stretched out, thinned, threatened to snap. At last she retraced her steps, close enough to look him in the eyes. "Whose life would ye trade, eh?"

He hesitated not a second. "A lost soul whose place on Earth is already forfeit."

The witch considered. "This companion of yours, how d'ye know him?"

"We have been trusted friends more than a year now. He is touched by the Divine, the voice of Uriel speaks through him."

"Does it now?" The witch snuffled again, not exactly a laugh. "Let me think on't. Away wi' ye." She made a shooing gesture with one hand that some might have taken for a warding spell.

He'd departed as bidden, but it wasn't a week before she'd sent word to him, with directions for finding a certain small passage tomb on the slopes above the Boyne Valley. She'd chosen Saturn's Day, a good day for a binding spell. He was warned to bring only his accomplice and the necessary offering and to speak of their plan to no one. The tomb was protected by charms that blinded ordinary eyes to its presence, but she would lift the veil over its entrance for this one night. He suspected what lay within.

A rook's caw and the flapping of heavy wings through the trees tugged his attention back to the present. He wet his lips. It seemed the witch had her own herald. Before long, the trees thinned and they emerged onto the verge of low grass-covered hills with steeper inclines beyond, forming the bowl of the great valley. Dee scanned the horizon, searching for the landmark that had been drawn on the back of the broadside scrap he'd received from the widow Ó Braonáin. And there it was, a distant outcropping in the shape of an outstretched wing and directly below it, as the raven flies, a small tumulus on a slope much closer to them.

"I believe this is the place." Dee carefully replaced the compass in his saddlebag, then urged his horse forward.

"A landscape of great beauty and greater desolation," murmured his companion, as if its rough contours were somehow familiar to him.

Yellow oat-grass and fairy flax clothed the flanks of the slope as they drew near the barrow, hiding calcareous outcrops and making their way uphill increasingly treacherous. Dee's horse picked its way hesitantly over the rock-scattered ground until at last they reached a flattened area in front of the barrow. It was typical of the smaller passage tombs built by the ancients who'd left their footprints up and down the land within the river's great loop. The low stone entrance was of simple post and lintel construction, framing the black tunnel leading into the mound. Around it in a careless arc were smaller stones marked with symbols potent to the ancient ones. There was no sound save for the gusting wind...no movement of animals, large or small, within their range of vision. The back of Dee's neck prickled as they sat their horses, watching and waiting.

He was about to offer his apologies to C for having made a fruitless journey when a draped figure stepped over the crest of the mound just above the tomb. For a moment the widow Ó Braonáin seemed a fair likeness of a banshee herself. Wind snapped at the edges of her voluminous dark shawl as long gray-streaked hair streamed across her face. Dee had been unable to guess at her age in their last encounter and today was no better. She could have been fifty years or fifty more.

"Have ye brought the exchange?" Her voice stilled the air around them, then tore away on the wind.

Stiffened from the ride, Dee got off his horse with less agility than he would have liked. "As you can see." He indicated the limp form in her dirty brown dress.

The crone pointed to a spot near the tomb entrance. "Lay her down there."

Dee watched, his stomach in knots, as his companion dismounted and gathered the young woman into his arms as lightly as if she were a sleeping child. He placed her gently on the bracken, and stood up. Taller and thinner than even Dee himself, in a heavy cloak with an ermine-lined hood, C stood silent and imposing.

The Irish witch stumbled backward, her breath sucked in with a hiss. The fingers of her left hand flicked a protective spell almost faster than Dee could discern it in the fading light. "*Namhaid!*"

Enemy. Dee held his breath for fear his companion had been insulted.

"Nay," C said softly, "I am not your enemy."

Dee sought a reassuring tone, although his own state of mind was less so. "Indeed, mistress, we have brought you the trollop I mentioned…a harmless wench."

"'Tis not her as I'm concerned over." She pulled her rag of a cloak across her breast. "My family's knowledge of 'Monsieur' reaches back some thousand years," she whispered to the wind, indicating the taller man with a jerk of her head. "Although I don't fancy ye were known by that name then."

C gave her a small bow and pushed back his hood. His features were gaunt but not unappealing, his eyes bright in the gathering gloom. Hair like spun gold framed his face and curled over his immaculate white collar. "Well met, m'lady. I am at your service."

At this the sorceress laughed out loud. "Aye, I've no doubt of't. 'Tis 'im as should be worried." She hooked her thumb at Dee, who regarded them both with a sense of dread. Cold as he was, sweat broke out over his brow.

Rain-dampened winds swept over the valley and up the eastward ridge, tugging at their cloaks. The horses turned their noses away, backs toward the approaching storm.

"When ye spoke of a cohort to aid in the spellcasting, I'd naught guessed y'meant this one." She retreated further behind the earthen rise of the tomb.

Dee wiped his brow. The damned hag, was she refusing to cooperate? "Monsieur's part in this is to seal the stone the moment the elemental has been caught."

"And what else is't he's here t'do, eh, once I snare the *bain-sídhe* for ye?"

Before Dee could form an answer, she veiled herself in mist. He blinked as light rain blew into his eyes, and then suddenly she was kneeling by the opening to the tomb.

"This will become your *buachloch*, your object of power," she said, pushing a rounded stone carved in spirals and sun disc emblems away from several others like it wedged partially into the ground, guarding the tomb's entrance. It was about the size of a human head.

Dee approached and knelt, reached out his hand. "May I?"

"Aye, thus far 'tis naught but a stone, though a *very* old one." She searched his eyes for a fleeting moment, then stood up, keeping Dee between herself and his tall compatriot.

Dee put his hands on the stone and believed he could feel its thrum under his fingers, gloved though they were. He was certain some power of the ancients lingered in marked stones like this, the bones of the earth. He nodded to C and said, "The stone will serve."

Radha Ó Braonáin stared down at the unconscious young woman in the grass. What thoughts may have passed through her mind Dee could not imagine, but his relief was visceral when at last she turned and went to the tumulus. Stooping under the heavy slab lintel, she disappeared into its dark maw. Moments later she reappeared, dragging a threadbare blanket weighed down by a body wrapped in funereal garb. She pulled the blanket up beside the drugged girl and unwrapped the body of her son.

Dee studied the young man. He might have been a pretty youth, possibly around age twenty, had not the wasting of disease overtaken him. The sunken cheeks, gray-white skin, and drawn lips masked a beauty that had just begun to flower before it was cut short.

"His life for hers, as we agreed." She touched the cadaver's hollowed cheek. Dee imagined he saw a tear slide down, but when she looked up her eyes were hard. She reached under her shawl and pulled out a small cloth bag. Rubbing it briskly between both palms, a pungent scent was released into the wind, riding moisture-laden gusts over the clearing. Dee's face was damp, although it wasn't precisely raining...misting, perhaps. The real rain wasn't far away. He not so much heard the distant thunder as felt it...a bone deep shudder he could not throw off.

The tang of the witch's herbs swirled in the air—he recognized hazel, monkshood, rowan, nightshade among other scents he could not identify. A practiced alchemist, this simple fact irked him and increased his sense of unease. He cut a glance toward C, who stood still as stone, an impassive observer for all he could tell.

The crone stood up and beckoned them closer. "Keep well inside the circle if ye value life and limb." Dee noticed this was addressed directly to him. Even more disquieting was the faint smile on the thin lips of Monsieur C. She then pointed at the grass a few steps away from them and it began to smolder in spite of the weather. She turned slowly widdershins, continuing to point, inscribing a complete circle that burned the grass to ash but never erupted into actual flame.

Then she began to hum, at first to herself and then more audibly over the din of the approaching storm. Dee took a breath and planted his feet firmly. The witch had begun her *foirteagal*, the spell of binding by names and words of power.

"To myself I bind this day the blood of the ancestors laid under these stones.

To myself I bind this day the breath of those who walked this ground.

To myself I bind this day the elements of earth, air, fire, water.

To myself I bind this day Bandia, Bbantlarna, Banrion, Mathair.

Goddess, lady, queen, mother, I summon thee!

Morrigan, Red Queen of Death, I summon thee!"

More followed, but in the ancient tongue of the Gaels. Dee caught a word here or there, but he didn't need to understand them. The effects of her incantation were evident.

Rain pelted the horses' backs and the two figures supine on the heather. Lightning split the cloudbank.

"*Néallta fola!*" she shrieked at the blackening thunderheads. *Clouds of Blood*. Dee knew that phrase, an ancient cry shouted at the onset of battle or in the thick of it, to prevent the tide of victory from turning. It was the invocation to slaughter.

Finally, faintly, the banshee's wail could be heard riding the wind, a keening scree just at the edge of hearing, then louder. Suddenly it was deafening, a sound so painful it could stop the heart, and it seemed to be inside Dee's own head, as if some raging animal were trapped there and clawing its way out. The storm broke over their heads in torrents of whipping wind and rain; he staggered to hold his stance.

Hovering above the tomb, mist coalesced into form, dissolved, formed again. At first it seemed one of the fairy folk, dangerous and beautiful, but then its features slipped and a terrifying corpselike mask froze Dee's blood where he stood, hands clapped over his ears.

The horses screamed and bolted, a flash of brown and black racing over the hillside back the way they'd come. He felt a rumbling of the ground under his feet. In terror he wiped rain from his eyes and scanned the scene beyond the witch's circle. Over the crest of the ridge above them came the Black Coach, a terrifying silhouette barely visible against the cloudbank. In the driver's seat, the fabled headless *dullahan* whipped a pair of horses so black to look at them was to see the emptiness of the starless night sky. Dee lost his breath and shook as if with a palsy. He'd seen many phantasmagoric manifestations in his studies and pursuit of the arcane, but never this. The carriage came to a stop beside the wing-shaped outcrop. Although he wished to turn away, he could not tear his eyes from the presence of Death's courier on the ridge.

"I advise you not to hesitate, my good doctor." C's friendly, collegial voice had taken a hard edge. "Once the Black Coach has been summoned to the land of the living, it cannot go back empty. Surely you don't intend to offer yourself? Sacrifice the trollop, as we agreed, and let us proceed."

Dee took an unsteady breath and let it leak out. He reached inside his cloak and found his pearl-handled athame, a blade sharp with a swordsmith's edge he'd used to perform many a symbolic ritual. It had tasted animal blood, but had never been asked to kill a human. It fit immediately into his hand, ready to do his bidding. His fingers closed around the handle.

Hands trembling, he took hold of the girl. Pulling her head back in a hellish mockery of Abraham slaughtering the sacrificial ram, Dee cut the big artery in her throat. Bright blood spattered over his hands and quickly bathed her shoulder. For good measure, he slit the veins in her wrists as well. Breathing in shallow jerks Dee completed the task, holding up her torso as she bled out over the stone. Somewhere in the maelstrom that threatened to cleave his skull, he heard the rough commands of the sorceress, bending the ancient elemental to her will. The roiling form of the banshee coiled and uncoiled around the slight form of Radha Ó Braonáin, obscuring her from sight.

A sharp thunderclap directly overhead was so loud Dee feared his eardrums had been blasted to ruin. For moments he could hear nothing at all. He let the dead girl's body fall where it would. Featherlight, he felt the touch of C's hand on his shoulder, and his hearing returned.

"Orin!" the witch cried, falling to her knees beside the youth. His eyes fluttered. The *bain-sídhe* was nowhere to be seen. Dee's gaze raked the clearing. Had the creature been trapped inside the stone?

Then dread fell on him like a shroud. The Black Coach sat still on the ridge, even though the girl was dead. For one terrified moment he entertained the thought that it had come to collect him as well, but then the witch spat out a howl. Her body began to stretch toward the stone, blood seeping from her eyes and nose and ears. In disbelief he watched as the flesh was shredded from her body. Then her muscles and finally the skeletal remains all disappeared into the stone in a carmine smear.

C leapt forward lightning-fast, grabbing Dee's blood-coated right hand and pressing it to the stone's surface. Dee screamed at the shock, feeling as if he'd pushed his palm with all his weight onto a hot anvil. His skin smoked and blistered, his field of vision narrowed and began to go dark as pain flowed over him.

"Claim the stone!" C's command vibrated through every nerve and sinew of his body.

Past rational thought, he repeated the words he'd rehearsed. "I, John Dee, do lay claim to this *buachloch*, bought by blood and sealed by fire. I bind myself to it and it to me until such time as I may pass it to another. *Go raibh amhlaidh*. So be it into eternity."

Immediately, the burning under his hand ceased. Shakily he inspected the skin, but saw no evidence of damage. He brushed the stone with his fingertips and found it shockingly cool to the touch.

"W-wherefore...?" He shook his head, unable to articulate his thoughts into a coherent question.

C reached down and took him by the elbow, lifting him to his feet. "Did I know the hag would be sucked within the *buachloch* alongside the elemental? Indeed not. Unplanned, but not nonfortuitous."

"The horses…"

"Waiting for us at the wood's edge. Come, we'll walk." C scooped up the stone as if it weighed no more than a cabbage.

Dee turned unsteadily and looked back over the carnage. The Coach was gone. On the rain-soaked ground, the boy who had been dead struggled to sit up. He clutched at the bloody shawl that had belonged to his mother and looked from Dee to Monsieur C with wild, uncomprehending eyes.

Dee whispered his name. "Orin."

"Aye, but…who be *ye*?"

CHAPTER
1

Friday, 6:30 P.M.

The mage crossed the darkened study, his scholar's robe pooling around his ankles. On the corner of a massive writing desk, a foot-high candle swathed in ripples of wax cast a yellow sheen over tumbled books and papers. Harried, he ran his fingers through his hair and turned to face the silent figure seated in shadow across the room.

Clearing his throat, the mage crossed his arms and hugged his thin frame. The seated figure regarded him with focused attention, and waited.

The mage wiped his brow. "Say to me again your master's words."

Low laughter, then a voice soft as powdered snow, but colder. "He said I should do for you whatever you wish. In other words, I'm yours to command." The seated figure stretched its long legs and made as if to stand. "It will cost you, of course—"

"Yes, yes, I know that." The mage waved his hand, a gesture of impatience. "One could hardly expect less. The nature of the spells you've taught me are unhallowed, by anyone's standard." He paced the narrow study, its vaulted ceiling lost in gloom. Satin bands on his sleeves and hem, emblems of his academic status, caught the candlelight.

His companion rose, tall in a hooded cape of blood-red velvet. "More is required than simply your word. You knew this, of course?" He stepped into the pool of light fronting the desk, his eyes bright sparks, boney hands pushing back the hood. Sharp creases ran jagged down his gaunt cheeks. Corpse-white fingers reached toward the desk and extracted a sheet of parchment, spreading it flat.

"You must write it out for me—your promise. My master requires the physical evidence, you see."

The mage hung back in the fringe of shadow that ringed his study. The specter tapped its booted foot.

"If you've changed your mind, I'll take my leave and not bother you again." He raised his hand as if in summons.

"Wait!" The mage lurched forward, stopped, took a breath, then stepped toward the desk. "Don't go. Tell me...what does your master want with someone like me?"

"You're a brilliant protégé, a valued accomplice. An enlargement, if you will, of his kingdom."

"And what about you? You don't mind being used this way? You appear to live well and act like a lord, but you do exactly what he tells you, like a common slave. You're quite willing to help me damn my soul forever, but what am I to you? Just another recruit? I had enjoyed your company these long months."

The velvet-clad shoulders shrugged and a smile split the pale lips. "Misery enjoys a companion."

"So you really are miserable? I thought you said your master would give me a life more incredible than anything mere men could imagine. Was that a lie?" For silent seconds, the two faced each other. At last the mage looked away. With eyes averted, he took the parchment, dragged a heavy, high-backed chair with clawed feet into the pool of light, and sat down. His writing quill lay beside an inkpot, but he left it untouched.

The emissary bent his tall frame over the desk, impatience in his voice. "Do you intend to sign or not? If you will do that, I can give you more things than you know how to ask for. I will be your slave in whatever schemes and adventures we two can conjure. If that is not what you want, then I've been wasting my time here."

The mage lowered his head and studied his hands. "I am yours," he said finally.

"Hah! Those are the words I want!" The tall figure reached an arm around the shoulders of his charge, enveloping him for an instant in a shroud of crimson.

"How...shall I do it?" The mage's head remained bowed.

"With your blood, of course," the figure said in a stage whisper. His white hand slipped inside his doublet and drew out a long, slender knife, its silver-white blade flashing. Its handle was pearl, its design from another time. He held it out in his open palm.

The mage stared, seemingly hypnotized by the blade. He wiped his brow again. "Then the old myths are true...it really must be done this way. I hadn't thought I would actually have to spill blood to bind myself to you."

"Just do it, and with the unleashed power of your vast learning, you may become as great as even my master. Anything is possible, after you sign."

"I'll do it for you, then"

"Nay, not for me. For the one I serve. Make no mistake."

"Give me the knife." The mage pushed back the folds of his robe and rolled up his linen shirt sleeve, exposing the skin of his forearm. He laid his arm, wrist up, across the sheet of parchment, put the point of the knife over the largest vein, and said, "Tell me what I am to write. Once I make the cut, I don't want to stop."

The figure jackknifed its long legs and knelt beside the mage's knee, one hand on the corner of the page. "Write, 'I give my immortal soul to Lucifer' and sign your name."

The mage hesitated yet again. "Should I use a pen to make it neat, or just dip my finger in and scribble the words?"

"What you will."

"Then hold the quill there ready for me." The mage put the blade again to his wrist. "So be it," he said and pressed down. Immediately, a bright red tracery rolled over his fingers and onto the page.

"SHIT!" The knife clattered to the floorboards. "Nobody told me the goddamned knife was sharp!" he screamed, tearing at the black robe and wrapping it around his dripping wrist. An oversized T-shirt and faded jeans showed beneath the folds of his scholar's gown as bright lights flooded the set. "Bayard! Where the hell are you?" he shouted at the lights.

Behind him, the spectral figure pulled off its cape and flopped into the high-backed chair. "Does this mean the end of rehearsals for the night?" he asked irritably.

A red-bearded man came swiftly down the aisle and climbed the low steps onto the stage. Kit Bayard, Mummers Theatrical Company director and owner of the aging Janus Theatre, took command of the scene. Solidly built and barrel-chested, he stood in a natural actor's stance and looked from one player to the other.

"What's happened?" he demanded and took the mage, now revealed to be a genuinely frightened young man in his twenties, by the shoulder. "How badly have you cut yourself?"

"It was supposed to be a fucking stage prop!" the actor yelped, his voice caught between anger and fear. "Who sharpened it like that? I'm bleeding to death, Bayard!"

"Calmly now," said the older man, unwrapping the actor's wrist and placing a folded handkerchief over the slice. "No one dies on my stage."

A young woman in Army-Navy fatigue pants and a faded green hospital smock came to the stage apron. "Should I call 911?" She put her copy of the script down and pulled a cell phone out of the holster on her belt.

"Everything's under control. But thank you, Claire, for your concern." Bayard turned to the stunned cast and extras seated in the front row.

"Rehearsal's over. Danny's all right, but if anyone knows how the weapons props got tampered with, I'd like to hear about it privately."

"What if he stabs himself on opening night, will the show go on?" asked the figure in red, smudging the greasepaint lines of his stage makeup with long fingers.

"Why is it that you make such a perfect Mephistopheles and such a shitty person?" Danny snapped.

"If you'd stop being such a drama queen for once I'd be happy to explain it to you."

"Stop this! I won't have fighting amongst the cast." Bayard glared at Morris, veteran company member, experienced Mephisto, and general pain in the ass.

Morris unfolded his lanky frame and stood up. "Hell, I'm going home."

Bayard's eyes tightened in his fox face. "Six-thirty Thursday evening," he called at Morris' retreating back. "Act three, all four scenes. Be prepared."

"I'm quitting this damn play," said Danny, tears glistening at the corners of his eyes. "You can find yourself another Faustus."

Bayard reached out and took the young man by the arm. "Shhh. It was a regrettable mistake, and luckily no lasting damage has been done. Come with me, I'll get you a drink and a bandage." He led the young man down the steps beside the wings and toward the double doors at the back of the auditorium. Claire followed at their heels, wearing an expression of concern. Bayard sighed and stopped, waiting for her to catch up. "Was there something else, Miss Porter?"

"Are you sure it doesn't need stitches?" She took Danny's arm in her hands and unwrapped the wound.

"Lucky break, us recruiting an EMT into the company, huh?" Danny said. "You wouldn't let me die, would you, Claire?"

She held his arm expertly. "Do you want me to bandage that properly—"

"No need," said Bayard, steering Danny toward the door. "I have gauze pads and tape in my office."

"I could use that drink. Jesus, I can't believe I cut myself." Danny cradled his right arm close to his chest. Slim-hipped and slightly built in just his T-shirt and jeans, he was no longer the imposing necromancer of Christopher Marlowe's invention.

Out in the lobby, the theater was dark and cool. Two yellowed bulbs over the front door marked the exit to the city street. Bayard gave Claire another careful look as she stood at the base of the wide curving staircase that led up to the second floor mezzanine. She was taller than average and lean but strong, from lifting people on stretchers, he supposed. Her thick straw-colored hair, caught at the nape and falling in Botticelli ripples down her back, was lovely, and there was a certain charm to the dusting of freckles beneath those earnest blue eyes. But he had no time for such niceties. He held her gaze, willing her away. A moment later, she turned toward the exit, following the rest of the cast and crew.

Kit Bayard led his Faustus to the mezzanine, which housed a local ballet company's rehearsal studio in a cavernous open room that occupied half the second floor. On the other side of the landing were the theater's administration and wardrobe storage rooms. His own cramped office and apartment faced the busy street below.

Unlocking the door, he motioned Danny inside. A jumble of the business and the personal rubbed shoulders in the narrow room: modern executive-sized desk, rollaway bed covered in a green velvet spread, liquor cabinet the size of a small refrigerator, a carved high-backed chair that appeared to be the mate of the one onstage, bookcases along all four walls. Leather-bound volumes, piles of aging scripts, hundreds of playbooks from Aristophanes to Shakespeare to Pinter crowded the shelves. In the far wall, a narrow open door revealed a white-tiled bathroom.

"This is some place." Danny sank down on the rollaway, his eyes wide.

"It's my retreat," said Bayard.

"Do you...live here, in the theater?"

"That I do."

He went to the cabinet and took out a tarnished silver goblet and a bottle of Irish Mist, an intoxicating blend of whiskey, honey, and natural aromatic spices. Pouring three fingers' worth into the goblet, he held it out. "Drink up. Steady your nerves." He leaned against the desk and watched as Danny emptied the cup in a few gulps. "Another?"

"Yeah, that was good." Danny blinked as the whiskey did its work.

"You might feel better if you lie down." A slight push to the young man's chest and Danny fell flat on his back. The empty goblet rolled across the floor.

Bayard picked up the cup and sat down beside him.

"Whadd are you...?" The actor's tongue sounded thick in his mouth.

"Did you know," said Bayard, his voice no more than a whisper, "that Marlowe had it wrong at the time he wrote the play?"

Danny's lips mumbled something inaudible, his eyes liquid-bright. Drunk or spellbound, his will was no longer his own.

"No one has to write anything or sign anything," the soft voice continued. "Think about it. How can you write a readable message in blood on a piece of parchment?" He touched the young man's lean neck where the lifeblood throbbed just beneath the skin. "If the blood's been spilled by the Master's blade, all you have to do is say 'yes.' Do you understand me?"

Danny gasped for air. "Y-yes..."

"Done." Bayard smiled. "And now, I think we'll just end this quickly, if you don't mind. She's hungry and not very happy with me of late."

He held the goblet ready, then swiftly produced the pearl-handled blade and opened the artery under the young man's jaw line. The bright red stream pulsed into the silver cup, filling it ruby red. Danny's startled eyes bulged, then rolled up, milky white.

Claire stood on the sidewalk in front of the theater in the crisp night air, frowning and watching the stream of headlights flowing across town. She was only the prompter and keeper of the master script for the Mummers, a role that didn't require much rehearsal preparation and accommodated her somewhat erratic work schedule. But that wasn't what concerned her. Danny should have received proper medical treatment for that cut. She knew it, and yet she'd let the director lead him away for a drink instead. She stood a moment longer under the theater portico, its fluted twin pilasters framing a stone archway upon which rested two immense faces, a product of the stonemason's art from over a century ago when the ornamented two-story playhouse had been erected, a monument to the muse in dark-red brick and white granite. She stared up at the sightless faces, one laughing, the other weeping. They faced away from each other, joined at the back of the head like Siamese twins: Janus, the two-faced god, depicted as Comedy and Tragedy. Claire reached for the door.

Slipping back inside the shadowed lobby, she waited for her eyes to adjust. Her intent was to go upstairs to Bayard's office, but then she froze—someone was coming down.

"I'm on my way, harlot!" The accent was unmistakable—aristocratic, with a touch of nasal London East End, blunted by years of living in the States. Had he spotted her? If he had, why address her like that? She didn't think she'd ever heard him use that kind of language to anybody in the five months she'd been part of the Mummers crew.

Claire hung back in a darkened corner of the lobby vestibule. The size and gait of the descending figure confirmed his identity, and she watched with curiosity as Kit Bayard quickly crossed the lobby to a small side door. She'd been told it led down to the basement where discarded scenery and broken equipment were stored. Holding what looked like a prop chalice in one hand, he unlocked the door with the other and disappeared into darkness, closing the door behind him.

Where was Danny? She'd watched while others of the cast headed for their cars or the pub up the street, but there was no sign of him. Her emergency medical training had kicked in at the sight of his injury and now kept her from abandoning an untended patient. Claire shifted from one foot to the other in the shadows, debating what to do. At a light touch on her back she whirled, swallowing a shriek.

She held her chest, gasping, the adrenaline flood almost painful. "Fuck it, Morris. You scared me to death."

"Well, obviously not quite." The faux Mephisto hunched his shoulders in a seeming apology. "I thought you might want a walk to your car. It's not the best of neighborhoods."

Claire was calming down, her heart no longer banging around inside her chest. Even so, he looked damned scary in the shadows, towering over her like that. "Christ, don't ever do that to me again. You just took a few years off my life!"

Morris took a step backward. "Sorry." He looked somewhat less intimidating as he held the door open to the street.

She followed him outside and sized up the shadowy side street where she'd parked. "Yeah, it *is* pretty dark. Thanks."

They fell into step, crossed at the light, and followed the cracked sidewalk toward her aging Honda a block away.

"I enjoy watching you rehearse," she said, making conversation. "You're good."

He laughed. "Well, they need somebody tall to be the villain."

"No," she said, "I can tell. You've had training."

"A bit." He stopped and seemed to be thinking something over. "Want to go for a cup of coffee?"

Claire smiled. "That sounds good." But then she remembered. Rehearsal had run overtime, and there was someone needing her at home. She backtracked. "Eh, I'm afraid I can't."

Morris nodded toward the row of shops along the sidewalk. "Café's just down the block. I'm going there anyway…wouldn't mind if you came along."

Not the most appealing of pickup lines, but that was Morris. Still, she was a little flattered that the scariest member of the Janus troupe thought he might enjoy her company, chatting over coffee. She didn't even know his first name. Everyone in the company just called him Morris and he didn't seem to mind. Maybe that was his first name. She'd never thought to ask.

"My mother's sick at home… I don't like to leave her alone too long." Claire hesitated. "I have an early shift tomorrow, too." She was already running late because of the situation with Danny, but as a medical professional she couldn't just ignore someone getting injured on the set. Stopping for coffee afterwards? That was verging on irresponsible. Calling home wasn't a viable option, either, because she knew her mother wouldn't be able to get out of bed and go down the hall to answer the phone. She wavered, wanting to take just a little time to socialize but feeling guilty as hell for it.

Morris gave her a thin smile and motioned in the direction of the coffee shop.

She followed him down the sidewalk. "One cup only, then I have to go."

Once inside, with a steaming cup of Mocha Java between her palms, Claire tried to relax into the cushioned barrel chair. "Nice little place—I've never been in here."

Morris nodded. "I come here to decompress. When I was starting up the newspaper, this was my office. Even got Bayard in here once."

Claire chewed her lip. That image of Bayard coming down the stairs was stuck in her mind.

"What do you think of him?" She sipped her coffee and watched Morris' narrow face. Black eyes regarded her over his beak of a nose, as he took a thoughtful breath.

"Not an overly pleasant person, bit too full of himself, but occasionally a brilliant director. Don't know why he's wasting his abilities in a small theater like this."

"Um." Claire nodded. She'd heard others say something similar. "What do you think happened to Danny?"

"Prop mix-up." Morris leaned back in his chair.

"No, I mean, do you think he's all right?"

Morris shrugged his boney shoulders. "Why wouldn't he be?"

"Well, that cut looked to me like it could use a stitch or two. I just wondered."

Silence followed, the buzz of coffee-shop voices surrounding their little table.

Claire cleared her throat. "Have you..." Her question hung between them while Morris traced the rim of his cup with a long finger, waiting. "How long have you been with the Mummers?" It wasn't what she wanted to ask but it was in the vicinity.

"About five years, off and on. Why?"

"Has anything else weird like tonight ever happened?" It was a lame question, and she was sorry it had popped out like that. She hated that it made her sound stupid when she was trying to be interesting and intelligent.

"Of course. Place is possessed. Didn't you know?" He wore his Mephistopheles face, with no trace of humor that she could see. With his short-cut black hair and eyes that looked right at you until you looked away, Morris wasn't someone you trifled with. At least, that was her impression.

"You don't really mean that. Right? I can never tell when you're being straight with people or pulling their leg."

"Dear Claire, I would never pull your leg. Except by permission." He actually smiled. "What's on your mind?"

"I just wondered...have you ever gone down into the theater basement?"

Morris nodded. "I've helped Bayard move flats and prop furniture down there for storage. Rancid smelling place. Thank god we don't keep the wardrobe there."

"Really."

"So what're you asking? It's just a stuffy, foul-smelling basement in a ninety-year-old building. No bodies buried down there that I know of." He was laughing, sort of.

"Yeah, good to know." She smiled back. "I was just curious." She wasn't sure if confiding in Morris about having seen Bayard descending the stairs with his silver cup was the smart thing to do. For all she knew, he and the company director were BFF's, although neither of them seemed the type to friend each other on Facebook.

She glanced at her watch. "Oh shit! I need to go." She scrabbled around in her purse for a couple of bills to leave for the coffee and stood up.

Morris leaned forward, his elbows on the table, chin in hand. "Too bad, I think we were just getting to the good part."

She gave him a look. It was so hard to tell if he was joking. "What good part?"

"The Janus Theatre and its resident ghost."

Claire stopped. Pulling her chair out again, she sank down and put her purse on the table. "So tell me."

Morris grinned at her. "We've all heard the stories. Hair like floating seaweed, dead silver eyes. If she laughs, it'll scramble your brains."

Claire was paralyzed. "And...she's in the basement?"

"I offered to hire a medium to prove whether the theatre was haunted or not, but nobody took me up on it. Too bad, would've made a good Arts & Entertainment piece for the paper."

"But you think there might be something to find?"

"I'm a non-believer. But it's a very old structure— probably best not to go down there by yourself. Vagrants, rats, that sort of thing." He wasn't smiling.

"I wasn't planning to," she said, clenching her hands in her lap. That was a lie—she'd been thinking of doing that very thing.

She stood up again. "I really do have to go."

Morris handed her money back. "My treat."

Claire hesitated, then took the bills. Money was tight. "Thanks."

"My pleasure, and Claire, don't worry about Danny. People come and go from the troupe all the time. If he quits, the understudy will take his role and after a few rehearsals nobody will miss him. He wasn't a particularly memorable Faustus, anyway. Can't imagine why Bayard cast him."

Claire gave him the slightest of smiles. "On the other hand, you're an excellent Mephistopheles."

"The part's an actor's dream. Villains are always more fun to play."

"You really didn't know the knife was sharp?"

Morris frowned. "No, I didn't. We have a box full of prop knives. I just pulled one out. Guess that'll teach me to take a closer look next time."

Claire took a few steps away. "That was a joke, right…about the ghost?"

He was getting up. "Walk you to your car?"

"No, really, it's fine. I'll walk fast." Somehow the idea of being alone in the dark with Morris had lost its appeal.

"See you at Thursday's rehearsal, then."

"Right." She wedged her way between crowded tables, heading for the door. When she looked back, he'd already pulled a newspaper out of his backpack and started unfolding it. Probably an issue of *Heads Up*, the inner city paper he owned and published. Claire wondered how good a living you could make as a publisher. Probably better than a paramedic's wage, with less chance of burnout. She trudged back to the car, her thoughts as bleak as the side street where it was parked.

CHAPTER 2

Friday, same night

Gwendolyn Porter lay in her damp bed, listening to the silent house. The bathroom was too far away, and she was too weak to make the long trip down the hall in the dark. Poor Claire would have to change the sheets when she got home.

Claire. The thought flushed warm over her chilled skin. Having her daughter back in the house after her husband's death was a comfort, almost a reason to live. Except she felt shamed at putting her daughter's life on hold while her own slowly flickered out. Claire had smarts, ambitions, a developing career…and a half-dead mother. It was a shame. Jimmie Porter's demise from unexpected heart failure had left them in a financial vise that grounded Claire's university studies in mid-flight and left almost no way to pay for her mother's medical needs. Such a shame. At least the mortgage on their small brick bungalow in Ormewood Park had been paid off for years.

She adjusted the nosepiece of the home oxygen support system and struggled for breath, the flow from the generator her bedside lifeline. She was cold. Even in summer she was never truly warm. The chill of diminished old age had moved into her bones and paid the rent up for life. Wheezing, she hunched over onto her left side. That was better. The pull of gravity was always worse if she lay on her back, even with half-a-dozen pillows propped behind her. Emphysema smothered you to death in slow motion as the lung tissue collapsed in on itself day by day, hour by hour, breath by ragged breath. Everyone agreed it was a tedious way to die. By comparison, she counted her husband lucky. A few struggling moments and he was gone. How easy was that?

Claire was their only child, unexpected when Gwen turned forty-one. They'd named her after Jimmie's mother, and she'd been their greatest source of happiness. But now, she was Gwen's only source of care. Poor Claire. It wasn't fair, but what could you do?

She was glad when Claire decided to join a local theater group. It sounded like fun with nice people from what Claire told her. Claire needed an outlet, something that had nothing to do with sickbeds and car accident victims, which was what her daughter saw most often in her job with the ambulance service that took calls from the Atlanta metro area and outlying neighborhoods. Although Claire had passed all her Paramedics studies near the top of her class, Gwen knew Claire would be better off in a research job. Moody all through high school and into Tech College, she'd seemed the happiest she'd been in a long time when accepted into Emory's chemistry program. She'd just started her first semester when Jimmie chose to leave them with no means of support. Ironic that an insurance salesman would have such a meager policy of his own. Gwen sighed, wheezed, and finally dozed.

"Mother?" Claire stood in the bedroom doorway, outlined by light from the hall. "Are you awake?"

"Just now, yes."

Claire came into the bedroom and leaned over her, offering a soft kiss on her cheek.

"You're my angel." Claire's hair was newly washed and smelled like flowers.

"Sorry I was late coming home tonight. Feel like getting up for some supper?"

A stab of guilt as Gwen remembered. Shame was on her lips. Finally, "The bed's wet." She could see the wince, even with her poor eyesight.

"Don't worry about it; I'll change the bed as soon as we've got you cleaned up."

"I hate for you to have to wait on me like this."

Claire made a dismissive gesture. "That's what I'm here for."

There it was, the bitter pill. Claire had come home to wait for her to die. She wished she could oblige by hurrying up. If she just quit eating it would go faster, but Doctor Curso's nurse had scolded her roundly for weighing in at ninety-four pounds on her last office visit. Anyway, she didn't have the courage. Even in the slow inevitable process of dying, the body still wanted to live.

In a clean dressing gown and seated at the round oak table in the small dining area, where in warm weather the glass doors would be opened onto a backyard patio, Gwen sipped at the chowder Claire had heated on the stove. The portable oxygen generator whispered softly behind her chair.

"I hate being a burden on you like this."

"Mama, will you stop?"

Was there a hint of resentment? Gwen wasn't sure. Well, it couldn't be helped. Who wanted to spend their youth nursing a dying old woman? "Claire, are you feeling all right?" Claire was massaging the back of her head and not paying attention to her supper.

"What?"

"You were frowning."

"I was? Sorry. I'm just tense. It's nothing serious."

"Are you sure? Your face looks pinched. Are you in pain?"

"Minor headache. Really, it's okay." Claire gathered up the dishes and took them to the kitchen, divided from the dining area by a long granite counter. She stashed them in the sink with her back turned to her mother.

Gwen noticed the hunch of her shoulders as she rinsed their soup bowls. Something was going unsaid, but she wouldn't pry. Claire would tell her eventually. She always did.

CHAPTER
3

Thursday, 6:45 P. M., a week later

"Before we get underway this evening, I wish to announce a slight cast change."

Bayard's voice carried all the way from the front of the stage to the back of the theater where Claire slipped in late through the double doors. He had a booming delivery even in ordinary conversation. She wondered what he must have been like as an actor. Probably the kind who stole the show every night.

"As most of you know, Danny has quit the play—and the company—which means that Tom will now assume the role of Doctor Faustus." Heads turned and the actor named Tom gave a thumbs-up.

Tom was Danny's understudy, which should make for an interesting tectonic shift in the play's dynamics. The two couldn't have been more different, in Claire's opinion. Tom, the near-skinhead who piloted a big chrome-covered Harley to rehearsals, was a couple of inches taller and at least twenty pounds beefier than Danny the whippet. In fact, Tom reminded her of a very young Henry Rollins, tats and all. Claire watched Tom interacting with the cast members taking up the front row of seats. She'd never heard him stand in for Danny since they'd begun rehearsals, or deliver any lines at all for that matter, so her interest was piqued. She rummaged in her tote bag for the script. They needed the most current marked-up version and it would suck if she'd left it at home in the rush to get here. Probably going to do a lot of prompting until Tom and Morris got used to each other onstage and the play found its new rhythm.

"I expect everyone to give Tom as much support as he needs to fit into the part," Bayard was saying. "Hello, Miss Porter, glad you could join us."

Claire's cheeks flamed as she slid into a seat on the third row beside doe-eyed Addie, the Mummers' go-to girl for all the sultry, slutty parts like the Evil Angel and Lechery in the Seven Deadly Sins grouping. Adelaide Murphy was one of the company's veterans, auburn-haired, green-eyed, somewhere in her thirties with a whisky-rough kind of voice. She was from New England, knew a lot about the arts, and for some reason, clicked right away with Claire.

All the heads turned toward them. Claire gave a quick tight-lipped smile. "Sorry, had a traffic accident to clean up."

Bayard nodded. "Yes, someone does have to protect people from dying. A commendable profession." He moved on. "So. For Tom's benefit, we'll begin from the beginning—act one, scene one, Faustus' study. Shall we take our marks and see who besides Morris is fully off the script now?" That was probably how Danny had scored a major part in the play. He was such a quick study as to be nearly off book by a second or third read-through. He was a great mimic, too. Could master any accent you wanted, if you didn't need it in a deep voice. She still wondered, just a little bit, why he hadn't been persuaded to stay.

The cast members taking part in scene one rose and headed for the wings: Faustus, his page Wagner, the Good and Evil Angels, and Faustus' scheming friends Valdes and Cornelius. Claire trailed them, feeling vaguely ill at ease. What was with that comment of Bayard's about preventing people from dying? She took up her position in the wings stage right, but couldn't stop frowning. This little venture into the acting world was supposed to give her some recreation and a creative way to decompress from her day job of making sure people got to the hospital more or less in one piece, but right now she wasn't having a lot of fun. Which, if she were honest, was her own fault. It wouldn't be the first time she'd been accused of being too nosey about other people's business and not knowing when to just let something drop.

Claire settled her butt on the barstool reserved for the prompter, positioned just out of the audience sight lines. They were running this rehearsal with full lighting and effects, but no costumes. She turned the script to scene one and got out her penlight.

Ruben the lighting guy, who sometimes moonlighted with the ballet company when they performed in the university theater across town, brought the house and stage lights down, with a single spot trained on Bayard where he stood center stage, in command of the ship. At least that's how she thought of him. He'd have made a great pirate captain, tiller in one hand and cutlass in the other, or maybe a bottle of whiskey, ordering his men into assault position as their lean, fast ship pulled alongside a slower, heavier civilian vessel where terrified ladies and their peacock gentlemen got an eyeful of their approaching fate. Claire blinked hard. Her eyelid movie vanished, and she tuned back into Bayard proclaiming the lines of the Chorus, a part he'd reserved for himself. It was easy to fall under his spell as Marlowe's "glorious blank verse," so-called by Addie, rolled off his tongue. He was *that* good. Claire had no clue what blank verse was until Morris, ex-English major and self-employed journalist, explained it to her.

"Unrhymed verse in iambic pentameter. Goes *dah-DAH, dah-DAH*, like that, five to a line. Christopher Marlowe was the first English playwright to fully exploit the form, and this play, *Dr. Faustus,* is the pinnacle of that expression. At least in my not-so-humble opinion." He delivered the explanation like a college lecture. Claire had felt appropriately stupid and uninformed, but now when she actually listened to the lines of the play beyond just looking for accuracy of delivery, she heard what Addie meant.

"...and now the good Doctor doth indulge in cursed necromancy. Nothing is as sweet to him as magic, which he does prefer before the dove of Heaven...and *this* the man that in his study sits." With a flourish, he strode off stage right, stopping just past Claire and positioning himself in the wings to monitor the action. A portion of the stage lights came up, revealing the set of Faustus' study, where Tom now sat in the high-backed chair instead of Danny. He faced the audience and launched into Faustus' opening monologue.

"...Put away your studies, Faustus, and begin to sound the depths of what you have attained..."

Claire sat up, more attuned to what was happening onstage. Where Danny had just inhabited his little area of the set, Tom owned the space. She wondered if riding a Harley had something to do with that. He spoke the lines clearly and confidently, with an air of authority that Danny had never got hold of. It was easy to believe this person could be the fabled scholar of Wittenberg who'd grown bored with his vast knowledge and wanted more. Intrigued, Claire suddenly couldn't wait to see how he played off Morris, who was also used to owning his portion of stage real estate.

"...Oh, what a world of profit and delight, of power, of honor, of omnipotence is promised to the studious artisan! All things that move between the poles shall be at my command..."

Tom was really getting into it. In fact, he was a natural. His voice had presence, and it was clear he'd memorized the opening lines to the point that there were very few mistakes. Claire lowered the script, more interested in Tom's complete takeover of the part than in helping him remember his lines. She wondered if he'd been madly practicing all this time, hoping for a chance to show his own approach to the role if for some reason Danny couldn't go on. She knew the understudy was always supposed to be ready to competently step in if need be, but in the nearly half a year she'd been with the company they hadn't had to promote an understudy until now. She slanted her eyes toward Bayard. He stood very still, watching the scene intently, his expression unreadable.

"A sound magician is a demi-god," Tom proclaimed.

The Good and Evil Angels made their entrance. Each had just a few lines with which to impress both Faustus and the audience.

"Go forward, Faustus....Be thou on earth like Jove is in the sky, Lord and commander of these elements." Addie played the Evil Angel to the hilt, her green eyes bright and her full mouth drawn into a bow that wasn't quite a kiss at the end of her line. Claire was sure that moment hadn't been nearly as provocative when she'd spoken those lines to Danny. This transformation of the play by a single cast change was going to be interesting to watch.

The scene played out, as did scene two, and they moved on to scene three, where Faustus has his first meeting with the management team from Hell—Lucifer, his lieutenant Mephistopheles, and a few assorted devils. Claire twitched in anticipation.

The scene-three scrim came down into place with backlighting to show the outline of a shadowy grove at night. Tom took his mark near the footlights, facing somewhat upstage.

"...I'll begin my incantations, and try if devils will obey my summons..."

Claire held her breath. What followed in the script was a passage in Latin that Danny had memorized syllable by syllable and repeated with ease, although she doubted he understood any of the words. A translation would be provided in the program for the audience's benefit, something to the effect of "May the gods of the underworld favor me; may the triple deity of Jehovah be gone; to the spirits of fire, air, and water, greetings...let Mephistopheles himself now arise to serve us."

The sound effects of thunder rumbled, and Tom took a breath.

"*Sint mihi dei acherontis propitii, valeat numen triplex Jehovae...*" Claire's jaw dropped. More thunder crackled and Morris entered upstage right. Her scalp prickled. This was really too good.

"Now, Faustus, what would you have me do?" Morris's voice was pitched low and seductive, yet projected well to the back of the theater. He advanced on the figure downstage and this time met an actor who was closer to his own height. Claire noticed the shift in Morris's body language, not hovering over his quarry as he'd done with Danny, but more like drawing himself up taller, sizing up this new persona who defied easy intimidation.

The actors went into the back and forth exchange in which Faustus demands to know whether his conjuring has forced Lucifer to send his chief lieutenant, to which Mephistopheles assures the scholar that he is merely curious and has come of his own accord.

"Did not my conjuring speeches raise thee?" Tom insisted, invading Morris's space. Claire was surprised to see Morris fall back a few steps before engaging in the famous repartee about Lucifer's fall from heaven with his attendant angels and the nature of Hell and whether the torment of being cut off from the bliss of paradise was worth the voluptuous pleasures of the underworld. Their voices rose and the exchange became more heated, a passionate argument instead of a scholarly debate.

Bayard came to life beside her and stepped out of the wings. "All right, let's take a moment, shall we?" Both actors surfaced from their personas with a slightly dazed look. Claire slid off her stool, straining to catch their words as the three of them conferred in lowered voices. She clearly heard Morris say "dial it back a notch" before Bayard turned to the rest of the cast and announced a short break.

"Faustus and his Mephisto are going to reblock the scene. Everyone else take a break and be back in twenty minutes sharp."

Claire advanced toward the trio. "Do I need to stay—"

Bayard dismissed her with a wave. "Not this time. Go on with the others. It's clear our new Faustus has his lines. We just need to fine-tune the delivery."

Claire nodded and headed down the stage right steps. As she caught up with Addie, a glance back at the stage revealed Bayard and the two actors having what seemed a good-natured laugh with some head-nodding. Tom was smiling a little sheepishly, Morris looked neutral, so it was all fine. Claire tried to relax that pinch she'd felt developing between her shoulders.

"Well, *that* was interesting," Addie said as they fell into step, heading up the aisle toward the lobby doors.

Claire stuffed the script in her bag. "Yeah, whole different play."

"Tom's hot, don't you think?" Addie the Evil Angel licked her lips, even if she might be a bit too old for him.

"I've never paid him much attention, to be honest. The Harley's cool, though."

"Well, he's a vast improvement over Danny." Addie pushed through the doors and held them open for Claire.

"It's weird about Danny. Gone—just poof, like he'd never been here. Sure, I'd be upset if I got hurt onstage, but I don't think it would make me quit the company. It's just..." Claire shrugged. "...Odd."

"C'mon, the whole place is odd, which is why I love coming here." Addie made a dramatic sweep of her arms, as if to embrace the Janus Theatre in its moldering entirety. "It has history, presence…and presences," She laughed wickedly.

"About that." They'd stopped in the darkened lobby. Claire considered getting a soda from the drink machine hulking in the half-light across the room, but changed her mind and headed up the wide stairs to the mezzanine where the lights were brighter and the ballet company was in rehearsal. "Morris told me the theatre's haunted. I think he was just trying to spook me."

"Worked, didn't it?" Addie was grinning. "That's Morris for you. Takes his Mephisto role a little too seriously. I wouldn't be surprised to find out he's a dabbler."

Claire stopped. "Dabbler?"

"In the occult. Oh, not like me. Not Wiccan. I mean, he probably reads Crowley or Anton Levay. For verisimilitude." She emphasized the '*tude*.

"Oh. You mean like method acting." They trudged side by side up the curved staircase to the second floor where taped music flowed out to meet them. "How's Wicca different from black magic?"

Addie made an exasperated noise. "Like day and night, that's how."

"I wouldn't know. I was raised Episcopalian." They shared a laugh.

On the mezzanine level, they stood in the wide entryway of the ballet rehearsal space. The cavernous room, with its rows of narrow floor-to-ceiling windows along the north and south walls and a bank of tall mirrors at the eastern end, was filled with twirling, leaping dancers. The music of David Byrne pulsed from speakers near the door. The air had a dry, dusty taste as jumping, landing feet pounded decades of dust out of the wood flooring. A dozen or so dancers not involved in the piece being rehearsed lounged or stretched in the corners or along the walls out of the way.

Peach City Ballet was a small company made up mostly of the better students from local studios and talented older dancers who hadn't made the cut over at The Atlanta Ballet, the city's big-league professional company. PCB's director was a lovely Brazilian man who'd danced in his heyday for the likes of Jose Limón and Alvin Ailey. PCB was his retirement project, a small but lovingly crafted jewel.

"I like watching them," Claire said. "Especially her." She pointed out a sinewy, athletic dancer, of medium height. "Jackie and I grew up in the same neighborhood, one street over from each other." With mousy blondish-brownish hair cropped in a short cap, slightly horsey facial features, ordinary brown eyes, Jackie was about as plain as they came, but Claire knew that once she was in motion, she was unmistakable. Most of the female dancers in the company had the willowy Swan Lake heroine look nailed, with their pale skin, long slim legs, and highly arched feet. But Claire preferred to watch Jackie, whose muscular precision and agility were more exciting.

They were rehearsing some modern piece, a mad perpetual-motion blur of bodies in motion. The ensemble of dancers, four men and six women, hurtled across the floor and back again in a nonstop blending, pairing, and unpairing. Claire had been watching in fascination their painstaking process of learning the piece over the past couple of months. Now it had become second nature, and they performed it with seeming abandon and spontaneity although in fact it was the pinnacle of precision.

"Awesome and then some," Addie whispered, settling herself on the floor near the entrance. Claire joined her. The floor could use a good sweep, but she was in her rattiest jeans, so it didn't matter.

"Yeah, Jackie told me who choreographed it, but I can't remember. Thorp or something."

"Twyla Tharpe. That's a section from *The Catherine Wheel*. I saw the whole thing performed when I lived in Boston. It's a demanding piece — this little troupe is very good."

Claire folded her legs Indian-style. "Jackie told me they're not doing a traditional *Nutcracker* this Christmas. The first half of the program is *The Skaters*, for all the patrons who need their dose of traditional ballet. They're ending the show with this." Claire nodded at the ebb and flow of leaping, tumbling, whirling bodies. "I don't know much about dance, but I like this a lot. Better than the classical stuff, I think."

It felt good, just leaning against the wall and letting the dancers whirl her exhaustion away. Jackie'd said it was okay, nobody minded the actors coming up to watch them rehearse. Likewise, she'd noticed some of the dancers slipping into the back row of seats downstairs during their own rehearsals.

Two male dancers tossed Jackie through the air, one to the other, in a move Claire found heartstopping. But Jackie was athletic and fearless. When they were kids, she was always the one you wanted on your team when it was choosing time, either at school or on a weekend game of slow-pitch in the open lot near their houses. She could hit a sandlot softball out of the park on any given day. They'd graduated high school together and Jackie had gone to a university out of state, while Claire signed up at a local technical college for an AA in their Health Services department. Jackie completed her B.S. degree in Movement Science and came back to their old high school to teach what they laughingly called "fizz-ed."

Claire finished her EMT Paramedic advanced certification in two years, and had worked with a large private ambulance service for nearly twice as long, but the burnout factor they were all warned about in these kinds of jobs was starting to kick in. If it weren't for Paul, her team partner, who was an island of strength and calm that she could only aspire to in her dreams, she might not have lasted this long. He was a little older than the average paramedic, having served in the First Gulf War. He told her he'd driven a tank. After her first trip out on a call with him at the wheel, she believed him. Nerves of absolute steel. Which brought up the memory of that first dispatch. Barely dawn, heavy traffic on the beltway, a motorcyclist hit by a truck and run over several times before police could get to the scene to divert the steady stream of early morning commuters and 18-wheelers around the scene of carnage. When they'd arrived, his body parts were strewn along a fifty-foot stretch of the highway. A bloody tennis shoe with the foot still in it, an arm with the hand barely attached, and the rest of the mangled body and the crumpled motorcycle further down. She'd almost lost her breakfast on the spot. Paul had just reached over, given her hand a squeeze and said, "Let's clean him up." Just like that. And they did. She'd gradually developed her own ways of coping over the months that followed, reveling in the lives saved and disassociating herself from the losses. It was easier now, but she'd never fully expunged that first horrific job from her memory banks.

She'd come to the conclusion that she'd be much happier in a laboratory doing medical research, looking at slides and helping develop a cure for cancer or whatever, but that required a chemistry degree, preferably at the master's level. She'd talked it over with her mom and dad, and they'd agreed it was going to be costly, but with some government loans it looked doable. Then the acceptance letter came from Emory and she enrolled in the fall term. But Jimmie Porter's heart attack had forced all those plans into reset.

Her mother told her he'd even had an insurance physical not a month before and was pronounced fit, for a man in his late fifties who smoked and drank and stressed too much. It was like he'd just decided on a whim to check out, no advance warning, no time for goodbye. The trooper who found his Buick angled off the highway into a ditch said he'd probably blacked out at the wheel. Claire wondered if she'd been with him whether she might have saved him; she wouldn't have been as experienced then as she was now, so probably not.

Claire watched the dancers glide and leap, twirl and turn. Jackie's strong, compact body curled and unfurled. Claire relaxed, letting her mind drift. After her father's funeral, her university plans had to be cancelled, and she found herself facing life trapped at home with an invalid mother to care for. At least she had a job, underpaid and stressful as it was. She supposed she should be thankful, but there were times when a black despair settled in her gut and she thought she might be close to losing it. There was a guy on the EMT staff who'd been let go recently for self-medicating his depression with controlled-substance pain relievers that were just too readily accessible. She understood all too clearly how it could happen.

"Hey." Adelaide was nudging her. "They're calling from downstairs, time to go."

"Right." Claire got to her feet and dusted off the seat of her jeans. They headed back downstairs to see what adjustments had been made to scene three. Claire hoped not much. She liked the new Faustus.

Stepping down into the shadows of the lobby, Claire couldn't help but glance across the expanse of hardwood flooring toward the closed basement door. She quickly looked away and followed Addie's shapely hips toward the auditorium. "Hey, you never did answer my question about Wiccans."

They pushed through the double doors to join the others taking their places onstage. "Tell you what," Addie said, heading for the stage left steps, "I'll bring my tarot cards to the next rehearsal and do a reading for you. Then you can ask me anything you want."

CHAPTER 4

Kit Bayard stood at his office window, looking down at the sidewalk. The evening's rehearsal had gone well, even with Danny's understudy over-acting the role of Faustus. And most of the cast had seemed willing to accept the explanation of Danny's withdrawal from the company. As far as the production was concerned, it was a stroke of luck—young Tom was a natural and already a much more convincing Faustus than his predecessor. Physically his presence onstage was more solid, although Bayard decided he might have to ask Tom to wear a wig for the actual performance...the skinhead look was probably not going to work. There was some awkwardness at first while Tom and Morris worked out their timing and delivery dynamics, but he could see there was potential for some really good theater. He'd anticipated a bit of prima-donna pushback from Morris, especially with Tom getting in his face like that, but they'd quickly worked it out with no apparent leftover snits. Bayard lit his pipe and inhaled its cherry aroma.

He felt keen anticipation toward mounting this particular play, even if it was a somewhat modernized version of the original. It was his own adaptation, preserving much of the original blank verse but substituting modern phrasing and vocabulary for passages that would otherwise be unintelligible to modern theater goers. Today's audiences, sadly, responded more enthusiastically to modern-English versions of sixteenth-century masterworks. And the company needed to fill the house for the play's run during the holidays. The Mummers Theatrical Company had its sponsors and donors, which included the Janus Theatre Preservation Association, but times were hard all over, especially in the arts, and the acting company's budget was tighter than it had been in years.

Watching the cast trailing away from the theater in twos and threes down the sidewalk, Bayard stood still as a shadow. Morris and the Porter woman were the last to leave. She'd annoyed him, asking about Danny and wanting to know how she could get in touch with him, to be sure his wounded arm had been properly tended to.

His fingers tapped a mindless jig on the sill as the seconds ticked by. Her ladyship was demanding payment again, but he wasn't ready to face her just yet. When it came right down to it, he was bloody tired of having to deal with her altogether. Four centuries was a long time to hold unrelenting control over a creature not even remotely human. Longer than he'd ever imagined when the proposal had first been offered him. Was he allowing himself a moment of regret? But without the stone, he'd have been dead and buried back when those assassin thugs of Walsingham's cornered him at Deptford. Government espionage in the court of Elizabeth I was a dangerous business, but more lucrative than playwriting, if one lived to collect. For all he knew, that still held true today. He'd been out of the spy business since his murder in 1593.

Bayard arched his back slightly and straightened his shoulders. He spread his listening fingers along the weathered casement…was the building empty yet? Wood and brick responded to him, telegraphing the answer to his query. No ballet dancers, no actors. Bayard sighed and headed downstairs.

He disliked having to put up with outsiders renting space in the Janus, which he'd bought outright with cash nearly a decade ago when he'd arrived in town, but it was a necessity in these tough economic times. His own group of actors was hand-picked and belonged there, although a few like Danny arguably less so. He hadn't really intended to sacrifice the boy, but the spilled blood on the rehearsal stage, fresh from John Dee's pearl-handled athame, had to be dealt with. He pressed the sheathed knife, deep in his trousers pocket, against his thigh. It was one of the few things that remained from his old life, from the moment at Mortlake where he'd taken possession of the stone. Carrying it over the centuries, it had served him well. Why it had chosen to sacrifice Danny he wasn't sure—the boy's life force was so pale it had gone into the stone practically unnoticed. Not much of a contribution, but not much of a loss, either. It all evened out.

Bayard reached the basement stairs and left the light off. His night sight was as good as any owl's. He mulled over the possibility that someone might accidentally discover the cornerstone in its current location, although that didn't seem likely. He kept the basement locked and rarely allowed anyone else access to it. Plus, what lay trapped in the stone had never established communion with anyone but Dee and himself in all its long years of servitude. He supposed for safety's sake he should weave a stronger net of deception over the area around that section of the masonry, what with more people coming and going upstairs. The last time he'd had to do that little bit of magick, it had cost him—the banshee had ripped at him more savagely than ever, and he'd been afraid their struggle might have been discernible to the outside world. He'd scanned the papers and television local news the next day for reports of earth tremors, insect plagues and whatnot, but all seemed boringly ordinary.

He hurried, surefooted, down the steps and into the gloom of the basement. Going immediately to the spot under the stairs where the cornerstone pulsed dusky red, visible to his eyes only, he put his own heartbeat in synch with the stone. Ignoring the dirt and grime, Bayard stretched out on the floor, his head under the stair risers and inches from the theater's foundation masonry. He closed his eyes and spoke the summons: *"Ecce signum."*

A response formed itself in his mind. *Acknowledged.*

"As master of the *buachloch*, I bid thee attend me."

As quick as thought, the answer filled his mind. *So full of yourself. We are here.*

Bayard opened his eyes and fixed his gaze on the stone's pitted surface. It was now black as obsidian, radiating the galactic cold of the void beyond the land of the living. He set his jaw and reached out with both hands. The moment his fingers brushed the surface, the stone became a glistening, pulsating heart, its truncated aorta spewing ventricular blood in a river over his hands and arms. The flood washed over his body, its spicy-sour stench filling his nostrils and engulfing the lowermost stairs.

Bayard struggled to keep his chin above the red tide and shouted, "Cease, damned crone!"

At once the river of blood evaporated, leaving a single drop quivering on the chipped tile beside his hands. Bayard got to his knees and glared back at the stone. "Such theatrics are wasted on me. I won't be intimidated."

The drop of blood smoked around the edges. *Take care an' ye not lose thy grip.*

"Don't threaten me," Bayard warned, anger rising like a flame. "I can send you away as quickly as you were summoned."

Aye, great one, with each libation thy vigor increases. Have I not kept ye hale and hearty these many seasons, while ye feed me the poorest of libations? A hag's sneering face hovered over the shining surface of the droplet. Her silver eyes followed his every move, shifting with the pulse of his own heart. *What is my master's will?* She infused the word "master" with such contempt that Bayard held his tongue for a heartbeat.

He recalled fleeting memories of Dee extolling the stone's powers and explaining how he and his mysterious friend had trapped the banshee along with the Irish witch who'd summoned her. He refocused his will, holding the specter at bay. "Servitude becomes you," he whispered. Wisps of acrid smoke curled around the hag's face, forming a writhing halo. "Hear me," said Bayard grimly. "If you place any value on your miserable existence, you will do as I require, and swiftly."

The basement was still as a mortuary.

"You have not adequately provided the wealth and fame promised me. If anything, my presence has diminished over the centuries. I want to see immediate improvement. And this too...I want to know instantly if anyone touches the stone besides myself. You will transmit this to me without hesitation. You will protect me from any source of danger at all cost."

The hag's face disappeared in a puff of smoke. Slowly the droplet congealed and stretched into a red line that coiled around Bayard's ankle. Scales began forming along its ridge.

"Stop! I forbid it!" The serpent lay half-formed, frozen in the moment. Keening laughter clung to the shadows and hugged itself in the cobwebs.

Bayard swept his hand over the malformation, erasing its near existence. He clambered to his feet and brushed dust from his trousers with trembling fingers.

"You *will* obey me," he whispered to the empty air.

CHAPTER
5

Friday morning

The alarm went off in the gloom just before sunrise, pithing Claire's brain with its high-pitched buzz. 6:05. That gave her barely enough time to stumble to the bathroom, get into her uniform, tie her hair back, cook a toaster waffle, find her keys, and drive to the emergency service center by 7, the start of her shift. The sky was just turning gray-blue when she pulled into her parking space. Yawning, she got out and headed through the automatic doors to the break room/lounge where the teams spent their between time, waiting for calls.

"Mornin', Sunshine." Paul was already there, watching the local news.

"If you say so." She gave him a weak smile. Just hearing his voice with its brotherly/fatherly everything-is-under-control vibe made her feel better. Maybe today the entire city would drive like sensible, responsible adults and all the looming heart attacks would hold off at least a week. How long had it been since they'd had a slow day? She couldn't remember. Four days of twelve-hour shifts that often stretched to fourteen, then three days off to recuperate, then back into it again. She lived for those days off.

A new hire was in the kitchen, trying to outsmart the coffee machine with no luck.

Claire took pity on her. "You got to lift the handle all the way up, so it'll reset. Then you can punch in the cup size, like this." A flick of the wrist, one quick poke, and the K-cup oozed its brown liquid into the new girl's cup.

"God, thanks. I was about to give up on it." The newbie had a slightly Hispanic accent. She didn't look a week over eighteen. Claire wondered how long she'd last.

"Rule number one. Never give up on your morning coffee." Claire tried to sound reassuring, remembering her first week on the job. "Everything going okay so far?" She poked a Jet Fuel K-cup into the machine and pushed the 10-oz button over her own cup.

"Yeah, so far." The girl was smiling.

"That's good. I'm Claire." She held out her free hand.

"Angela."

"If you, like, need anything or have any questions, just ask me." Good grief, she was sounding like the nurse at her mother's doctor's office. Feeling old as Methuselah, she took her coffee and went back into the lounge area.

She was just settling back against the couch cushions with a gulp of Jet Fuel in her mouth when the first call came in. Paul was on his feet, pulling his jacket over his brawny shoulders. "Time to roll. Bring that with you."

They settled into the ambulance cab, Paul in the driver's seat. Claire snapped a lid on her cup and nestled it securely in the holder, then buckled up, listening to the dispatcher describe the situation over the dashboard radio. It was a vehicular accident, on Piedmont Avenue near the beltway intersection, involving a motorcycle and one or more cars. Claire's stomach tightened.

"Traffic's moderate to heavy, police just now arriving on the scene," the dispatcher's voice was measured and precise.

Paul turned on the siren and the lights and stomped the gas. "Here we go."

Claire nodded.

Paul plowed through the traffic as if the great lumbering beast that was their class III ambulance had an invisible cowcatcher attached to the grille. Claire focused on the dispatcher's voice, continually feeding details as they homed in on the accident site.

"We have one person on the ground, condition unknown."

Paul crossed lanes and flew around an SUV that hadn't pulled over.

The radio crackled. "We have a car overturned, occupant trapped inside."

"Gonna need the Jaws of Life," Paul commented.

Claire said nothing. The morning was off to a great start.

They pulled up to the crash site, cordoned off by a bank of cop cars, lights flashing. Cars and trucks streamed past, slowing for a few seconds as drivers gawked and then sped away. Paul parked the ambulance on the shoulder of the highway as close as safely possible to the point where the crash had taken place. Claire could see the cyclist, still in his helmet, lying on his, or maybe her, stomach. Hard to tell gender from this distance. At least the person seemed to be all in one piece. A small gray car sat on its roof, wheels in the air, a hundred feet or so down the side of the road where black skid marks left the pavement. The motorcycle lay on its side not far from its rider.

Paul killed the siren. "Take the guy on the ground, I'll check the one in the car."

"Right." Although both were licensed paramedics, seniority made Paul the team leader, which was just fine by Claire.

She jogged past an apparent eye witness, telling his story to one of the policemen, a note of awe or admiration in his voice.

"His cycle blew the back tire and instead of flipping, he just laid it down on the grass of the shoulder nice as you please. I ride a bike, too, and that was a pro landing. Hardly any damage to the bike. Dunno about the guy, though..."

Claire reached the crumpled cyclist just as he rolled over onto his back. He fumbled with the chinstrap of the visored helmet.

"Hey, let me do that," she told him, pushing his head gently but firmly back to the ground. "Don't move a muscle—just let me do the lifting. Everything's all right now, you'll be okay." She slipped into the comforting mantra that she used with accident victims to keep them still and not freaking out.

"I'm just going to lift your head now and slip the helmet off, okay?" She heard a muffled response that sounded a little dazed, but not freaked.

She eased the helmet off, put it aside, and stared.

"Tom!"

"Hey, Claire." His voice was shaky, but he didn't seem traumatized.

"Just lie still..." She checked for broken bones.

"I'm okay, how's the bike?"

"Better than you should be. Do you hurt anywhere?"

"Just my head."

"How many fingers?" She made a V sign.

"Two."

"What day is it?"

"Friday. Trust me, I'm fine. I need to call the bookstore—"

"You aren't fine until I say so. Just stay still, please." She went through her protocol checklist and finally decided everything was in working order. Only then did she allow him to sit up. He groaned and looked around at the flashing lights and people in uniform milling around the upside-down car. Claire could hear Paul, asking questions and giving orders in that steady no-nonsense voice she relied on.

"Holy shit. Is that person dead?"

"Doesn't sound like it." Claire stood up and took a good look. Paul was on his knees, his arm reaching through the smashed driver's door window. He must have released the handle because at that moment the door fell open.

"Are you okay to just sit here for a few minutes? I need to go help over there."

Tom waved her away. "Sure, you go." He felt around inside his leather jacket and pulled out his cell phone. "I won't go anywhere, just need to make some calls. Looks like I'll be late for work." Well, if he could joke around, she decided there couldn't be much damage done.

It didn't take too long to get the college student extracted safely from her silver Nissan. They strapped her to the backboard with her broken collarbone stabilized and loaded her into the ambulance. She was weepy, but not hysterical. Tom was on his feet now, looking down at his bike and frowning. Claire scanned his stance, still alert for anything off. He knelt and put his hands on the flattened back tire, probably looking for the nail or whatever had caused the blowout.

"You sure you won't come back with us to the hospital? Just sit around for a bit and be sure there's no residual sign of concussion?"

Tom looked up, his expression friendly but determined. "Don't worry about me. There's nothing wrong."

"Well, would you mind signing this waiver stating you refused further treatment?"

"No problem." He reached for the clipboard, quickly scanned the sheet, and signed his name, Tom Brennan, in big looping letters. "You're a good medic, Claire. I appreciate that."

Nonplussed, she retrieved the clipboard. "I-I try to be. If the situation was reversed, I'd want somebody competent to work on me." Self-conscious, she shrugged but couldn't quite muster a laugh. "Well, I need to go. You'll be all right?"

"Don't worry. I'm just gonna sit down here with the bike until the wrecker shows up." He frowned again. "That was a new tire."

Claire allowed herself to look at him more closely than she'd done in the theater. She'd always been somewhat put off by his shaved-head-leather-jacket look, but now she saw a young man about her age, maybe even younger, with clear gray eyes under dark brows. She guessed his hair might be black if he allowed it to grow. High cheekbones and a thin, tight mouth gave his face an intense expression. But it wasn't just bone structure. There was something else going on with him. Something repressed...maybe that was where he was pulling his performance as Faustus from, some dark well of angst. Then she really did laugh—what a romance novel scenario. Tom would likely be mortified if he knew what she was thinking.

"Something funny?" The skin around his gray eyes crinkled just a little.

She heard Paul crank the ambulance. "Nothing worth mentioning. Well, I'm out of here. You be careful...I don't like leaving you by yourself after a fall like that."

"*Das macht nichts.*" He waved a dismissal.

What? He did German as well as Latin? Claire climbed into the back of the ambulance with their patient, her head full of questions. The Mummers had a company full of strange people, no joke. Maybe that was why Danny'd chosen to leave—he was too normal.

CHAPTER 6

Saturday night

Tom shifted his butt in the high-backed chair onstage. His side was stiff, and when he'd showered earlier he could see his left hip and shoulder were purpling where he'd hit the ground in yesterday's accident. Nothing broken, which was lucky, because he didn't need something like that slowing him down. Good to know, though, that if he *had* been in bad shape Claire and her laconic teammate could have ably taken care of him. She knew her stuff, and his estimation of her had gone up as a result of the encounter.

He'd wondered why she wanted to join the company since she seemed to know so little about acting or the theater or dramatic literature. She was very detail oriented, though, which made her the perfect choice for prompter and keeper of the master script with all the performance notes. For his part, Tom relished the role of Dr. Faustus. There was latent magic in those lines—and it wasn't just the beauty of the language. He could feel it when he spoke the words extolling the virtues of the underworld, greeting Lucifer and his minions as an equal, and especially the invocations that summoned the King of Hades' second in command, Mephistopheles. The first time he'd said that passage in Latin, what flowed through him was indescribable, even better than a hard-on. Raw power that flayed flesh off the bone. It had taken him a couple of minutes to recover. Morris had felt it too, he could tell. In fact, it had scared the shit out of him—he'd seen it in the man's eyes. The moment passed as soon as Bayard stopped the scene, but Tom felt the lingering sensation well past the end of rehearsal.

Now he was being careful to, as Morris put it, dial it back, holding that undercurrent of electricity in check, creating dramatic tension onstage but not letting it overpower the acting itself. This particular scene they were rehearsing, in which Faustus has a fleeting repentance for selling his soul so easily and requires a visit from Lucifer and the Seven Deadlies to renew his commitment, was fast becoming one of Tom's favorites.

Tom allowed his thoughts to drift as he waited for rehearsal to begin, first back to the accident where he'd felt his body shift into protection mode moments before it hit the ground, and then further back to the time he'd discovered the Janus Theatre and the Mummers Theatrical Company. He'd only been in town a few weeks when he'd spotted the auditions display ad in some arts newspaper he'd picked up in the metro rail station downtown. Following his instinct, he'd come here, tried out for a few parts, offered his services for some non-acting jobs, and had been accepted into the fold. He was intrigued by the people in the company, and in particular its ginger-bearded director, who was brilliant and overbearing in an old-world, European royalty sort of way. It was Kit Bayard who'd suggested he look for a paying job at The Rookery, a large used bookstore on the south side frequented by the city's academics and literati and specializing in hard-to-find, even rare, books. A number of Bayard's valuable first-edition playbooks had come from there.

"Places!" Bayard's baritone cut across the backstage chatter. Claire watched Tom get up with a flinch and take his mark. Silence descended, and Ruben adjusted the spots to focus on the figure of Faustus standing beside his desk. Lucifer, a portrait photographer in his forties who said he'd wanted the part because he got to wear red face paint and horns in costume, entered and commanded Faustus to have a seat and observe a little show cooked up by the underworld entertainment board.

"Go, Mephistopheles, fetch them in." He waved grandly.

One by one, Pride, Covetousness, Envy, Wrath, Gluttony, Sloth, and Lechery paraded across the stage as Faustus questioned each regarding his or her particular talents. When he inquired of "Mistress Minx" what manner of apparition she was, Addie oozed voluptuousness that ensured no one would miss the double entendre of her answer: "I am one that loves an inch of *raw mutton* better than a plate of fried stockfish"—a line guaranteed to draw laughter from the audience—"and the first letter of my name begins with Lechery." Tom leered at her appropriately.

The mage's allegiance to Hell firmly reestablished, Lucifer turned and led the Sins offstage, calling back to Faustus, "I will come for thee at midnight." The lights dimmed to a single murky pool encircling Faustus in his ornate chair with Mephistopheles hovering at his shoulder like a vulture.

"Farewell, great Lucifer," Tom said, signaling their retreat with an upraised hand. He then got up and turned to his companion. "We twain shall be off as well. Come, Mephistopheles!" Linking arms, Hell's lieutenant and Faustus exited stage left, like mates off to a rugby match. The lights winked off, but for a second or two a murky red haze lingered around Faustus' chair instead of plunging the stage into the intended blackout. Claire put the script down and rubbed her eyes. No, the effect was gone. The house lights came up. She cut a quick look at Bayard standing in the wings beside her. Although he chewed the end of an index finger as he stared at the chair in Faustus' study, there was no other sign he might have seen anything amiss. But then he pulled out his cell phone and called someone. Claire listened intently as he talked to Ruben.

"So what was that just now?" Bayard turned and faced the lighting control booth nestled in a small balcony above the back row of seats. "Is that so? No, everything's fine." Bayard walked out onstage and stood beside the chair, seeming lost in thought. He didn't ponder long, though.

"All right, everyone. Gather round, please." He addressed this to the empty rows of seats in front of him, but his voice carried well enough that within a minute or two the entire cast and crew had gathered.

"Very well done," he said, sweeping his gaze over the assemblage. "The play is in brilliant shape, so we'll call it a night. Go home, get a good night's sleep. I needn't remind you full dress rehearsal is in two weeks. This is the first time the Mummers Theatrical Company has mounted a production of *The Tragical History of Doctor Faustus*, so donors and patrons will be attending the opening night performance, and I feel safe in saying they are in for an amazing evening of theater."

The guy playing Lucifer—Dave? Drew? Claire couldn't remember—initiated a brief round of applause, followed by laughter and heated chatter as the troupe dispersed. Bayard stayed onstage, conferring with Ruben. Claire would have paid good money to stay and eavesdrop, but that wasn't happening. She collected up her things, went to the back of the theater, and stood around by the double doors, waiting for Addie. There was that business of a promised tarot card reading and the building's so-called resident haunt she wanted to ask about. She also wanted to compliment Addie on her interpretation of Lechery, which was both campy and chilling, probably exactly what the great Marlowe'd had in mind. Being one of the Sins looked like it would be a fun part—you got all dressed up in an outrageous costume and only had one or two lines to learn. Claire had dallied with the notion of trying out for one of those parts, but was so certain she'd screw up the dozen or so words allotted to her, in the end she'd backed out of the audition. Still, it was fun to watch Addie vamp it up. She wondered if there was a subtle difference in meaning in Marlowe's use of the term Lechery, as opposed to Lust, the name moderns applied to that particular Sin. She'd have to ask Morris. Of anybody in the cast, he'd be the one most likely to know.

She'd also noticed Tom seemed a little stiff moving through some of the more active scenes. Maybe she ought to question him about it, although admittedly if she hadn't seen him on the ground yesterday, she'd never have guessed he'd been in a traffic accident.

She supposed the bike was in the shop and wondered how he'd gotten to rehearsal.

Addie was coming up the aisle with Tom in tow. He seemed to be moving okay from what she could see, but as they drew closer she could tell he was favoring his left side.

"...and I think this play is just the most exciting thing I've been involved in for ages—" Addie was gushing. Which she did better than anyone Claire knew. Tom had a pinched look around the eyes that Claire instantly recognized.

"You should have come with us to the hospital and at least gotten a pain prescription," she said, reaching out for his injured arm almost without thinking. He flinched away.

"It's just bruised."

Addie looked from one to the other. "What are you guys talking about?"

Claire bit her tongue. Maybe it wasn't her place to tell anyone about the accident since Tom hadn't shared that little piece of excitement with the cast.

"Dropped my bike in traffic yesterday," he said. "Claire came to my rescue." He gave her the briefest of smiles.

"Wow." Addie was bugeyed. "You're really lucky you weren't killed!"

There was an awkward silence in which the strangest expression passed over Tom's face. Like that illusion onstage tonight...Claire was sure she'd seen it, but when she blinked it was gone.

"So," Morris said, coming up behind her. "Who's up for a drink in honor of the brilliant Mummers' acting society?"

Addie grinned and raised her hand. "Me!"

He looked at Tom, who shrugged. "Why not?"

"And the lovely Miss Porter?" Morris cocked his head and rocked back on his heels, hands in the pockets of his wool blazer.

"Well..." There she was again, caught between duty and guilty pleasure. She felt like Faustus tempted by the Seven Deadlies, only this time there were just three of them. As far as she knew, she was the only one who lived at home with a parent and had a compelling reason not to stay out late. Addie was divorced from some guy in Boston, where they'd been patrons of the arts and attended a lot of galas and parties for ballet and drama until he'd cheated on her with a very young ballerina. Morris was a bachelor, but as to whether he had a significant other, who knew? And Tom? She had no idea what his story was, but he'd become more interesting with each rehearsal.

Addie looped her arm through Claire's. "She's in. Who's driving and where are we headed?"

"I've got a rental car…might as well use it," Tom offered.

"Driver picks the place," said Morris.

Tom wrestled the keys out of his jeans pocket. "I know a good biker bar not too far away."

Addie squeezed Claire's arm. "I'm definitely in."

Morris looked skeptical. "You're not serious."

Tom cracked a smile. "Nah. It's just a neighborhood pub with really good stout." Claire wanted to giggle—it was clear two could play at this dead-pan humor thing. Funny how fascinated she'd become over the dynamic between Tom and Morris, on and now off stage.

"Okay, I'll tag along." Once again, her mother would need to wait while she spent some time just for herself. She felt guilty as all hell, but had no willpower to turn her new friends down and go home.

* * * *

The pub, Doyle's Tavern, was exactly as Tom had described it—hidden away on a side street with roomy padded booths, dark-paneled walls, dim shaded lamps, and a heavy-duty wooden bar with beer on tap and a brass foot-rail that ran its entire length. The tables between the booth seats appeared to be made of lacquered, and much scarred, solid pine planks.

On the tableside menu, the food list offered fare such as seafood chowder, haddock smokies, lamb stew, and a cheese board with Irish and French cheeses served with bread sticks or cracked-wheat crackers. The special of the day was smoked ham, Stilton cheese, tomato, and onion piled on toasted pumpernickel bread. The beer side of the menu was arranged into stouts, ales, and lagers with names like Guinness, Murphy's, Beamish, Harp, and Smithwicke's. Claire felt as if she'd stepped through a time-tunnel leading straight into downtown Dublin.

Though a Saturday night, the pub was nearly empty, with just two older guys on stools at the bar and a couple of college students studying in a booth near the door. Tom steered his group to a big round booth at the back of the room.

"Wow, I had no idea this place was here." Addie was checking out the bartender topping up the mugs of the stool geezers. "How'd you find it?"

"Instinct, I think. I have a taste for imported stouts and porters." Tom lowered himself carefully into the booth and Claire followed. Addie slid in from the other side, followed by Morris.

The middle-aged pony-tailed bartender showed up and nodded at Tom as if to an old acquaintance. He then offered to explain the wide range of imported beverages to the rest of them. After much discussion, Addie chose something called Killian's Irish Red, which the bartender assured her was light and refreshing. Morris went for a Guinness pub draught from the bar, and Claire ended up choosing a bottle of Samuel Adams because it was the only name on the menu she recognized. Tom was asked if he wanted his usual, which turned out to be O'Hara's Irish Stout, a wicked pitch-black brew with a roasty, winelike aroma.

"Do you come here much?" Claire asked.

"Only enough for George to remember what I like." Tom leaned back against the padded backrest. Claire could almost see his trapezius muscles slowly unclinching.

"How's your motorcycle?"

Tom made a face. "Bent handle bar, kickstand broken off, bent back fender, blownout back tire. Fix all that and it's back on the road."

"You were really lucky," Addie said, licking her tongue around the lip of her beer bottle.

"So are we. Recasting that part twice would be royal pain in the ass." Morris didn't sound like he was trying to be amusing, but with him you never knew.

Addie jumped in. "That part was *made* for Tom. You wouldn't be able to recast it." She gave him a radiant smile, as if that ended the discussion.

Claire sipped at her beer and then remembered. "Morris, what's the difference between Lechery and Lust?"

His eyebrow went up. "Well, that's splitting hairs, isn't it? And why, Claire, would you want to know? Big plans coming up?" Addie laughed out loud.

Claire flushed. "No. I mean, in the play. Why does Marlowe use the name Lechery instead of Lust?"

Morris sighed. "You're just no fun, are you? If you must know, it's a subtle bit of wordplay on the part of the bard. Think about it. One encompasses the other, doesn't it? Lechery is the excessive indulgence in lust, which we can define as unfettered sexual activity. You—well, maybe not *you*—can lust for anything...power, knowledge, wealth. Lechery applies specifically to sexual lust, ergo..." He shrugged as if the answer should be obvious to the average knucklehead.

"Okay, but what I don't get is why everybody calls her Lust now, instead of Lechery."

Morris leaned toward her, elbows on the table. "You can thank those Protestant Reformation chaps for that. They used the word 'lust' in their sixteenth-century non-Latin translations of the Bible. Dumbing the Scriptures down for the masses. No offense to those religiously inclined."

Addie gulped at her Killian's. "Well, that's obviously nobody at this table. I'm Wiccan, Claire's a lapsed Episcopalian, Morris is a terminal atheist." She turned to Tom. "What about you?"

"Buddhist."

Morris snickered. "I do like your sense of humor."

"So is there really a ghost in the Janus Theatre?" Claire figured she might as well drop that bomb while she had the chance.

Maybe it was the beer. She wasn't used to drinking, but she'd nearly finished the bottle.

"Of course there is." Addie's bottle was empty, too. "Old buildings like that always have some kind of presence attached to them."

"Have any of you actually seen it?"

"No." Tom's answer was quick. The tone of his voice and his body language, arms folded over his chest, were hard to misjudge: nonbeliever. Claire wasn't surprised, even if he did make a convincing German necromancer.

"Not seen it, no," Addie said, "but I've felt it plenty of times."

"Felt how?" Claire didn't seem to be getting the right details from them. It also occurred to her they might be stringing her along.

"Like a cold breeze down your back," said Morris. "Or a noise, a screech maybe, just on the edge of hearing. Something you thought you heard, but when you paid attention to it, it's not there. Like quantum physics. You can only see those particles moving if you glance at them sideways. If you look directly, they freeze."

"So we have a quantum ghost."

Morris laughed and chugged the rest of his beer. "That's very good, Claire."

"But seriously. What's in the basement?" Silence settled around the table.

"Nothing but junk. I've been down there." Morris caught the bartender's attention and held up four fingers for another round.

Claire took a breath. "I think there's something fishy down there."

Morris leaned back. "Well, it doesn't have the most pleasant smell, that's for sure."

"I could do a reading on it." Everyone looked at Addie, who started digging around in her bag. "Got my cards with me." She pulled out a black mesh drawstring bag containing a well-worn deck of cards. "I don't mind doing a reading here. I like the vibe— it's benevolent. And we practically have the place to ourselves."

She was wiping moisture from the space in front of her with her napkin, feeling with the flat of her palm to be sure the surface was dry before placing the cards down on it. She shuffled the oversized deck three times and then held it face down in her left hand. The cards were black on the back, with a small silver pentagram in the center. "What's the first question?"

"Who's in the basement?"

"Oh Morris, you can't ask questions worded like that. It has to be something like, 'comment on the energy in the basement of the Janus Theatre'...something that doesn't require a specific name."

"Why don't we each pose a question?" Claire said. "Just go around the circle."

"Perfect. I'll pull four cards, one for each question." Addie was all smiles. "Claire, you go first." Addie put her right hand over the deck and closed her eyes.

Claire swallowed the last of her beer. "Comment on the energy down in the Janus basement."

Addie pulled one card off the top and placed it face up on the table. They all leaned in.

"Three of Wands."

"Is that good or bad?" Claire crooked her neck around, to get a better look at the image of three women, one young, one middle aged, and one silver haired, each holding a stick of wood with leaves growing from the end.

Addie moved the card to the left of the open space in front of her. "It generally means that the thoughts of the querent—that's us—have taken form and direction. It's the card for understanding, seeing one's way clearly."

Morris did not look impressed. "We could all use some of that. But the card didn't comment on the basement, it commented on the person asking the question. I guess the deck has a mind of its own, eh?"

The next round arrived and the bartender cleared away their empties.

Claire pulled a small note pad out of her purse and jotted down the first card info.

Addie laughed. "Looks like we have an official record keeper. Tom, you're next."

"Skip me."

"Then I'm next." Addie cut the deck, placed her right hand over it, and closed her eyes. "What is the nature of the presence we feel in the Janus Theatre?" She pulled a second card and placed it face up. "The Horned One."

They all stared at the new card. Two naked figures, a man and a woman, crouched in an attitude of flight before the towering muscular torso of a manlike creature with antlers and furred goat legs.

Morris squinted at the card. "Oh, I get it. That's the Wiccan version of the devil. More benign, I suppose."

"It's not the devil," said Addie. "Pagans don't believe in a 'devil.' This card represents the male aspect of deity, the counterpart of the earth mother."

"Cernunos," said Tom.

Addie shot him a look. "That's one name for it. Anyway, the card means empowerment, earth magick."

"Or the Devil, if you want a Christian interpretation," Morris added, "which would be appropriate, given the context of the theater and the play being rehearsed there."

"I like the pagan image better," said Claire. "You're next, Morris."

"Why does Claire want to know about the ghost in the basement?"

Claire flushed. "Hey, that's not fair. Addie isn't doing a personal reading."

Morris grinned at her. "Rephrase. What is Claire's connection to the entity haunting the Janus Theatre?"

Claire sulked. "That's not much better."

"Shhh." Addie held her hand over the cards. "They want to answer." She cut the deck and pulled a third card. They all leaned in again. On the card a young man in a red robe was placing four gleaming daggers into a square formation. "Four of Swords."

"Looks ominous," said Morris.

Addie was thoughtful. "Not necessarily. Swords usually indicate direct action or decision making. The number four is positive, which I would take to mean directing one's energy toward a constructive goal. It could also mean thinking things through before taking effective action."

"That sounds like Claire." Tom took a long pull at his second stout.

Addie nodded. "It does, doesn't it?"

Claire squirmed, self-conscious. "Well, sorry, I don't think being spontaneous is in my DNA. I'm methodical, always have been. Last question is yours." She turned to Tom, who'd slouched down in the booth.

He was silent, just looking at the cards. Claire wondered what was going through his mind.

At last, he sat up with an effort. "Assuming there's a presence in the Janus Theatre, what does it want?"

Addie cut the deck and pulled the final card. "The Tower." She pushed the card forward for all of them to see. The image depicted a round three-tiered tower with bright red and yellow light blasting out all its windows, the top cracking apart and falling, and its foundation stones crumbling.

"Destruction," said Morris.

"Massive change," corrected Addie. "Illumination or revelation. The truth comes to light, in a forceful way."

Claire's skin tingled, looking at the image of the exploding tower. "Comes to light how? Does it mean the ghost wants to do something physical, like destroy the theater?" She looked around the table. "Are we in danger just by being there?"

Addie made an exasperated noise. "Of course not. The picture on the card isn't meant to be taken literally. The interpretations are metaphorical, suggestive. It's just there to give you an impression of energy being released."

Morris held up the card for a better look. "That's some energy blast."

"Let me see." Tom reached out for the card.

Claire gulped at her second beer. "Now you guys are getting me spooked."

Addie swept up the cards and stowed them back in their mesh bag. "I think you're looking at this all wrong. My feeling is that we have an unhappy spirit that for whatever reason is unable to move on. We should all flood the place with white light and feelings of love and peace when we go there—reach out to the entity and help it let go of this earth plane and head to the light."

"What if we don't believe in the light? Should we suggest it go toward the dark?" Morris was in irony mode.

Addie sniffed. "Well, you can do what you like. I'm going to try to help the poor soul move on."

"Do you think Bayard knows he has an unhappy spirit haunting his building?" Claire was wondering how his "you harlot" remark squared with a poor unhappy spirit that needed help.

"I doubt it. He doesn't strike me as the spiritual type." Tom's expression was dour, but it might have been his post-accident aches and pains setting in. Claire had a half-empty bottle of Lortab in her medicine cabinet at home she could give him, if he'd take them. She made a note on her pad to bring them to the next rehearsal.

"I wonder if he'd have a cow if we did a cleansing ritual on the building, like with incense and smudge sticks." Addie was fishing for encouragement.

It was obvious to Claire, if not the rest of them, that Addie was already making plans to do that very thing, no matter what the consensus was. She wouldn't mind going along with it, just to see what happened. If it got her into the basement for a look around, so much the better.

Morris finished his beer and dabbed at the edge of his mouth with a napkin. "You're on your own, I'm afraid. This

Mephisto plans to keep his otherwordly interventions confined to the stage."

"Same here," said Tom, maneuvering his wallet out of his back pocket. "Much as I like sitting around here I need to get home and stretch out." Since he was driving, obviously they all had to leave.

Claire woke from the comfy alcohol daze she'd slipped into. "Absolutely. You should be in bed." She quickly got out of the booth and stood up, pulling on her jacket. Morris and Tom split the tab, refusing to let either of the women pay. Claire made no objection, and Addie gushed about chivalry not being dead and buried.

Wedged in the back seat of the tiny rental car with Addie, Claire felt a moment of panic as they approached the empty theater. All its lights were off, even the ones over the entrance. It looked like an empty shell. At least she'd managed to park out front this time — a rare bit of luck. Normally the parking slots along both sides of the road were filled all day and often past dark.

Tom stopped and kept the car idling as Morris unfolded his long legs and got out. He helped first Claire and then Adelaide maneuver out of the cramped back seat. They stood on the sidewalk together, his arms draped companionably around both women. Tom nodded to them and drove away.

"Must be hard on a cycle kind of guy to be stuck driving a four-cylinder minicar," Morris remarked. "I heard him mention an accident?"

"Yeah, he was nearly killed!"

Claire gave Addie a look. "It wasn't that bad. He got bruised up but nothing broken or damaged. The car that swerved to avoid hitting him lost control and turned over. That driver was lucky, too. Just a broken collarbone. We got her to the hospital in good shape."

"I don't know how you do the work you do," Addie said. "I have such a weak stomach when it comes to blood."

"Likewise. We stand in awe of you, Claire." Did he really mean that? Claire scanned his face under the streetlight. Hard to tell. She found her keys and headed toward her Honda.

"I guess I'll see you next week."

"Drive safely." Morris hunched his shoulders against the wind that picked up as they'd been talking. It had been a fairly mild winter so far, with December just a few days away. But there were warnings of an approaching cold front with temperatures in the teens and twenties. Claire shivered in her thin jacket. Maybe she would get to wear her wool overcoat this season after all.

She cranked the car and eased away from the curb, letting the few cars still on the street go by. In her rearview mirror, Adelaide and Morris stood on the sidewalk watching her drive away. This was the first time she'd done anything social with a group from the Mummers. They turned out to be people she'd gladly call friends, people she would consider investing time in beyond her theatrical connection with them. Even Tom, who was unforthcoming and somewhat taciturn. Thinking about them made that sinking feeling in the pit of her stomach ease up.

She didn't have many friends these days, which she knew was part of her problem. Most of her circle of pals from high school was gone, scattered across the country. Jackie came back, but she'd brought with her a girl friend, as in *serious* girl friend. They bought a small townhouse together in a newer housing development and Claire didn't see much of Jackie after that, except at rehearsals. Who else was there that she could call friend? There was Paul, whom she'd trust with her life, but he wasn't really the kind of person she'd go hang out with or confide her darkest fears to. Although maybe that wouldn't be a bad idea—he'd been through some genuine hell of his own in Kuwait and Iraq and somehow seemed to be coping with it.

Claire drove the remaining miles toward home in a kind of road amnesia, her thoughts drifting back through images of high school and earlier, times where small moments of significance stuck up above the cloudbank of a nondescript life. She turned off the main road into the old neighborhood where she'd lived all her life. A few newer houses were scattered among the Craftsman cottages and bungalows and brick ranch-style houses that had been there since the 1920s and 30s, but mostly it was an old neighborhood, drowsing in its decline, where memory lay thick along the tree-lined narrow streets. The weathered picket fence marking the small front yard of the house she'd grown up in came into view. Even in the headlights she could see how soot had stained the tall chimney and vines encrusted the brickwork arches over the front porch. The house needed some work, but there was no money for it.

Tendrils of that black creeping emptiness she associated with clinical depression, which she held at bay most of the time, crept into her thoughts and tightened the lump in her throat. Only then did she realize it had been completely absent for that cozy hour and a half she'd spent in the pub with Addie, Morris, and Tom. They'd taken her out of her usual routine and caused a shift in her psyche, somewhat the way Tom's takeover of Faustus had shifted the play into new territory. It was something to think about.

CHAPTER
7

Friday, a week later – after midnight

A cold wind blew across the tracks of the beltline near Piedmont Park. It was an undeveloped section, the rails long abandoned and overgrown, with trees and underbrush thick on one side and a steep bank sloping down to the park on the other. Bayard walked between the tracks, a shadowy form in black, barely visible to anyone who might have looked. But the woods and the long stretch of railroad tracks were empty.

He was hunting, as he'd done at least once every couple of months for the past…four centuries, give or take a decade. There was a homeless campsite below the Woodward Bridge. He'd hoped to find a tramp in the woods or on the tracks, passed out and sleeping it off, but no such luck tonight. Buckled to his belt was a 61-ounce stainless steel, wide-mouth thermos. It would hold nearly four pints, which was more than enough to placate her ladyship for a month or so. A zippered pocket of his jacket held the necessary blade.

He'd discovered a number of things during his tenure as owner of the *buachloch*. The most critical was the fact that like the stone, Dee's ensorcelled blade had a thirst. Not just for sacrificial blood, but for the soul as well, which meant merely draining a little from someone and leaving them to recover did not work. The blade had to take a life for the libation to be accepted by the *bain-sídhe.* Whether the witch Radha Ó Braonáin had any say in the blood sacrifice as well he didn't know—he supposed they'd worked out a coexistence of sorts over the centuries.

He'd also discovered that substitutions didn't work. A blood bag purloined from a local Red Cross office had no effect when he'd bathed the stone in its contents. It was as if he'd tried to flip on a light switch where there was no electricity. Once he'd even offered animal blood from a slain deer instead of a human, and the resulting sparks had burned the hair off the backs of his hands. Being an elemental, the banshee clearly had issues with him shedding the blood of wild creatures for his hell-spawned ritual. So he'd come to accept that only the intentional blood sacrifice of a human from Dee's blade could preserve his hold over the stone. When he let that task go too long, untoward things happened, like that fiasco with Danny. Getting rid of his body after the libation had been tedious and time-consuming, secret access to the landfill near Buckhead notwithstanding.

A low growl off to his left pulled him up short. He cast about and then saw it, there in the tangled underbrush of kudzu and poison ivy—a large stray dog with its teeth bared and its short rough coat bristled along its back. It crouched in indecision, drilling him with its eyes. Bayard looked into its animal brain and saw the territorial aggression, but more than anything else naked fear. It poured off the dog's body in waves that Bayard tasted on the air rather than saw with his non-human eyes. He supposed the beast saw him as a zombie of sorts, something alive, but somehow not. A suspended life, if one wanted a precise definition. But dogs knew nothing of defining. Its trembling haunch bunched to spring as its growl went deeper.

"I wouldn't if I were you," Bayard said, touching the feral brain with his mind.

Immediately the cur dropped its coiled charge and galloped off into the trees as if the hounds of Hell were at its heels.

Bayard sighed and turned around, heading back the way he'd come. Hunting here was a waste of time. There were other places he could try.

An hour later he found what he was seeking at the southbound entrance of the graffiti-riddled Krog Street Tunnel. A trio of painters, two boys and a girl, busied themselves with spray cans, covering someone's message and adding their own. From their explosive laughter and slurred voices he assumed they were drunk or high, which worked to his advantage. A shadow against darker shadows near the entrance, he watched and waited. The girl, probably a runaway if he was any judge, turned and puked painfully over the rail of the tunnel walkway onto the cracked pavement. Bayard inhaled the smell of vomit along with the familiar pungent stink of urine. He actually liked the old tunnel for its ugly industrial style—built in 1912 according to the date incised into its foundation stone, it ran for several hundred feet under a railroad with rows of squat, squared-off pillars, every inch of its dank cavelike walls covered in urban art. It drew the curious, the appreciative, and the unwary. It wasn't the first time he'd found prey here.

Their task done, the unsteady trio exited the tunnel and wove their way across the highway and down a narrow sidewalk canopied by a steep bank of overarching trees and underbrush. Bayard followed discreetly. It didn't take long for one of them to drop out, collapsed against the low retaining wall while the other two left their companion lying there. He waited long enough for the girl and still-vertical boy to get well out of sight around the next corner before pulling the comatose figure into a narrow footpath between an abandoned building and the wooded part of the block.

The teenaged boy mumbled and struggled fitfully as Bayard turned him onto his back and pulled his dirty sweatshirt away from his neck. Before he could properly come to his senses and scream out, Dee's knife had done its work and his red life's blood was pumping into the thermos. Bayard's knee planted firmly on the boy's sternum kept him from trying to sit up, and within moments the thin body went limp. Capping the thermos and clipping it to his belt, Bayard pulled the body into the tangle of brush and vines. Eventually it would be found, maybe even identified, but no trace of its silent attacker would ever be discovered. Her ladyship would see to that, concealment being part of her job description. If Bayard were somehow prevented from tending the stone, she would go unfed, so it behooved her to ensure he was able to carry out his part of the bargain. He often wondered what would become of her if indeed for some reason he ceased to attend to his duties. Would she stay trapped, powerless and shriveled, into eternity?

Once he'd dreamed that Death had come to her rescue, cracking open the stone, freeing his minion, and claiming the witch's soul. He'd startled awake in a sweat and lain as still as if the Janus were his tomb, listening and straining his heightened senses. It had only been a dream, but sleep had not returned that night nor for several afterward.

Bayard unlocked the back entrance to the theater, crossed the basement quickly, entered the lobby, and climbed the staircase to his private quarters. Once inside with the door locked and bolted, he removed several books from a shelf against the wall beside the tiled bathroom and pressed a hidden spot. The bookcase rolled inward a foot and then slid sideways behind the wall, revealing a tiny kitchenette. Bayard put the thermos on the shallow counter beside a stainless steel sink. He took an apple from a basket and consumed it in a few ravenous bites, then pulled a chunk of Stilton from the tiny efficiency fridge and wolfed that as well. Hunting made him hungry, but oddly, he'd gone vegetarian over the years. No red meat or poultry, very little fish. Dairy he could still stomach, but eggs he could not. He'd once eaten an entire basket of Comice pears after a foray into the night. Bayard took up the thermos and unscrewed the cap. The sickly sweet aroma rose from the lip of the container, but Bayard paid it little attention. Reaching into the cabinet over the sink, he brought out a different cap with a metal spout like a built-in drinking straw and screwed it onto the thermos. It had proved to have the perfect angle necessary for reaching the cornerstone in its present location.

He went to his desk in the main room of his quarters, retrieved his pipe, filled it, and set it alight. Then he sank into the high-backed chair and smoked the entire bowl in the mostly dark apartment, just listening to the building and its immediate surroundings. All was quiet, but tense, waiting. Bayard drew on the pipe. The bowl glowed red momentarily, and he blew the smoke out. It perfumed the close quarters with a smell that reminded him of another room, high-ceilinged, heavy-timbered, and chill, where he'd first been introduced to the pleasures of the pipe. Bayard enjoyed another languorous pull from the pipe, savored the taste and scent of the cherry-flavored tobacco. She knew he was coming down, but she could wait in Hell until he was good and ready.

He watched the bowl glow red and dark again. And then he remembered. What in the name of all unholy had he seen onstage in that scene between Faustus and Lucifer? Ruben swore it was nothing he'd done, although he liked the idea and asked if he could try to recreate the illusion for the show. Bayard demurred—that had been no illusion. Had Tom been aware of anything *outré* during that moment when he'd uttered Faustus's lines and exited with Morris? His sharpened senses now scanned the stage area of the theater downstairs, but it was cold and empty.

He sat and smoked and when his pipe was done, he knocked out the ashes and fetched the thermos. It was time. He headed downstairs in the dark, unlocked the door to the basement, and snapped on the staircase light in case any lurking rats might want to be warned beforehand. His footfalls clumped down the narrow steps till he reached the black and white tiled floor. Bayard gathered his focus and sat down facing the alcove under the stairs.

CHAPTER
8

Friday, same night—1:30 A.M.

"I'm gonna go tally up the receipts and reconcile the register, can you lock up out front?" Nanette, owner of The Rookery and purveyor of all things used and esoteric in the book buying world, tossed Tom the keys, which he caught one-handed.

"No prob—I'm on it."

"Thanks. Sorry to keep you so late, what with your accident and all. But we have to stay open later during the holidays and you're the one I trust the most..."

Tom sorted through the keys on the master ring, looking for the one he recognized as the front door key. "I don't mind. Nowhere else I need to be." At nearly 1:30 in the A.M., that was true enough.

Nanette winked one kohl-ringed eye at him. "You're a love." Her flirtation with him was harmless—she was longtime married to the bookstore's co-owner, a man her age who also ran a successful personal business as a practicing stage magician, which might explain the store's extensive tarot card section. He wondered idly if Adelaide's deck had come from here. The cultivation of a sultry mystique was part of Nanette's persona and added to the bookstore's atmosphere. He watched her straight bottle-black hair sway across the butt of her skin-tight leather pants as she made her way with the money pouch through the crowded stacks to the back room. She wasn't his type, being too brassy and painted-woman extrovertish, so any flirtations returned on his part were mere courtesy and of no consequence.

Since coming to Atlanta, he'd not allowed himself any entanglements, emotional or otherwise, except for his involvement with the Mummers. Instinct, again, had led him there and he did not question the rightness of his being accepted into their little congregation, as he thought of them. Bayard played Pope to his acolytes, who hung on his words and worshipped his brilliance, or so it seemed to Tom. But that assessment of Kit Bayard was for himself and no one else.

Tom went to the front door, pulling the doorknob tight. He was fitting the key to the lock when a tremor went through his hands as if it were coming from the door frame or the floorboards under his feet. His body tensed and muscle memory telegraphed the sensation to his brain—earthquake. Which was ridiculous because as far as he knew, the great state of Georgia was not an earthquake zone. That being said, he'd lived in Greece where quakes large and small occurred too often, and his body remembered. He held the doorknob and felt the tremor subside. What. The. Fuck. Tom locked the door and turned off the lights in the store front.

He stuck his head in Nanette's office. "Did you feel that?"

"Hm?" She pulled her attention out of numbers and sales figures. "Like...what?"

"Like a rumble, in the building."

"Oh, sort of…I thought it was a big truck going by or something."

Tom stood for a moment, unsure, replaying the sensation and not coming up with answers.

"Everything all right?" Nanette was looking at him funny.

"No, I mean, yeah. No problem, everything's fine. Front is secure." He came in and handed her the keys.

She took them and regarded him from under iridescent-shadowed lids. "I know you have a lot on your mind, nearly getting killed in traffic and having to put your baby in the shop. Go home and go to bed."

Good advice. He'd heard it from someone else recently, too.

"Thanks, I will." He slipped out the back door and into the employee parking lot behind the bookstore. It was dark as pitch. No moon, faint stars. Letting his eyes adjust before walking across the lot, he allowed himself a moment of dismay at the sight of the tin can rental car squatting in his parking place. The only thing it had going for it over his Harley was it was warmer. But not by much.

He was about to get in when he felt the tremor again, a faint shaking under his feet as if the solid earth had suddenly gone fluid. Automatically he started counting the seconds…one-one hundred, two-one hundred, three-one hundred…the tremor stopped. Definitely not his imagination. He got in the car and sat in the dark for a few minutes, waiting to see if it would happen again. When it didn't, he started the engine and eased out of the parking lot.

He drove slowly most of the way home, and passed few cars on the highway. Everything seemed normal. Tom's mouth settled into a tight, thin line. Normal his ass. A cast member inexplicably injured in rehearsal, the new back tire of his bike blowing out for no reason he could find, red mist onstage that the lighting guy hadn't programmed, that stupid tarot card reading forecasting destruction and exploding towers, and now earthquakes where to his knowledge there had never been any. No, things were not the hell normal.

The street where he'd rented a one-room studio apartment over a garage was completely dark this early in the morning, even though its neighborhood edged up against the Georgia Tech campus. Normally you could hear the typical background noise that afflicted most student housing blocks—loud music, parties, groups of people standing around on sidewalks, and continual sounds of cars coming and going. But tonight, all was dark and quiet. The garage was a freestanding wooden car barn set somewhat behind the main two-storey house to which it belonged. He parked the rental car in one of the bays under the apartment and climbed the outside wooden stairs up to his room.

Although billed in the real estate ad as "spacious studio housing near campus," it was in reality one largish sparsely furnished room with an adjoining smaller room the size of a closet containing a tiny shower stall, sink, and toilet that could have fit comfortably into a mobile home. There was a clothes rack against one wall for hanging things like suits and coats (which he didn't own) and an old, scarred chest of drawers for everything else. Built-in cabinets above a six-foot kitchen counter on the eastern-facing wall were designed for glassware he also didn't own. The counter contained a sink and a small apartment fridge under it, but no stove. He'd bought a second-hand microwave at a yard sale, which so far served his needs adequately. He ate a lot of ramen-in-a-cup.

The view of the green tops of oaks and elms from the eastern window over the sink was pleasing enough to make up for any missing amenities. Tom was accustomed to living frugally, and when he was on the move, he carried his worldly belongings in a bedroll strapped to his bike. In the far corner, a queen-sized mattress and box spring took up a large chunk of the floor space. A card table with a folding chair against the opposite wall served as a desk. His backpack and bedroll were stashed underneath.

He pulled a Guinness from the fridge, kicked off his boots, and stretched out on the bed with the pillows bunched up behind him, determined to find out if anyone else had felt the tremors. He didn't have a computer or television, but he'd recently acquired a smartphone as his means for staying connected to the outside world. He powered it on and thumbed through his Internet apps for local news. He didn't really think he would see any mention of earthquakes and got exactly what he expected. Nothing in his email, either. He took a long gulp from the Guinness and set the bottle on the floor beside the mattress. In the local forums where he was a lurking presence, he also found nothing, except one lone topic posted about an hour ago.

Hotlanta trembler – u feel it?

Pulse pounding, Tom clicked on the link and read a brief but astonishing exchange between two forum members.

yeh thought it was an explosion

i werk at Allnite Pizza. glasses shook n everthin

awesome where r u

N Highland got 2 fotos

Where on North Highland? He clicked on the image icon and a grainy photo filled the tiny screen in his hand. A deep crack ran all the way across the street. He clicked and saved the image. There was a second photo, taken less close up so part of the sidewalk and the buildings beyond were visible. Tom caught his breath—clearly discernible in the background was the façade of the Janus Theatre.

CHAPTER
9

Friday, same night — 1:30 A.M.

"Ecce signum."
Acknowledged.
"As master of the *buachloch*, I bid thee attend me."
We are here. We have been waiting.

Bayard tipped the thermos just enough for a thin red line to trickle over the spiral sun signs cut into the stone a thousand years ago. The blood sank into the rock and was consumed at once, leaving no trace.

A young one, by the taste. The soul is both bitter and sweet. Give us the rest.

"All in good time." Bayard let another trickle wet the top of the stone. "I have questions." That didn't begin to describe what was in his mind at that moment. He had much more than questions — call them misgivings, forebodings, suspicions, apprehensions. Things were not right and he wanted to know why.

We might answer. The voice was nectar-sweet laced with the prickle of venom. *What could we offer that the great Christopher Marlowe, acclaimed playwright and master spy, does not already know?*

"Why did the blade seek prey of its own choosing, without my knowledge or agreement?" He tried to keep the anger out of his voice, but wasn't sure he succeeded.

The basement was utterly still, the tiles on which he lay cold as a glacier. Seconds turned to minutes...it was as if the stone had gone dead. Bayard allowed a thicker stream from the thermos to coat the surface.

"Was my question not stated clearly enough?" He might have the patience of that fool Job, but it would do him no good if the banshee refused to cooperate. She was bound to serve the master of the stone, to suspend his death and preserve his life, but she did not have to make it easy.

Aye, we heard thee. Silence followed.

She was becoming more recalcitrant lately, and that was the main query that he needed resolved. When she was in this mood, he would have to cajole, and if that failed, threaten. He bathed the stone again.

"I was told by the previous master of the *buachloch,* the great magister John Dee, that if I desired, I could speak with shades whose souls have been claimed by the lord of the underworld...is this indeed true?"

Screechy laughter filled the basement cavern and ricocheted off its hard planes and surfaces.

Who would ye wish to bespeak, yer worship? Great Lucifer himself? Or perhaps a lesser demon who will most certainly attempt to deceive ye.

Bayard waited for the laughter to subside. "I would bid Doctor John Dee himself appear before me." A long silence ensued as he lay unmoving, head under the stairs, right arm angled in to reach the stone with the thermos spout. A faint scent of smoke came to his nostrils. Was she going to burn the building down around his ears? Not likely. Who else would she get to bring her offerings of blood and souls?

He poured the remainder of the thermos over the stone. "I command the *bain-sídhe* to bring me the shade of John Dee!"

Smoke filled his eyes and lungs and he jerked back, banging his head on the stair risers. Before he could even utter the most choice sixteenth-century oath he could remember, a loud crack shook the basement and popped his eardrums. On his hands and knees, Bayard stared into the gloom and then caught his breath. Stretching full across the basement floor, from one end to the other, was a foot-wide crack.

He scrambled to his feet, ignoring the painful bump swelling at the back of his skull. Smoke burned his eyes and coated his tongue. He coughed violently, as the building trembled around him. He half expected to see the cliché of fire and brimstone wafting up from the crack, but that wasn't happening. Instead, the actual air in front of him split. Bayard rubbed his hand over his eyes, but the image held. A vertical line nearly as tall as the ceiling formed and hung right in front of him. Slowly it widened as if the fabric of reality that was the Janus Theater on a city street in a southern metropolis were slowly being ripped apart. Bayard began to shake—into the rift he saw only void, flat black with no light or shadow…only the soul-freezing cold of empty space.

But within the gradually widening rip in his universe, something was coalescing, a vague form materializing at the center of the gap. A man-shaped figure.

A second deafening boom shook the building. The support pylons groaned and debris fell from the ceiling—Bayard feared for a moment the theater might come down on top of him. The rift in space-time had disappeared, but a tall, bearded man stood where it had been. A tight black skullcap covered his head from his hairline down to the nape of his neck. His beard and mustache were white with streaks of gray, the manicured beard reaching halfway down his chest and tapering to a point. His heavy black scholar's robes were cut in the style of a Cambridge don. Staring down the length of a long straight nose, his dark eyes raked the face of his summoner.

"Fie!" Bayard's voice was a croak. His vocal cords had forgotten how to function.

"I am come, as I was bidden." The voice sent icicles forming along the rafters.

Bayard took a step forward. "Is it really you?" The specter looked for all the world like the scholar and alchemist who'd somehow duped him into trading his immortal soul for the promise of suspended death. But he knew well that the minions of Hades were devious, and perhaps this was not the person he sought at all.

Shivering like a plague victim, Bayard faced his unwelcome patron. "D-do you remember me?"

"I ne'er thought to return to this realm," said the icy voice. "What wouldst thou of me, sweet Marlowe, that I am untimely plucked out of oblivion?"

Bayard's throat constricted. It *was* the man he knew, no doubt. How to voice his apprehensions without making it sound as if he'd lost all control over the banshee? In a flush of anger he'd bent her to his will, but hadn't thought out how to articulate his queries if she could actually bring Dee to him. He'd seen unfathomable things since he'd given up his mortality, but some small corner of his once-human mind chattered in terror at this apparition from beyond the grave.

The sepulchral voice continued. "By human reckoning, 'tis been nigh on four-hundred twenty years since we two met. The fact of thy continued life should be evidence enough that what I promised thee has come to pass. The Black Coach has not come for thee, yet thy visage is of a man of thirty."

"Twenty-five." Bayard found his voice. "Let's be accurate."

Stalactites of ice reached down from the ceiling as the specter responded. "Death's Herald remains ensorcelled within the *buachloch*. Thou art still the master. What is thy question?"

Try as he might, Bayard could not stop his tongue from stammering. "Something is d-different...t-things are not right. Your knife—"

"This?" Dee held out his left hand and the pearl-handled athame appeared. "What of't? I did give it into thy care for safekeeping. Wherefore question its power?"

"To...to what end did it choose a victim without me?"

"Mayhap it hears the mistress's voice more clearly than thine."

Bayard flushed. "I hear her right well enough! Always there if I listen, always demanding. You never warned me it would be like this!" He felt an angry tirade building and clapped his jaws shut.

The knife vanished from Dee's outstretched palm, and Bayard felt its weight in his trousers pocket. He tried again. "Something isn't right. She fights me, and..." He dreaded to say what was really in his mind. "There are omens. Signs...of something I don't understand. Has your master changed his mind regarding our bargain?"

The cold voice frosted the stair rail. "Thou'rt bound fast to thy fate."

Fury bubbled over. "I saw the red mist onstage—what was *that* supposed to mean? Just paying a friendly visit, to see if the play represents your lord's interests to his liking?"

"I ken naught of that."

"How can you not know?" Bayard was feeling beyond exasperated at this verbal fencing. "Don't demons and spirits know everything that happens on the earth plane, once they cross over?"

The floor of the basement became an ice sheet. "Thou'rt a fool, if that is what ye believe."

"Tell me the truth." Bayard's voice shook with fury. "Can she force me to turn control of the stone over to another? Because that's what I think is going on here. There's a plan being hatched behind my back, isn't there? Mutiny? Maybe she's looking for a new master, but you promised me the stone would be mine until I myself chose to give it up. I command you to tell me!"

Silence fell like a pall over the basement. Then, "Death's Herald is not the only presence within the *buachloch*. Thou'rt a clever wag—think on't for thy answer."

For a split second, Bayard felt the airless vacuum of empty space, cold beyond measure, and despair so achingly pure he would have slit his own throat with Dee's knife if he could have moved his limbs. Then he gasped in air and fell forward, hands touching the gaping crack across the floor. The shade of his tormentor was gone.

What the hell, the bastard had just told him to figure it out for himself? Bayard was beyond fury. He scrambled back down on his belly and put his hands on the stone.

"Radha Ó Braonáin. Attend me!" He was also beyond cajoling. As master of the cornerstone, he was taking charge and demanding a proper response.

This time, instead of the dead silver eyes his mind always saw when he touched the stone, a woman's face of indeterminate age framed in iron gray hair wild as a storm over the heather took hold of his imagination. He'd not seen that face since the day he'd claimed the stone as its new master. He'd shed blood and smeared the stone with it while Dee spoke the words of power, sealing the transfer of ownership. The banshee had appeared immediately when summoned, a horrific presence swaddled in gray shrouds that billowed in an unseen wind. Behind her lurked another, a human figure, a woman. He'd had no interaction with the latter during the claiming ritual, but Dee had identified her for him.

"What are you scheming?" Bayard demanded, stretched out on the cold tiles of the Janus basement.

"Master Marlowe." Her low voice was a counterpoint to the faint background scree of the banshee. "Well met, indeed." Her laugh was guttural, all tricksy and not to be trusted, which he absolutely did not.

"I command you to reveal to me what is in your heart and mind."

Her voice dropped to a near whisper. "I am yer obedient servant, so I am."

In his mind's eye, the witch reached out to him, drawing him into her skinny arms and pressing him with an iron grip against her boney breast. As she held him, she began to squeeze tighter, to the point of discomfort. His body lay on the floor, but he felt every pressure point of her deadly embrace, pulling him ever tighter. And then it wasn't just her arms wrapped around him—an aura of malice enveloped them both, pressing against him from all sides. His bones began to crack as pain wracked his body, both on the floor and in the illusion playing out in his mind. She cackled and wrapped him in her hatred, slowly and deliberately crushing every bone in his body.

"I cannot slay thee," she whispered, almost below hearing, "but I can indeed shew thee what is in my heart."

Blood leaked from the eyes and ears and mouth of the body on the floor. Bayard screamed into the void. At last she released her hold and withdrew, sinking back into the stone. His mind was blank with pain, barely able to process the fact that his ribcage was crushed against his spine, his arms and legs pulverized to shards, his neck broken...not as a dream or hallucination, but real time, in his flesh and blood body.

He stared at the stone in white-hot agony, feeling his bones slowing finding their way back together, knitting with excruciating, glacial slowness, relentlessly mending the damage done. He saw the corpselike face of the banshee with its fish-silver eyes watching him writhe.

"I remind you," he gasped, choking on the blood in his esophagus, "that you ...must...conceal evidence of our little party..." His vision was tunneling, his consciousness shutting down.

At that moment thunder boomed outside, and a downpour like to the original Deluge drowned out all else. Before he passed out completely, Bayard had a brief mental image of the street outside the theater. Torrents of rain obscured a gigantic crack in the pavement that was gradually repairing itself.

CHAPTER
10

Saturday, dawn

Pain is relative, isolatable. If one focused on a single small point, the rest retreated into the background—not gone, but reduced to a low-level drone in a symphony of shrieks. Bayard embraced this observation first-hand as he lay on his bed, concentrating all his awareness on his left arm, feeling muscles and tendons repairing around knitting bones. If he paid total attention to the returning mobility in those particular fingers and that specific wrist, he could ignore the greater misery going on in the rest of his body.

The reversion process was well along by now, which was why he was lying on his back in his upstairs quarters instead of crumpled face down on the basement floor. The long bones had fused first, allowing him to drag himself up both sets of stairs—a teeth-gritting ordeal, but once he'd collapsed onto the bed and stretched out flat, the rest of his body had realigned itself so the repair job could go swiftly. Nothing he could do but wait for it to finish, which gave him plenty of time to think.

With more than four hundred years to refine his technique, he'd learned what it took to control the banshee. An uneasy truce had existed between them for centuries: he provided her with the required libation and she preserved his life, and helped him prosper when he was able to situate the *buachloch* under the foundation of a theater. He'd never directly confronted the other one, the Irish sorceress, and so had mostly forgotten about her. But this night's disaster brought home to him how vastly he'd underestimated what powers she might be mistress of. It simply never occurred to him she would be a threat to his safety. And that, ultimately, was the problem. As master of the stone, he'd expected her to obey him when called, but instead she'd attacked him. She couldn't kill him, of course, but perhaps, unlike the banshee, she wasn't spellbound to protect his life. He wasn't surprised that she'd harbor malice toward anyone who controlled the *buachloch*, being trapped in it. Bayard wasn't clear on whether turning her spellcraft against her had been an accident or a sly deceit on the part of one or both of the other parties involved in the entrapment. He'd assumed witch and banshee alike required the periodic sacrifice, maybe even shared it somehow, but now he thought probably not. Would it matter to her if he were dead and there was no one to continue the ritual? And why now, after centuries, had she come into the foreground and confronted him? He replayed Dee's warning in his mind — *Death's Herald is not the only presence within the buachloch.* Indeed.

Bayard lay in the dark and pondered these things. Gradually the pain in his body began to fade and at last he sat up, shaken, but whole. He stripped off his bloody clothes and went unsteadily to the white-tiled bathroom. He got in the shower and turned on the water as hot as he could stand, scrubbing crusted blood from his face and hands. Eventually he felt clean, but even then he lingered under the shower head, letting hot water pelt his face and chest, standing once again hale and hearty in his twenty-five-year-old body.

Wrapping himself in a floor-length bathrobe, Bayard returned to bed just as pallid, rainsoaked daylight was beginning to frame the windows facing the city street.

Exhausted, he lay back on the pillows and closed his eyes. His soul felt ancient, desiccated. He was like an insect sucked dry by a small, innocuous-seeming spider wielding a deadly poison. After this night's demonstration, it was clear he'd need to approach the stone with utmost caution. Although he'd survived the witch's onslaught, the damage done to his etheric body was soul-deep, abrasive and less quick to repair. Even the idea of dealing with the day's plans and evening rehearsal was more than he could stomach. He reached for his cell phone on a bookshelf beside the bed and thumbed Morris's number from memory.

When Morris answered, Bayard didn't bother to identify himself. "I require a favor."

Morris responded after a few seconds' silence. "Why? Should I be concerned?" His tone was dry, possibly ironic, definitely aloof. Bayard allowed himself a smile. Morris didn't disappoint.

"Let's just say I find myself indisposed. Tonight's rehearsal is canceled. Can I rely on you to pass the word?"

"I can make an effort. You're serious, aren't you? Are you ill?"

"Nothing a day's rest won't cure."

"Should I come check on you?"

"No. Call Adelaide, she can contact everyone else. She has the master phone list."

"And yet you called me first. I'm flattered."

"Don't be a prick. Just do this for me and consider yourself owed in kind."

"Oh, I will." Morris' voice was desert dry.

Bayard punched END and put the phone down. Biggest mistake he'd made in his recent human interactions had been his one-night stand with Morris. They'd both realized it was a mistake and agreed without speaking to carry it no further. It was just that the man had reminded him of someone else, too many years ago: the tall, sharp-faced son of spymaster Walsingham. He'd been part of a threesome with a young woman as beautiful as a sea nymph. Ah, well...an old man's folly that wouldn't be repeated. He wondered what Morris would think if he knew the truth.

Bayard rolled carefully onto his side and half slept for another hour or so, listening to the deluge coming down outside, until morning began to spill through the rain-streaked windows. He got up, stretched carefully, and was relieved to find everything in place and apparently in working order. He went into the bathroom to relieve himself and stopped short.

His face in the mirror over the sink revealed something that hadn't been there before last night. His ginger hair, especially that of his goatee, was streaked with white.

CHAPTER
11

Saturday morning

It was raining like hell. Had been since the wee hours of the morning and showed no sign of letting up. Well, maybe not like hell. If the production of *Doctor Faustus* was any standard to go by, traditional Hell was all fire and burning, not curtains of water. Standing at the kitchen window, watching it come down in sheets off the steep edge of the roof and pound onto the backyard patio, Claire wondered where a stupid expression like that had started anyway.

Exhausted from a long shift yesterday that had been non-stop—they'd barely had time to clean and restock the ambulance between calls—she'd fallen asleep as soon as her head hit the pillow, but hadn't slept well, and was jerked awake some time after midnight by a sharp, sudden thunderclap and sensation of falling. Heart thudding, she lay awake listening to rain pummeling the roof. Finally, she had let the noise lull her back to sleep where troubled dreams of windswept moors and galloping horses outrunning a thunderstorm left her tired and yawning when she got up the next day.

And here it was almost noon, but still the rain came down. Most people would be pissed to be stuck inside on their day off, but she didn't mind. Her shift varied with the weeks, and this was the first time she'd had Saturday free in months. Dressed in an oversized faded navy sweatshirt and baggy sweat pants, her hair pulled back in a quick messy braid, Claire was ready to be holed up for the day. With outside temps hovering around 39, it wasn't quite cold enough to snow, but it was a chilled miserable day that nobody wanted to be out in. She was more than grateful that today's rehearsal had been called off. Apparently Bayard was under the weather. He'd called Morris who'd called Addie who'd called everyone else, so their next rehearsal would be toward the end of the coming week. Just as well. Everyone knew their lines, and the production itself was pretty smooth in terms of costumes and lighting. They could actually go live with the play today if they had to. Happily that wasn't on the agenda.

She watched the rain and waited for the tea kettle to whistle. The idea to bake some biscuits or cookies crossed her mind, but that would involve more work than she was willing to get sucked into. It would help heat the house, but she could just as easily turn up the thermostat. Either way would add to the utility bill. The kettle shrilled and she turned off the burner. Looking through the basket of tea bags on the counter, she pulled out raspberry and green with lemon. Then she went around the long granite counter, through the small dining area, and into the main room of the house.

The living room was warm, and her mother dozed wrapped in a comforter on the loveseat in front of the small fireplace. The remodeling job done on the house over a decade ago had installed central heat and air (and the granite countertop), but they'd kept the working fireplace for its cozy factor. Below a narrow oak mantel, it had a wide squarish brick façade that made the entire room toasty when a fire was blazing in the grate. Her dad used to buy logs for it, but now Claire made rolled-up paper logs from a stack of newspapers and brown grocery bags that had been collecting for months on a spare dining room chair. Maybe they weren't as aesthetically pleasing, but they got the job done. She'd planned to scour the tree-shaded back yard for fallen twigs and small branches to use as kindling, but that was out of the question today.

She touched her mother's shoulder. "Mom? You want some tea?"

Her mother stirred and smiled. "That would be nice."

"What flavor?"

"Raspberry."

"Coming up."

Claire padded in her stocking feet back to the kitchen. It was these small things that put them in synch and made Claire's chest ache. She loved her mother so much at times like this, it was painful to think about how it was going to be when the respirator failed to be enough. When that inevitable death came, Claire would be alone. Completely. Well, there was an aunt across the country and a cousin whose name she didn't remember, so technically that wasn't true. And the neighborhood was full of families she'd grown up with, people who considered her as much one of their kids as their own. Jackie's mom had always treated Claire as a second daughter, and she'd spent more nights than she could count at their house, curled next to her playmate in Jackie's single bed. But that particular train of thought—death and the relentless passage of time—led down into the black hole of despair she fought to avoid by doing external things like joining a theater company and going to pubs with friends. The abyss retreated as she carried the mug of tea in one hand and a TV tray table in the other out to the living room.

She set the table up in front of her mother, careful not to get the oxygen generator line tangled in its spindly legs.

"Sugar, or maybe some honey?"

Her mother shook her head and took a few sips from the cup. "This is fine."

Claire went back for her own cup and then curled up on her side of the couch, feet underneath her. They sat together without speaking, just listening to the rain and watching the fire burn down. Finally, Claire got up and pushed the coals around with a poker, bringing the flames back to life. She put on a few more paper logs, which caught and blazed up.

"Your rehearsal got cancelled?"

"Yeah, Addie said Bayard was sick or something. That's pretty rare—the man's never missed a single rehearsal in all the time I've been in the company."

"I wish I could see the show. It sounds exciting." Her mother sighed and readjusted the comforter around her feet. They'd never carpeted over the original hardwood floors, which helped retain the value of the house but meant the floors were cool underfoot during the winter.

"It'll be videotaped. I'll bring you a copy and we can watch it together."

Her mother smiled and nodded. Claire had gotten so used to these limited responses that it was easy to forget how voluble and talkative the mother of her childhood had been—a sociable woman so opinionated and eager to discuss or argue any point that got tossed into the conversation that she usually dominated the exchange.

"Could you..." Claire waited while her mother gathered enough breath to say what she wanted. "...get my sweater?"

Claire supposed that, no longer having the breath to adequately express what she thought, her mother's mind must work overtime. In a way, emphysema seemed a karmic joke of some kind for a person who'd expended so much breath explaining what she thought, and what she thought others should think.

She got up and went to her mother's bedroom and retrieved a well-worn gray cardigan from the bed. Helping her mother sit up straighter, she slipped the old sweater in place, making sure it hadn't bunched up in back where it would make an uncomfortable lump.

"Better?"

Her mother nodded. She looked small and folded in on herself, partially wrapped in the coverlet, with the sweater draped around her stooped shoulders. Hard to remember how she'd looked when Claire was in grade school. Gwen Porter had delivered her only child at the late age of forty-one, early middle-age by some standards, but Claire's memory produced the image of a slender, elegant woman with dark bobbed hair and large luminous eyes.

She settled back in her spot at the end of the couch, wondering if she really ought to turn up the thermostat. She felt guilty for keeping the house at bit cooler than she'd like, just to save a few pennies on the heating bill. Her mother looked cold. Not the level of comfort Claire knew her mother had grown up in. Gwen's family had been wealthy, her father an investment banker, but he'd lost a bundle somehow; Claire wasn't sure of the details. Gwen had gone to college and married late, far beneath her station to Jimmie Porter, a young insurance salesman. He was a friend of her brother and came around the Porter household a lot because, according to Gwen, they'd instantly hit it off. Once married, they'd struggled financially, trying to make it on their own. Gwen's family helped them occasionally in the early days of the marriage, but as the family became increasingly impoverished themselves, those infusions of cash came less often and finally stopped. Claire had a picture in her mind of Gwen going from living a privileged childhood to a barely lower-middle class married life. Her mother's brother, Jimmie's pal, died in his fifties of lung cancer as had their father, a weakness of the lungs apparently running in that side of family. Claire assumed it had skipped her because she was tall and sturdy, with a strong constitution—her problems were mostly mental.

Her mother coughed slightly, then started to choke. Claire was on her feet in an instant. Her trained hands went to work, massaging the middle of her mother's back between the shoulder blades.

"Just lean forward." One hand on the shoulder, the other on the back, as much for comfort as for therapy. Gradually her mother relaxed and the coughing spasm passed.

Claire remembered being told that her mother had started smoking at a very early age, which, her doctors informed everyone, was the reason she'd developed emphysema. The wasting disease in Gwen's lungs had really taken hold when Claire started middle school, and by the time she entered high school her mother had become an invalid. Now, at age 66, Gwen had marginal lung function left, requiring her to stay tethered to the portable oxygen generator that hissed softly to itself, artificially sustaining its patient in the land of the living. These days she spent most of her time reading and dozing, dependent on the gray box the size of a small ice chest. There would come a time, though, when the collapse of lung tissue and inability to expel oxygen would take its toll and the patient would suffocate, or end up with a breathing tube down her throat. Dread settled around Claire's shoulders—not a way anyone would choose to make their exit. There were times when her black mood was on her that she wished she could help nature along. Then she'd feel guilty for having even entertained such a thought.

"Whatever happened…to the one who got hurt?"

It took Claire a second or two to figure out what she was talking about. "You mean Danny?"

Her mother nodded. "Sounded like you should have treated him."

"Yeah, I know. But Bayard wouldn't let me. He didn't seem to think it was that bad. Then the next day he told everybody that Danny had decided to quit the play *and* the company."

"And his replacement is better?" Gwen sipped the last of her tea.

"Yeah, by light years. I wouldn't have thought changing one character would make such a difference, but in this case it really has." Claire thought about it. The play had momentum, excitement because of Tom's presence onstage. He'd managed to push Morris to a higher level as well, and the two of them sparred as Faustus and Mephistopheles in a way that made the play come alive. She'd never seen the play as anything other than running lines and marking stage positions while Danny had been Faustus. But now it had become a real story, the tragic plight of the worldly scholar risking his immortal soul for fame and fortune—a story of greed and regret as gripping as any soap opera. And in that moment, she decided to give Danny a call.

Claire got up. "Mom, I need to go call about the rehearsal schedule. I'll use the phone in Daddy's office so it won't bother you. Want me to heat your tea while I'm up?"

Gwen shook her head. "Go talk. I'm fine." She bunched the sweater up under her neck and closed her eyes.

"I'll leave the door open...call me if you need anything."

Claire headed down the hallway toward the tiny back bedroom that had served as her father's home office. Its single window looked out over the fenced-in back yard. A large business style desk took up most of the floor space, with a couple of gray metal filing cabinets pushed into corners.

Jimmie Porter had a real office downtown in the suite maintained by the insurance firm that employed him, but a lot of the time he'd worked from home to be near his ailing wife. Claire was touched when she thought about it. Hard as their lives may have been, Gwen and Jimmie Porter never ceased to care for each other, at least as far as Claire could tell. Their cozy little bungalow on the narrow residential street in their southside neighborhood of old friends encompassed a world they'd built for themselves that had little to do with the brief socialite life her mother had led in college. When they'd gone looking for a house, for Jimmie it had been love at first sight over the small Craftsman with its arched doorways, neat brick fireplace, and pecan floors. Claire remembered going with her parents to see the house when it was on the market and walking though the unfurnished rooms, hanging onto her father's hand. She'd been four, or maybe five…preschool, anyway. What she'd liked most was the fenced back yard with its big trees, one of which had a tire swing.

Whatever Gwen may have thought of it, given the house she'd grown up in, she'd never challenged Jimmie on his decision to buy the bungalow, at least within Claire's hearing. Her mother had plenty of opinions about how to furnish the house and insisted on putting a small birdbath fountain in the front yard "to dress it up," but once they'd moved out of the tiny upstairs apartment of which Claire had only shadowy memories, the family settled in with no complaints. Claire had her own bedroom, so what wasn't to love? Their first year in, Jimmie added a two-person wooden swing under the arched supports of the open front porch. Claire well remembered him varnishing the pale wood with its cutout heart design across the back. These days the swing was terminally weathered with too many slats missing. It should probably be replaced, but since Claire had no plans to swing in it any time soon, that particular task sat near the bottom of her priority list.

She eased down into the well-worn leather chair behind her father's desk. It had been all she could do to go through the drawers and piles of papers right after his death. Reading his correspondence and pulling everything out for inspection felt embarrassing, invasive…as if she were plundering through someone's private life without their knowledge (which, of course, she was). But the deed had to be done because there were things like unpaid bills, letters from clients, insurance contracts waiting to be executed, and so much business trivia to sort through that it made her head ache. She'd sucked it up, though, because there was no one else to do it. At least the one thing she'd especially been dreading—unearthing a stash of porn mags or something worse, like love letters from someone who wasn't her mother—hadn't materialized. She thought perhaps there might be a God.

Now, the surface of the desk was mostly clear and she'd started using it herself. She found Addie's number among the entries she'd added to the rolodex and then hesitated, her hand on the receiver. She could imagine Addie's reaction to the call. *Holy crap, Claire, give it a rest! What is it with you and this obsession over Danny?* She grimaced and dialed the number.

Addie answered on the sixth ring, slightly out of breath, just as Claire was about to hang up.

"...'ello?"

"Hey, it's me. Claire. Sorry, did I catch you at a bad time?"

"No, no. I was in the laundry room downstairs. Had to run to catch the phone. What's up? I hope that rat Bayard doesn't want us to come in after all."

Claire laughed. "Not a chance. The reason I called, I just wondered...since you have the cast phone list...if you could give me Danny's number."

There was a beat, then two. "Um, okay. Give me a minute." Claire heard the receiver clunk down on a hard surface as Addie went to retrieve the list. She returned shortly and read out the number. Claire jotted it down and wondered what the bloody hell she was doing. This was none of her business, but like an itch she couldn't quite reach, she couldn't let it alone.

"Mind if I ask why you wanna call him?"

"I just wanted to ask him if he got his wrist properly treated. I don't know if he lives alone or what..." Lame. Completely lame. Addie must be rolling her eyes. Claire sighed and leaned back in her father's chair, quietly despising herself.

"Well, I can tell you that he lives in an apartment near Inman Park. Don't know if there's a roommate."

"Ah. Well, thanks for the info."

"So, why do you *really* need to call him?" Addie had switched to her legal assistant's voice, which told Claire she wasn't buying any part of the checking-up-on-a-patient excuse.

What to say? "I just have this gut-level feeling that something's not right."

Instead of laughing, Addie said, "I could do a card reading on him. Hang on, I'll go get them." The phone clunked down again. Claire ground her teeth. She didn't want a bloody card reading predicting falling towers and whatnot. She just wanted to hear the guy's voice and satisfy the rat-gnawing worry she couldn't shake off.

But Addie was back—Claire heard the cards shuffle.

"Okay. Claire, just picture Danny in your mind, if you would, please?" Her voice went up, like a question. Claire sighed. She'd gone this far, might as well play along.

"Are you visualizing, Claire?"

"Yes. Go ahead."

"So...here we go. I'll pull three cards. Show us the energy surrounding Danny. Is he safe?" There was silence, then, "Hm. All three cards are reversed."

"How bad is that?" Claire felt a tension headache starting at the base of her skull.

"Depends. Reversals can mean barriers or blockages, or it might just show delay in the resolution of something. Doesn't necessarily mean bad luck...usually the interpretation is more complex. Anyway, first card is The Seeker, reversed. My guess would be it means a delay in learning or understanding, or there is a barrier preventing enlightenment."

Claire made quick notes. "Could it refer to something secret, or maybe something that's preventing us from finding out what we want to know about Danny?"

"It might."

Claire added that to her notes. "What's the next card?"

"Six of Swords, reversed. Hm, not so good."

"Why?"

"Well, swords generally have to do with actions or physical events, and the number six has to do with the self. So I'd interpret the card to mean selfishness or a failure to do what's right, a misguided sacrifice maybe."

Claire's scalp prickled. "A what?"

Addie's voice was thoughtful. "The sacrifice of another, for one's own selfish interests. Not literally a sacrifice, you understand...probably like undermining someone's well-being to further your own ends...or something like that."

Claire realized she was holding her breath again, a nervous habit when things she didn't want to hear came out anyway.

"Claire? You there?"

"Yeah, I was just thinking. Keep going."

"Last card. Eight of Wands, reversed. Dishonesty, falsehood, communication failure."

Claire put her pen down. "We're being lied to. I *knew* that story about Danny quitting the company was bullshit."

"Huh? But, he did quit. I think." Addie seemed genuinely confused.

"We only have Bayard's word for it." Claire was annoyed—the truth seemed blatantly obvious. He knew what really happened to Danny, but he wasn't sharing.

"Well, yeah, but why would he lie? I mean, what's his motivation?"

Claire bit her lip. "Who knows? I'm just suspicious by nature. Do your cards ever give you wrong information?"

"Not wrong information, per se. Sometimes I might misinterpret what they show me, especially if it's a complicated reading. But looking at this spread, it's actually pretty straightforward. Three reversals, all having to do with blocked communication and lack of information. It does sound like something being kept secret, doesn't it?" Claire thought she might have heard a whiff of fear in Addie's voice. Maybe she remembered that other reading she'd given in the pub.

"Your question was worded to get an answer specific to Danny, and not just in general, right?"

"Yeah..." Claire could almost hear the gears grinding.

"You want to help me follow this up?"

"Absolutely."

That went better than she'd hoped. Addie was on board. Claire wished she could have pulled Tom and maybe Morris into her little private investigation too, but Addie would have to do for now.

"Tell you what. I'll give Danny a call. Then we can decide where to go from there."

"Now you've got me worried. What are you thinking?"

Claire chose her words carefully. "I think we've been lied to about Danny. I can't imagine why Bayard would do that, unless he has something to hide. Something bad. And...it bothers me that nobody's looking into it."

"You know something, Claire, I really admire you."

"Why? I'm just doing the right thing."

"You're a brave person. To be honest, I've had some misgivings myself, but didn't have the nerve to go poking around in Bayard's business. He can be a little intimidating."

"More than a little."

They both laughed. "Maybe it's nothing, and we've cast him in the villain's role by mistake."

Addie agreed. "I would love it if you were totally wrong on this."

"Well, let me try to call Danny, and I'll tell you what turns up."

Claire disconnected and dialed the number she'd written down for Danny, and held her breath. It rang once, twice, four times, then a recorded message came on. "Hey, Danny Ward here. Obviously I'm not home or you'd be talking to me right now. So, leave me a message, won't you?" Chipper sounding. Claire wondered how old that recording was.

"Danny, this is Claire...from the play, remember? Just wanted to see how that cut was doing. It looked to me like it could have used a suture." She waited, but no one picked up. "Well, if you wouldn't mind, just give me a call when you get a chance." She let her breath out and hung up. *Shit!* She'd forgotten to leave her number. Claire fumed for a couple of minutes, then called again. To her surprise, a voice answered. It wasn't Danny.

"Yeah?" A male voice, not too old, probably a roommate.

"Ah, hi. This is Claire Porter? I'm...trying to get in touch with Danny Ward."

"You and everybody else. Haven't seen him." Claire tried to gauge the voice. Irritated? Curious? Couldn't care less?

"When did you last see him, then?" She felt less self-conscious with this stranger who didn't know her from Adam.

"What's it to you? You a girl friend or something?" Claire frowned. Maybe not a roommate, who would surely know if Danny had any romantic attachments.

"I'm just a friend, a medic...I'm checking up on an injury he received about a week ago."

"Don't know anything about that. He's skipped out best I can tell. His rent was due two weeks ago, but he hasn't paid. Another two weeks and I'm putting his stuff out on the street."

Claire's brain went on high alert. "Who am I talking to?"

"Apartment manager. Used my key to get in right when you called. You wouldn't happen to know where else I might track him down, would you?"

Claire gulped air. "No, I wouldn't. Thanks for your time." She put the receiver down and sat very still, thinking. There were any number of probable explanations for his absence—the improbable part was not taking care of his rent. Danny was, in her experience, much too detail oriented to let that happen. She wondered if there were any relatives who could be contacted and then decided that wasn't a road she wanted to go down. Leave that up to missing persons and the police, if that's what it came to.

What bugged her worse right now was the idea that Bayard had kept something from them. Once again, she imagined him coming down the stairs, heading for the basement, and once again, she really wanted to go down there and have a look. But not alone. Maybe she could get Morris, or better, Tom, to go with her. Common sense warned her this was folly, possibly dangerous, but the worrywart in her was itching irrationally to see for herself that Bayard hadn't somehow let the boy bleed to death and then hidden his body. What she wanted most in the world right now was to discover the secret Addie's cards described. The scariest thing was that the foolhardy part of her brain was already on steroids trying to figure out a way, short of breaking and entering, to make that happen.

CHAPTER
12

Thursday night, following week

Tom piloted the Harley through evening traffic with an ear on its distinctive engine growl and an eye on the cloud of vehicles in several lanes around him. The bike seemed to be working fine since coming out of the shop, but Tom wasn't taking any chances. The bike was his lover. He'd gone through withdrawals the few days he'd been without it.

He could see the Janus Theatre up ahead, dominating the corner of the block with its two-storey art deco façade, a little shabby but still demanding respect. Its namesake, the two-faced Roman god of beginnings and transitions, looked north and south along the street. The Gatekeeper. Tom pondered the significance of that particular epithet most often associated with Janus. He knew from his travels through Italy and down the Iberian peninsula that Janus was a part of much local mythology, having jurisdiction over doors and passageways as well as the power to open and close them. He wondered about the doors he'd opened by joining the Mummers Theatrical Company. Of more concern was whether or not he'd be able to close them, if it came to that.

Tom thragged around the corner at the light and up onto the sidewalk in front of the theater and then cut the engine.

Rolling the bike into the entrance alcove, he dismounted, pulled off his helmet, and chained the wheels. Taking a deep breath, he stood for a moment facing the street, watching cars and trucks roll over its asphalt surface. Not a crack or crevice to be seen. He'd come straight out here as soon as the bike was repaired to get a close-up look at the roadway, but there was nothing unusual. Maybe he'd hallucinated those earthquake shocks. But he didn't think so—he had a copy of a photo on his cell phone that said otherwise.

He turned and went into the theater lobby, wondering what had caused Bayard to call off last Sunday's rehearsal. Addie had been a little vague about the reason for the cancellation, so she probably didn't know either. One less rehearsal really didn't matter to Tom. He knew the part as if he'd lived it and could recite the lines as if he'd written them himself. Onstage, he wore the part of Faustus like a second skin. He relished the moment when they would have a live audience to respond to their artifice of words and stage magic, to sense them falling under the spell of the story unfolding in front of them. Opening night couldn't come soon enough.

In the dim lobby others of the cast and crew were milling around, shooting the shit and waiting for the call to places. The upstairs area was lighted and busy, with the ballet company holding their final rehearsal classes before relocating across town for the next two weeks to the university theater where they would be performing. Near the base of the staircase he spotted Adelaide, Morris, and Claire in a huddle, deep in some discussion that looked serious, a fact telegraphed by their expressions and body language. Well-meaning and earnest, Addie was easy to read...the Porter girl not so much. She gave off a steady, reliable vibe on the surface, but he sensed a jumpiness underneath, an edginess she kept a tight lid on. She had hidden issues, which made her more interesting. Morris he thought he understood pretty well—intelligent, educated, moderately ambitious, closeted. They played off each other with appropriate intensity onstage.

He started to approach them, then hung back for a moment, just observing. It looked like the two women were trying to talk Morris into something, and he was resisting, a skeptical expression on his face and his hands jammed deep in his pockets. Maybe he needed a rescue.

"Oh, here's Tom." Addie waved and beckoned. He joined them, wondering what he was about to be roped into.

Morris glanced at the helmet under his arm. "Got your bike back, I see."

Tom nodded. "If I ever buy a car, I know what I'm not getting." They laughed. A cosmetic reaction, covering more serious business. He waited for them to broach whatever it was.

"I was going to smudge the building—"

"But we talked her out of it—"

"Wouldn't want to set off the fire alarms." Morris had adopted an air of benign amusement, but Tom read something else as well. The faux Mephisto was uneasy, but not admitting it.

Tom filed that away and turned to Addie. "Why would you want to do a cleansing ritual?"

"I thought we went through this. To release the restless spirit, or spirits, trapped in the building."

"Has anybody actually seen this so-called restless spirit?" Tom looked from one to the other.

Claire turned to Morris. "You're the one who first mentioned it to me. You even gave me a description…hair like floating seaweed, I think you said?"

Morris shrugged. "Yeah, well, it's just what I've heard. It's been the rumor around here for years."

"I've felt its presence a number of times," Addie said, rolling the smudge sticks between her palms. "It's frustrated."

"I would be too, if I were forced to live in the basement." Morris's mouth quirked into a sort-of smile.

"You don't have to be a believer in the supernatural to feel its effects, you know." She stuffed the smudge sticks back in her bag.

Tom shifted his booted feet. "That's not the real issue, is it?" He'd been reading the tells of people with secrets for way too long for these three to fool him. He was certain they'd been plotting something a little more worrisome than spreading lemongrass smoke around the lobby.

"I did a card reading for Claire...well, it was really for Danny...and the message was loud and clear. Something's being kept secret."

Claire spoke up. "I'm suspicious that something bad has happened to Danny, and I think Bayard knows what it is, or at least he knows that Danny is missing."

"Who says he's missing?" Tom was pretty sure Claire was the real instigator of the "plan," whatever it was, and not Addie.

Claire laid it out for him. "His landlord says his rent's unpaid, and nobody's seen him since the night of the rehearsal when he got cut."

Tom licked his lips. Now they were getting to it. "Maybe you should call the cops and file a missing person's report. If what you said's true, he's been off the radar longer than forty-eight hours."

Claire backtracked. "I didn't want to go that far, just in case there was a legitimate explanation, like an out-of-town family emergency, something that would make him drop everything and leave."

Tom couldn't help smiling. "You won't call the police, yet you're intent on doing something. Don't tell me you're going to confront Bayard and accuse him of removing his lackluster Faustus so I could have the part."

Morris stifled a guffaw. "Good one. I concur."

"Of course not!" Claire's cheeks flushed—a fleeting effect but he'd seen it—and her blue eyes narrowed. She was exasperated, a look that appealed to him. "I just thought it might be worthwhile to look around, maybe in the basement, if we can somehow get in there."

"We?" Morris rocked back on his heels, another tell Tom recognized, which likely meant Claire would have to count the journalist out of whatever little scheme she was trying to sell them.

"You told me Bayard let you go down there before," she said. Stubborn, single-minded. Tom could see she wasn't going to give up on this idea any time soon.

Morris parried. "So what do you want me to do, dear Claire? Ask him for the key and his blessing to conduct a thorough search of the premises? What shall I say we're looking for?"

"I'd rather look around without him knowing about it."

"So we're back to secrets," Tom said, cutting a look toward Addie.

She met his eyes. "I don't want to get anybody in trouble, but I think Claire has a point. Danny's missing, and the last person who may have seen him is Bayard."

"Hey, you guys. Places!" Drew, Tom's Lucifer, was waving at them from the auditorium double doors. The lobby was empty. While they'd been talking, everyone else had gone inside for the final rehearsal before dress.

"Coming?" Morris headed toward the theater doors. Addie trailed after him, and Claire followed, a scowl on her face Tom had no difficulty reading.

He wondered how long it would take before Claire figured out a way to snoop around on her own. Not a smart move—he didn't know what might be hidden from prying eyes, but he wasn't fool enough to think the building was completely safe. Maybe he should hang around after the rehearsal to see what foolhardy thing she would do next. He was starting to like Claire, in her baggy sweatpants and oversized sweaters. Too bad he had no intention of getting involved with her...it might have been interesting.

Light pooled around three figures in Faustus' study: an elderly academic, the doomed scholar, and his satanic companion. In a desperate voice, Faustus addressed the audience.

"Damned art thou, Faustus, damned. Hell claims his right and with a roaring voice says, 'Faustus, come, thine hour is almost spent." He fell to his knees, face upturned to the old man, who stretched a hand toward him.

"Stay these desperate steps, good Faustus. Even yet the angel of mercy hovers o'er thy head. Call for mercy, and grace may yet be yours."

The tall figure of Mephistopheles with his billowing cloak stepped between them. In his white hand, a dagger caught the spotlight. "Traitor! Disobey my sovereign lord and I'll tear thy flesh in pieces."

The old man backed away, terrified at the emissary of Hades yet reluctant to abandon his friend. The crouched figure of Faustus turned his back on the old man and reached for the blade held out to him.

"Sweet Mephistopheles, entreat thy lord Lucifer to pardon my unjust outburst." He took the dagger and held it up at eye level, facing the audience. "With my blood again I will confirm the vow I made before."

Mephistopheles stood behind him, caped arms outstretched like a carrion crow.

"Do it then, Faustus, with a truthful heart, lest greater dangers may attend thee."

"Cut!" Bayard stepped out of the wings. "Bend over him more, as if you mean to swoop down on him and carry him away."

Morris stooped and curved his arms. "Like so?"

"Exactly. Otherwise, gentlemen, the scene is excellent."

"Are we taking a break?" Tom put the dagger on the floor in front of him and sat back on his haunches. He'd made sure it was dull as a butterknife before handling it.

Bayard rubbed the back of his neck. "We can, if you like. In fact, I think it's a good idea." He spoke to the cast in the wings. "We'll commence in twenty minutes. Act Five, scene two, at the point where Faustus sees the end and bids his university friends farewell." With that, he turned and went down into the theater, striding along a side aisle toward the back without stopping to chat with anyone. Tom sat on the stage, watching his receding back. The man seemed tired, his shoulders held stiff against absent but remembered pain. Tom knew this body language well, having experienced it himself recently. He stretched, flexing the muscles in his arms and back.

"Serious tats you got, man. Fierce." It was Ruben, the lighting guy, marking the spotlight for Morris's crow effect. "What's that design, barbed wire?"

"Vines with thorns. It's a climbing rose...the loops connect in a Celtic knot. Here." He held out his arm to give Ruben a better view.

"Does it go all the way around?"

"Yeah, it does." Tom pushed up his T-shirt sleeve. The trail of thorns wound around his bicep and up, presumably, onto his shoulder.

"Sweet." Ruben crooked his head approvingly. "Where'd you get that done?"

Tom got to his feet and noticed Claire watching him from the wings. "Not in town. I've had 'em a long time."

"I got these done down at a shop down in Little Five Points. Guy I know there is the best in town." Ruben displayed a pair of crossed swords on his forearm. Italian, sixteenth century, Tom guessed, looking at the details—diamond section blade, hilt cuspidate in the center with arms bent downwards, floral motif on the pommel.

He nodded approvingly. "That's nice work."

Ruben beamed. "Gerrara blades, if you know anything about sword history. I'm getting a German longsword, early sixteenth century hand and a half, on the other arm. Gotta get enough money saved up, though. These babies aren't cheap."

"I know that's true." Tom caught Morris's eye. He seemed to be finding this macho comparing of tattoos highly amusing. Whatever. Tom didn't make a big deal of his body art, but he didn't try to hide it, either. It was what it was…a part of him.

Morris turned toward Claire and addressed her directly. "So what do you make of our director's new fashion statement?"

"The white streaks in his beard?" Claire bookmarked the script in her lap. "It's no mystery. He explained it to Addie. Told her that he'd been coloring his hair and beard to look younger, but now he's decided it's too much trouble. He washed out the dye, and that's how it really looks."

"*Au natural*, how charming." Morris looked anything but charmed. Tom sensed issues there as well, but he wasn't interested. He focused his attention on Claire and joined them in the wings.

"Just for the record, I don't think it's safe for you to poke around the building on your own."

Claire's steady gaze challenged him. "Who says I was going to?"

Morris snorted. "Well, if either of you runs into a ghost, I want a full account. It would make a great local interest story. We could add the Janus Theatre to the Haunted Houses Tour next Halloween."

"I don't think Bayard would be too happy about that." Tom wanted to question Claire alone, but since Morris seemed determined to hang around, he touched her hand and said, "Don't leave tonight without talking to me." Then he went back to his mark onstage and stretched out flat on his back, pushing his spine into the floorboards and breathing slowly, letting his thoughts go idle until the rehearsal resumed.

Bayard returned exactly twenty minutes later and walked down the center aisle to the front.

"Is everyone rested? Good. Commence please, at Act Five, scene two." He took his customary place beside Claire in the wings, and the lights dimmed. They ran through the final two scenes of the play with a couple of adjustments, and then Bayard took center stage as the Chorus to deliver the Epilogue.

"Cut is the branch that might have grown full straight…"

Tom shivered. Those famous last lines always got to him.

"…Faustus is gone, look ye well on his hellish fall…"

Tom stood upstage in shadow with Morris on one side and Drew on the other, backlit and barely visible to the audience as Bayard's rich baritone filled the theater all the way to the back row, bringing the play to a close. It was powerful stuff. The stage went dark, and he imagined thunderous applause as the houselights came up. He doubted anyone in the audience on opening night would leave the performance unmoved—such was the playwright's genius. It was a pity, all the critics said, that Marlowe's own branch had been cut short by his untimely death, leaving just six plays on which to build his literary legacy. Tom was inclined to agree.

Bayard pronounced the rehearsal concluded, and bid them good night.

"I won't see any of you again until dress rehearsal next week, so get some rest, relax, and arrive next Friday ready to perform straight through with no stops, as if the audience were in place." Several cast members gathered around him, asking last-minute questions about the play's more mundane issue—how many comp tickets would they get for family, and so on. Bayard steered them toward the stage left steps, chatting away. He was clearly in a good mood.

Tom went backstage to the green room to gather his helmet and leather jacket.

"Hey, you got a minute?" It was Drew.

"I guess so." Tom hoped he sounded noncommittal. He wasn't keen to get into one of Drew's tedious analyses of the interaction between Faustus and Lucifer. Lucifer was there to collect the soul of his newest recruit. End of discussion. If there was any nuance going on, it was to make sure Mephistopheles executed the blood contract as signed, with no weaseling or last-minute concessions. Tom could appreciate Drew's enthusiasm for the dynamics of their repartee—it was a small but important role—but his attention tonight was elsewhere.

"Do you think Lucifer regards Mephisto as a colleague or a slave?"

Tom sighed. "It all depends on your definition of *minion*, doesn't it?"

"Well, see, I've been thinking about that." Drew settled in.

Tom leaned against the wall, keeping an eye on the clock. He hoped he could catch up with Claire before she did anything stupid.

Claire was dying for something to drink, but she'd be damned if she was going to pay several dollars for a can of soda from the machine in the lobby. More inviting was the tall distilled water cooler on the second floor, put there mostly for the convenience of the dancers. She didn't see Tom anywhere, but he was probably trapped by Drew or somebody else who wanted to talk shop, or maybe Ruben wanted to see more of his tats. She climbed to the top of the stairs, got her cup of water, and then spotted Jackie lounging against the doorway of the ballet rehearsal room.

"How's it going down there in the bowels of Hell?" Her husky voice was comforting, like old times. She was still in her leotard and tights with shapeless sweatpants slung low over her hips and a thin dance sweater draped around her shoulders.

Claire joined her, sipping at the water. Jackie smelled of sweat and honeysuckle. The flowery undertone was her shampoo, if Claire remembered right. "It's okay. Are you done for the night?"

"Um hm." Jackie nodded."Wait a sec while I pack up, and I'll walk you out to the car."

"Sure." Claire sat down in her usual spot, putting her keys and purse on the floor beside her. The room was mostly empty, with just a few stragglers hanging around. Jackie went to a pile of *pointe* shoes, soft ballet shoes, towels, water bottle, and snacks in a brown paper bag in the corner and began stuffing them into her oversized dance bag. She wiggled her feet into a well-worn pair of Doc Martens, pulled on a flannel jacket, and hoisted the dance bag strap over her shoulder. It looked heavy.

"Ready?"

Claire grabbed her purse and got up. "Ready." They went down the stairs together and crossed the lobby. She didn't see Tom, but she knew he was still there. Just outside the front doors she could see his black motorcycle, big and mean and well-broken in, dominating the entryway, awaiting its owner's return in aggressive silence.

"Nice ride," Jackie observed as they went out past the Harley.

"Yeah, it belongs to our star player."

"I'd kill for a bike like that." Jackie looked dead serious, but laughter colored her voice. "Where are you parked?"

"Had to use the parking lot in back."

"Cool. Me, too." The half-smile appeared on her face again. Jackie readjusted her bag and started walking.

They rounded the corner of the building, went down a narrow alley, and came out behind the theater into an asphalt lot where a low stone fence marked its boundaries.

Claire followed Jackie to a late model Jeep Wrangler, which wasn't the old Ford she remembered Jackie owning since high school. Maybe it belonged to her partner. Sylvia? Something like that. Claire wasn't good with names, but faces she could peg at forty paces. Jackie unlocked the door and tossed her bag inside. "You look tired. How's your mom?"

"Hanging in there. Not too good, I guess."

Jackie leaned against the front fender of the Wrangler. "Too bad about your dad."

Claire smiled and nodded. No need for explanations—Jackie understood the situation as well as anyone could.

"Jacks..." She wasn't sure how to frame what she wanted to ask. "You spend a lot time here, right? In the building, I mean."

"Um hm."

"Anything ever creep you out? I mean like stuff you can't explain?"

Jackie pushed her thin fingers up through her hair, pulling it away from her face. She studied the laces of her boots. "How weird do you want? We've had light bulbs come unscrewed from their sockets, things like that. I think the cops came out here once because we kept complaining about the bulbs—our director assumed it was vandalism. The police told us to just glue every last one of them in their sockets. Didn't do any good, though. The bulbs just unscrewed themselves loose again a week or so later."

"Is that a true story?"

Jackie grinned. "Yeah. But that's nothing. You should hear the theater people talk. They got some stories will curl your hair. Well, not *yours*." They both laughed—Claire's hair was a thick mass of straw-colored waves.

"I've heard some tales. That's kind of why I asked."

"But you haven't seen anything yourself, have you?"

"No..."

"Well, there you go. Until it gets personal, nothing to worry about. Oh, speaking of personal, I wanted to let you know. We'll be leaving after the first of the year."

Claire snapped out of her funk. "What? Who's leaving?"

"Me and Sylvia. She's got a new job in North Carolina and I'm going with her."

Claire's stomach dropped to her knees. This news trumped anything she'd been chewing over about the stupid theater. "Oh. Well, I guess I won't see you again, after the show's done."

"I guess not." They stood in silence, letting the fact of separation settle in.

"Damn, Jacks. I'll miss you." Claire forced the bile in her throat back down where it properly belonged, in the pit of her stomach.

"C'mere." Jackie reached out and wrapped Claire in a tight hug. Finally she let go and swung herself up into the driver's seat of the Jeep. "I'll send our new address, once we find a place to live."

"Where in North Carolina?" Claire's voice sounded squeaky.

"Greenville. It's a college town."

"I'm sure it's nice." Claire stepped back as the Jeep rattled to life. "Take care." She waved as Jackie backed out of the parking space and aimed toward the street. A sense of numbness settled around her shoulders. If someone had asked her name at that moment she might have had to think about it.

Jackie rolled down the window. "Take care of your mom, and give her my love."

Claire gave her a tight smile and nodded. Jackie drove away. Claire headed across the lot to her Honda, all thoughts of meeting up with Tom blasted from her mind. She stood with her fingers on the door handle, stupidly trying to think what to do next, when it dawned on her. She didn't have her car keys.

She stood still, hardly breathing. Then she searched through all her pockets, which were empty. With trembling fingers, Claire thrashed her hand all over the inside of her purse, but couldn't feel anything that resembled her key chain. In a flash of anger, she dumped the contents of her purse out on the hood of the car. No keys.

"Damn! *Damn!*" She threw everything back into her purse, trying hard not to scream just for the pure hell of it, and then she remembered. She had been sitting on the floor of the rehearsal hall waiting for Jackie. Her keys were probably still lying right there in the dust. She leaned against the car, shoulders sagging. As much as she hated the idea, she would have to go back inside.

The theater was empty when Tom finally disengaged himself from Drew and came out into the lobby. No sign of Claire, so he hoped that meant she had given up and gone home. Just to make sure, though, he checked the street out front, but there was no sign of her. He went upstairs to the ballet rehearsal room. The door was closed but not locked, so he poked his head inside. It was dark and empty. Tom stood at the head of the staircase, debating what to do when he became aware of someone behind him. Close, invading his space.

"Mr. Brennan. Can I help you with something?"

Tom turned. "Maybe. I was looking for Claire."

Bayard glanced over the banister at the darkened lobby. "I haven't seen her since rehearsal ended."

Tom angled for a closer look at the director in the dim mezzanine lighting. He had the fleeting impression of a face lined and creased with age, but when he blinked the illusion was gone. He tried to read the presence of the man before him and sensed weariness beyond endurance, caginess, a dab of curiosity, and above all, a vast capacity for deception. Addie's big secret? He shifted his attention from Claire—she could take care of herself, at this point—to the man in front of him. Bayard met his gaze without blinking. Friendly on the surface, but clearly on guard.

"I expect she's gone home," Tom said. "I think she has an invalid mother who needs tending."

"Sounds reasonable, Claire being our resident Good Samaritan." They faced each other in the semi-dark, neither moving to leave. Bayard seemed to be weighing something in his mind. "Would you care for a drink, Tom? Relax, and talk about the play? I'm quite taken with your interpretation of our poor tragical Doctor Faustus."

Tom nodded. "I'd like that, but just a small glass. Can't pilot a Harley under the influence."

"I'm certain." Bayard turned and walked across the landing toward his office. Tom followed. He widened his senses, questing. Yes, this was where he needed to be.

Bayard opened the door to his apartment and motioned Tom inside. A floor lamp in a corner cast soft incandescent lighting over the director's desk, chairs, bookshelves, and neatly made bed.

"Make yourself comfortable. Sherry, Pinot Noir, or something more pedestrian?"

Tom sat down in the carved high-backed chair. He'd spent much of his rehearsal time in its mate, so it felt familiar. "Irish Mist, if you have it."

Bayard chuckled. "I do, indeed. Excellent choice."

Tom shrugged out of his leather jacket and settled back in the chair. "Heather wine, brewed and drunk a thousand years ago by Ireland's heathen chieftains, or so the advertising says."

Bayard's eyebrows went up. "A man who knows his liquor. I'm impressed, indeed I am." He chose a cut-glass tumbler from the wine cabinet and poured it half full, then handed it to Tom. He served himself the same and took a seat at the desk, where his pipe and tobacco resided. "Mind if I smoke?"

"Not at all." Tom didn't mind if Bayard wanted to fill the small apartment with pipe smoke—he'd already taken in the scents of the place. Old paper, old wood, old leather, cherry tobacco, ceramic tile cleaner, and yes, under everything else, the sharp tang of blood.

Tom felt the blended liquor fold itself around his tongue. "I like your adaptation of the play...keeping the feel of the original but updating some of the wording for modern audiences."

"You're a connoisseur of Elizabethan drama? I wouldn't have guessed, especially not from someone so young. I suppose it's true, what they say."

Tom looked around the small study with its wraparound bookcases. "What do they say?"

"That looks truly can be deceiving."

Tom inclined his shaved head toward Bayard. "I'm not as young as I look."

Bayard laughed. "Nor am I." He smoothed the streaks in his goatee. "What, exactly, excites you about this play?"

Tom swallowed more of the whiskey. "It feels real to me. That setting, those characters, especially Faustus himself. It rings true."

"I agree. The language is evocative, filled with sensory detail. Can you imagine British life in the 1500s? You have Queen Mary burning martyrs. I've read the stench of burning human flesh is unique. No other smell quite like it. Then you have Protestants reforming everything and suddenly a dreary Catholic monarchy becomes awash in unfettered philosophy — you have Luther's proclamations, Calvinist ideology, the writings of John Dee where science and sorcery are equally pursued. And on top of that imagine a visceral city life with the odor of slaughtered cattle in the air, streets clogged with butcher's blood, discarded rubbish, carts loaded with offal from cattle markets. Rich and poor jostling each other along crowded narrow streets, on horseback and on foot. And cold, clear church bells breaking over the sleeping city every morning at daybreak. To distill all that into mere words is no small skill."

"How do you know what it was like, in that much detail?"

"I've done my research." Bayard leaned back in his chair and lit his pipe.

Tom emptied his glass. "I've read all Marlowe's plays, and his collected poetry. You could say I'm interested in the man himself, his wide-ranging ideas on philosophy and the teasing way he treats religion. There's something...personal... in the way he retells the old German Faust tale. It's like it came from the point of view of someone who knew first-hand what he was writing about."

Bayard made a scoffing noise. "You think Christopher Marlowe sold his soul to the Devil? Come now, you don't strike me as a superstitious fellow. Our friend Adelaide, yes, but not you."

"I don't mean literally, with horned demons flying in through the window on a fire-breathing dragon. I mean someone who's compromised his honor, his ethics, even his beliefs to attain something that maybe he shouldn't have, but once he's made those choices they can't be taken back. The ripple effect of those actions spreads out into the future regardless of what else he may do."

Bayard was silent, just staring at Tom with his dark eyes.

"If you could speak directly to Marlowe himself, what would you say?"

Tom did not hesitate. "I'd ask how closely he identified with Faustus. How much of his own thoughts and aspirations and fears were poured into the character's personality. Did he believe Faustus deserved his fate? That's what I'd ask. "

Bayard drew on his pipe. "Well, the idea of someone with enormous talent and capability throwing it all away for a false reward is compelling, isn't it?" He downed his own glass and stood up. "If you don't mind, it's been a trying week for me and I'm tired."

Tom was on his feet in a second, pulling on his jacket. "Sorry. I've taken up too much of your time, especially if you're not feeling well—"

"Let's just say certain sponsors have been difficult. Diplomacy was never my strong suit."

Tom went to the apartment door and let himself out. "Thanks for the whiskey, and your time."

"Likewise. It has been most enlightening." Bayard pushed the door shut, and Tom heard the lock click in place. So much for his interview with the director.

He turned and quickly went downstairs. For a moment he stood in the lobby, just listening. "What's your secret?" he whispered to the shadows, but the building was still and silent, with nothing to tell him.

Tom pushed the front door open and stepped out into the cold. He figured he must have missed Claire while he was in the green room listening to Drew go on and on or upstairs playing at philosophy with Bayard. Most likely she'd got tired of waiting on him and gone home. Just to make sure, though, he straddled the bike, hung his helmet over the handlebars, and lit a cigarette. He waited and smoked, to see if she'd catch up with him after all. By the time he'd smoked the cigarette down to the filter, he felt annoyed with himself for wasting time and cranked the engine. The Harley roared to life and he backed out of the alcove. With one last look up at the darkened windows of the Janus, he goosed the throttle and tore down the street.

CHAPTER 13

Thursday night, continued

The theater was tomb-still. A few lobby lights were on, but the bulbs in the ceiling fixture and over the stairwell landing were low wattage, so their light was dim and scattered, penetrating the shadows as effectively as a penlight through dense fog.

Claire chewed her lip. Somehow she'd missed Tom. She'd intended to meet him in front of the building, but it hadn't worked out. It didn't seem like she'd spent that much time in the parking lot with Jackie—her mood plummeted at the mere thought of that farewell scene—but by the time she'd come back to look for her keys, his motorcycle was gone. The lobby was cold and Claire held her arms tightly across her body, shivering in little spasms. She headed for the stairs. Hating to go up there, but knowing she had to, produced a sensation of slow motion where movement was dreamlike, as in those pre-waking moments when consciousness hovers just out of reach.

She got to the landing and walked as softly as possible to the ballet rehearsal hall. The door was unlocked so she slipped inside. It was empty and dark, although the mirrored panels across the room reflected streetlights outside, producing a disquieting sense of watery movement along the walls. Claire tried to shake off the feeling of tense awareness that pervaded the room as she came all the way in. She scanned the floor and quickly spotted her keys, right where she'd left them. The tall windows watched her like so many pairs of eyes. She stood perfectly still, her breathing shallow, listening for sounds of anyone moving around. Pocketing her keys, she hurried out and down the stairs, heart thudding against her ribcage. Then she heard a door opening and closing on the second floor, followed by footsteps coming toward the stairs.

Crouching in the shadows, she pressed herself against the wall beside the stairwell. This time Bayard seemed in no hurry as he came down, sauntered across the darkened lobby to the street doors, and locked them. Then he checked his key ring, found another key, unlocked the basement and went in, leaving the door open behind him. And why not? He was the only one in the building, as far as he knew. Claire waited, breathless, to see how long it took him to do whatever it was he did down there and come out again. Minutes slipped by, and then more minutes, until she was certain she'd been hiding for at least half an hour. Had he gone out a back door? The worst part was that now she was locked in, which meant the only way she was going to get home was to find him and ask to be let out. The thought of her mother at home, panicking because Clair was late, pushed her into action.

She crossed the lobby and stopped at the head of the narrow basement stairs. Bayard had switched on a light at the bottom, and its grime-encrusted bulb flickered as if it was not seated firmly in the socket, and every creak and sigh running through the walls and floors of the building threatened to short the tenuous connection. Peering down, she could see green-painted concrete walls, their pitted surface flanking steps that pitched steeply for maybe a dozen narrow wooden risers, then jogged right and went down a few more.

Claire descended step by step, heart jumping out of her chest, hand outstretched against the wall to steady her balance.

The air in the cramped stairwell was stale and left an unpleasant taste on her tongue. Reaching the bottom step, she expected to find Bayard but saw no one. She hesitated, breathing and listening.

"Hello?" Her voice fell softly on the deadened air. The cavernous space of the basement stretched away from her, its walls lined with painted flats, piles of used lumber, broken furniture, and storage crates stacked one on top of another. Cobweb-encrusted shadows filled its corners, while square concrete pillars transected the room at regular intervals in stark relief from the bare bulb.

Claire stepped onto the basement floor, then walked out a few steps, her Reeboks squelching over the tiles. Holding her breath, she heard nothing but the pounding of her own heart. Silent seconds passed, as she fought the urge to run back up the stairs. Then she spotted ascending steps barely visible across the basement. They were set in the far wall, leading up to a metal door. Guessing it must open into the alley behind the building, Claire could only assume Bayard had exited that way. If the door could be opened from the inside, she would be free with quick access to the parking lot.

At that precise moment, a tower of filing boxes some distance away toppled with a heart-stopping crash, spilling papers and file folders in a jumble over the floor. Claire fled halfway up the stairs, and then dared to look back. The skitter of feet and a flash of a skinny naked tail gave the culprit away.

"Fuck...rat..." She could barely catch her breath her heart was pounding so hard. "Get. A. Grip." She headed back down.

The far door was a long way across the basement and deep in shadow, but it really was her only option at this point. She stepped down onto the tiled floor again, resolute.

That was when the stench hit her. A rotten smell, but with a nauseous, sweet bite to it. Claire gagged and clamped her hand over her mouth. The last thing she wanted to do was throw up in the grubby basement of the Janus Theatre. Trying not to breathe in, she wiped sweat from her face and held her nose. The fetid odor was worse near the stairs…a dead rat, or something worse?

It was making her sick to the point of passing out, which didn't make sense, given her occupation. She was quite used to the smell of blood, but this was something different. Pulse roaring in her ears, her vision narrowed to pinpoints and she fell with arms splayed out, catching at anything to break the fall. Her head struck the tiles and she half-bounced, half-slid with her shoulders wedged into a narrow crawlspace under the steps. Her open palms hit the row of foundation stones mortared in crumbling concrete, scraping the skin of her palms. Gasping, Claire lay still, her senses on overload. The stone closest to her face was eroded and irregular, unlike the others, which were finished and square. Its rough surface oozed something darker than the shadows. She touched it with trembling fingers, and then scrambled onto her hands and knees, leaving bloody prints.

"Shit…!" Claire's fingers began to pulse with tiny electric shocks that flickered around her wrists and then went racing up her forearms. She clung to consciousness just long enough to note that both arms had gone numb to the elbow. Points of light whirled in front of her eyes, slowly coalescing into a gaunt, vaguely female face with wild, tangled hair. A screech split her eardrums as her field of vision went bright red and then black.

For one marrow-freezing second, she lay on the basement floor unable to breathe, but with the next gasp a warm, damp breeze blew over her face. Head aching and vomit threatening in her throat, Claire waited agonizing seconds with eyes clamped shut for the world to stop doing its tilt-a-whirl. Slowly the nausea retreated and she pushed up on one elbow, opening her stunned eyes. Impossibly, she found herself sprawled on a mud bank, the gloom of an overcast sunset settling over the tidal flats of a wide river. The stench still filled her sinuses, but it had shifted to a fishy, raw-sewage smell—the gag-inducing scent of blood had disappeared along with the Janus Theatre.

Claire groaned and tried to sit up. Her head ached beyond belief and even the faint light stabbed at her eyes. Likely a mild concussion. And possibly something worse; why the hell did the theater basement look, and smell, like the world's worst polluted river? She closed her eyes and sat perfectly still, trying to make the pain subside. She'd never experienced a shock-induced hallucination before and wondered how long it would take to wear off. None of the clinical definitions and descriptions of head injury delusions she'd read gave any indication this kind of tactile sensory overload was possible.

She opened her eyes again and was dismayed to see the foul-smelling riverbank had not disappeared. She stared, disbelieving, at the stagnant water lapping at low tide along its banks. On the near side, small boats lying on their sides clustered like clam shells on the mudflats. A pair of swans drifted downstream, pale and incongruous. A man's voice called to a boatman out on the water, and then Claire saw with a shock the dark outline of a city sprawling along the opposite bank and up onto the higher ground. As darkness began to fall, she saw soft lights sprinkled all over the hillside: candles in the windows of narrow houses, torches bobbing along the bankside road. Claire caught her breath—torches?

She rubbed her eyes, her dazed brain unable to account for what she saw. Even more disturbing, it looked vaguely familiar in a second-hand way, as if she'd seen it in a photo or something. Staring across the water, it came to her—the scene was on the front cover of the Shakespeare anthology Addie had loaned her. Impossibly, she was staring at the live version of the Thames, as seen from the Elizabethan theater district of Southwark. Shivering to her very core, Claire recognized the stinking, teeming body of sixteenth-century London hulking across the river like a great scabrous beast.

Dumbfounded, she couldn't stop shaking. She put her hands to her face, then yanked them away. Her fingers and the creases of her palms were caked with blood. Stifling a retch, she wiped them on her sweat pants, but the stains wouldn't come off. Staring at the evidence, she tried to remember how it got there. She hadn't scraped her hands that badly on the stones under the stairs. In forcing her mind back to the blackout moment, she failed to see the two men struggling along the muck of the strand until they were too close to avoid notice. They dragged something heavy between them—as they drew closer, she saw it was a body.

She watched, frozen in terror, as the men hauled the body to the water's edge and dropped it with a loud slosh face-down in the shallows. Their guttural voices echoed across the slow-moving current in accents so thick Claire barely recognized it as English.

"...give 'is bloody plague germs to the fishes."

"...was you as drunk after 'im last—be catchin it yerself next off—"

"Whisht!" The first speaker slapped his hand across his companion's chops and stood looking at Claire like a pointer that had just flushed a quail from a hedgerow.

"What is't?" queried the second man.

"Tis a maid, don't ye see? All by 'erself there..."

Adrenalin flashed through Claire in a great white wave of alarm. Gulping air, she scrambled to her feet and turned to run up the bank, mud sucking at her shoes, but the taller man was too fast. He caught her in no more than half a dozen leaping strides, and clamped his filthy grease-coated arms, thick as oak branches, around her waist and held her squirming until his companion could catch up. Her mind rebelled—the immediate danger was overwhelming, but more compelling was the fact that this creature of her hallucination was solid. It held her as firmly as any live person could.

"Oh god," she squeaked, pushing and kicking against the man. Her hair came loose, falling in a wheat-colored tangled mess over her shoulders.

"Wot we got 'ere?" queried her captor, grabbing her by the hair and pulling her face back for a better look, which allowed her the same. Crude patch over one eye, stiff stringy hair near shoulder length, stubble of beard, and half an ear, over which a thick whitened scar pulled the skin tight on either side of its zigzagged line.

"Hold 'er, mate, I'm coming," called the second man, stumbling in an awkward, club-footed gallop like a hobbled donkey. "Wot is she, then?"

One-eye hawked and spat onto the dirt, then laughed in loud barks at Claire's appalled face. "Somebody's cast-off. Got on naught under 'er coat but a bodice of some sort and pantaloons, as yer can see."

"Aye, I see that fine enough," shouted the other at close range, as if his hearing were none too good. His chest heaved with labored breathing, and his shoulders sloped off-center from his twisted torso.

"Please let go," Claire pleaded, knowing in her gut such entreaties were useless, as was struggling in the man's iron-hard grip. He was built like an ox, and smelled like one as well. She was holding her breath, trying not to breathe in the man's overpowering aroma of carious teeth, musky sweat, badly tanned leather jerkin, and pants stiff with feces or stale urine. "I don't have anything worth taking, no money, no jewelry..."

One-Eye laughed in her face. "She says she dunt 'ave anything we want...'ere's what I want!" He ripped her sweater and medic's smock off her shoulder, exposing her breast and engulfing it with four blackened fingers. The ring finger was missing at the knuckle. Claire screamed and tried to jackknife her knee into his groin. The hand released her breast and smashed across her nose and upper lip so fast she hung, stunned, across his arm for several seconds, lights arcing across her brain, before she fully understood what had happened. Testing her lip with her tongue, she felt a tear and tasted blood.

"Aw, why'd ye want to smash 'er face, Fergis? Now she an't so pretty as she was," whined the twisted man, pawing at her shoulder.

"Would ye be trying to tell me how t'handle a wench?"

"Nay, but—"

"Whoreson, ye'd not even know wot to do wi' the leavin's when I get done with 'er, you bloody sod." Claire swung, dazed, as the man sidestepped a lunge from Club-foot. "Dog's body!" laughed One-eye.

"Son of a plague-gutted whore, I'll kill ye!" screamed the twisted man, pulling a short knife with a blackened blade from his jerkin.

"Come at me then, swine," barked One-eye. He tossed Claire aside like a bundle of rags and took a fighting stance. "I'll slice up yer liver an' make to sup on't, then I'll have this skinny maid's arse all to meself. Avast, filth!" He crouched, laughing between broken teeth.

Club-foot lunged at his companion, shrieking incoherent curses. Off balance, he careened into the pit of One-eye's abdomen, where he punched vigorously at the stained codpiece.

"Arrrgh! I'll rip out yer lights for that," the big man bellowed.

Blind with pain and fear, Claire inched her way over a heap of rocks and rubble, expecting rough hands around her throat with each breath. But as the sound of their scuffle escalated, soon she was scrambling up the sloping bank and over a low stone wall. At a stumbling run, she crossed a rutted road and ducked down a narrow dirt lane between clusters of thatch-roofed houses. A gurgling scream in the direction of the river sent her sprinting over a cloud of chickens and on past the last house in the row to an empty cattle byre under the canopy of an ancient oak.

The dry, clean hay smell was heaven. Crawling under a head-high drift, Claire lay still, listening for sounds of pursuit. Instead, she heard two male voices in soft discourse—clearly not the two from whom she'd just escaped. She guessed the speakers to be near the trees on the far side of the byre.

"T'would seem the stone may needs be moved shortly, if he's of a mind to keep it." An old man's raspy voice. His breathless, halting speech revealed his cardio-pulmonary disease to Claire's trained ears. Her mother sounded that way.

"You made a clever choice in your successor, my dear doctor, appealing to his artist's lust for fame and fortune, although why you chose not to keep it longer yourself after all the trouble it cost you—and me—to make it I cannot fathom." The second speaker sounded younger and foreign, his voice silky, yet resonant and elegantly enunciated.

"Aye, 'tis true enough." Footsteps crunched over dry grass and twigs as the pair moved closer. "For all my learning, there was no wisdom in this matter. But I suspect you knew...have known all along...how I might best be used to your own ends."

"Nay, not my ends but those of my master. Relinquishing the *buachloch* to another does not absolve you from our original bargain." The voice was smooth as satin, with undertones of something else... Claire couldn't put her finger on the exact quality that made her skin prickle but she was suddenly trembling far worse then she'd been during her encounter with two of London's finest lowlifes. The fear was nameless, but palpable.

"I knew that." The old man's voice was resigned. "I simply could not continue, e'en though it meant a swift decline in health and fortune once ownership'd been given away. The fact that 'twas you and not the Lord Gabriel who did come to fetch me on my deathbed was no surprise." His voice sounded threadbare, worn thin and infinitely sad. Claire shivered. What was he…a ghost? She must be full-blown, completely delusional to even be thinking such a thing.

The honeyed voice laughed softly. "You were not entirely forthcoming with our Master Marlowe about her ladyship and her needs…how if he failed to feed her, old age might o'ertake him in a most unpleasant way. He'd not be shielded from the arrival of the Black Carriage in that case."

"If I'd told him all, he'd not have taken possession of the stone. No sane person would."

"Indeed. I thank you, Professor Dee, for your recruitment of our illustrious playwright. I have enjoyed a fruitful, if reluctant, connection with him in your stead these twenty years past, despite the fact of him carelessly getting himself murdered—albeit temporarily. In his present guise he's sent many a sacrificed soul down the path straight to Hell, for which I am most obliged. But as you see now, the threads of Fate pull taut. A choice looms."

"I wonder if he will choose to retrieve it."

"If not, then I shall collect his soul and you needs must find Mistress Banshee a new owner. A small but necessary request from my master." Silence fell between them. "How shall I serve thee, my good doctor, once this task is done?"

"I would see the Great Library of Alexandria, before the fire…"

"Be assured, I shall be your perfect companion." Soft laughter encircled the byre and sent a wintery chill over Claire's skin.

Dee's voice took on a sour tone. "I find no mirth since I was laid in the ground. Not e'en my daughters mourned long my passing."

"Mirth is where you find it. I have enjoyed eternal amusement in tangling the skeins of human lives and then standing aside to see how they struggle to get the snare unraveled."

The old man's voice softened. "I suppose 'twould explain why ye chose not to interfere when the boy came to me at my deathbed. I revealed all our secrets, y'know. What we twain had done together."

"I care not, nor does my master. But it does add sauce to the game." There was silence, then the same voice again. "Ah, see where the moment arrives." The footsteps headed away from Claire's hiding place. She hardly dared to breathe.

Inexplicably, a swell of clapping and voices charged with excitement rose on the breeze and died away. Puzzled, Claire dragged herself out of her hiding place. It was nearly dark outside as she struggled to her feet, unsteady and lightheaded. More cheering and shouts, punctuated by loud guffawing laughter. A carnival?

Holding onto the gate of a stall, she touched her face—it felt puffy around the mouth. The split inside her lip where One-eye had smacked it against her teeth stung like crazy, but at least it wasn't bleeding much now. Claire took a deep breath. The evening air carried scents of the river and night-blooming flowers. Hallucinations complete with smell-o-vision. Why couldn't she wake up? She tried to work her way back to what had happened before she'd landed on the bank of the Thames, but at that moment an explosion of cannon fire pounded her eardrums like thunderclaps. A loud hurrah rose with the shots, cheers and shouts that suddenly shifted to shrieks and wails of terror. Something violent and terrible was taking place just out of sight.

Claire stumbled away from her sanctuary and through the grove of oaks behind the byre. Coming out into a small clearing, the source of the commotion filled her field of vision. Flames and a pillar of smoke infused with swirling sparks climbed from the circular roof of a round, windowless building hulking just beyond the line of trees. Shocked, she watched in fascination as tendrils of red-orange and magenta writhed under and over wood shingles with their dry thatching, dropping sparks and smoldering planks down on the heads of a crowd of people now pushing over each other through a narrow door in the wall facing her.

Horses screamed and thundered away from the building, knocking bodies down and trampling them in their panic to escape the growing inferno. Strangely, Claire felt a flicker of recognition igniting in her brain as flames encircled the timber and plaster walls, clawing toward the heavens.

The sickening, pungent smell of burning flesh mixed with the stink of pine resin slapped her face on the quickening breeze. Unable to look away, she searched her memory for the scene, and suddenly she had it. Here in living color was the event she'd read about in the Shakespeare anthology: it was the Globe Theatre, in Shakespeare's London, burning to the ground from cannons fired during a performance of Henry *VIII*. Claire's mouth fell open. No longer consumed with how she happened to be here or why, she gawked, paralyzed, at the three-tiered tiring house that sat above the roofline with its curtained balcony and flaming pennants smoking in the light breeze. With an inevitable rending noise, the structure tore loose from the support posts of the upper gallery and crashed down out of sight, presumably onto the stage and all the groundlings, actors, and patrons unable to escape to safety through the single narrow exit.

Claire stood transfixed, taking it in, watching the green and argent halos given off by flames and smoke that now defined the theater walls. She was seeing first-hand the destruction of the famous landmark.

Claire stumbled out from under the trees and into the melee of crazed animals and frightened people, the heat of the blaze at their backs. They jostled and shoved at Claire in their panic, their burnt hair and seared skin terrible to see. Abruptly, a heavy body fell against her, shoving her off balance. She stumbled in terror, but an instant's glance revealed it wasn't One-eye come for his wench—it was something much worse, something barely human.

"H-help me, damn ye!" it rasped in a strangled voice, a sound like sandpaper scraping an open wound. It was a man, but only barely so. Its burned, shriveled skin spoke of fire and the grave; one eye seemed damaged beyond repair. Claire felt light-headed. Stars danced in front of her eyes.

"I...oh god," she squeaked, staring into the dark pool of the fellow's good eye. Red flickers danced in the iris, reflecting the hell exploding behind her. There was something horrifyingly familiar in that look.

"Verily, mine eyes doth deceive me...'tis *you!*" burbled the man-thing. With clawlike hands it clutched to its sunken chest what seemed to be a heavy, round object wrapped in animal hide. Leaning against her, the creature sent a reek of roasted flesh sweeping over them both. She vomited instantly and violently.

Sagging with its weight, the creature shifted the object clumsily into the crook of one arm and latched his free hand around Claire's bicep with appalling firmness. The fingers were filthy and the nails split, as if they'd clawed through solid earth.

"Let go of me!" she screamed, the heat of the inferno baking her bruised face. Terrified, she dragged the man-thing toward the line of trees and the river. The wattle-and-daub with which the exterior theater walls had been sealed roared with such heat Claire imagined the lashes searing from her eyelids. The tops of the nearest trees were starting to smoke. Fleeing peasants and ladies in ruined finery surrounded them as the air filled with cinders and cursing voices.

"Come on wi' ye," yelled a woman running toward her from one of the timbered houses beyond the oaks. "Every hand's needed!" She tossed a crude leather bucket at Claire's feet. It dawned on her that a bucket brigade was being formed to haul water up from the river. It was a futile effort, of course, if this place followed the course of history as she knew it. The Globe would burn to the dirt on which it was built, claiming a number of lives among its ashes, and would be reconstructed the following year on roughly the same spot.

"It won't help..." she said to the woman's disappearing back. Beyond the trees and between the row of houses she saw the bucket line forming; already sloshing containers were coming hand over hand toward the front of the line where people with handcarts and wagons waited to receive them.

The charred man clung to her arm with an iron grip. "Help me," he gasped. Claire forced her way toward the shadows under the oaks, the creature dragging heavily behind her. "I cannot hold the stone...ye must take it yourself, Mistress Porter."

"*What?*" Claire stopped. Her mind stalled.

At that moment, the stone tumbled from the man's grasp and landed with a crushing thump on Claire's instep. Yelping in pain, she knelt and grabbed at the rounded rock surface with both hands. Lightning flashed through her fingers and up her arms as her vision went white hot, then cold and black as empty space. A woman's face both beautiful and terrible swam into her field of vision, and cold eyes scoured her brain. She felt naked and flayed alive under that dead gaze. A screech rippled through her mind. Crying in pain, she wrapped her arms around her head.

"Miss Porter? Claire?" A familiar voice, very far away, then closer, brought her awake. "You seem to have got a nasty knock on the head." Firm hands took hold of her shoulders and helped her sit up. Opening her eyes a crack, she saw the bearded, ruddy face of Kit Bayard. Haloed in a sweep of soft fox-colored hair, his face hovered just above hers.

"Here, let me help you up. Can you stand?" He hauled her to her feet and slid his arm around her waist for support. "I was just making the rounds of the building before retiring, but imagine my surprise to find you lying down here. The floor is filthy. If you'd like to wash your face and hands, I can unlock the lobby restroom." His eyes were wary.

Claire's mind raced. "I was looking for Tom. I thought he might have come down here. I…think I tripped on the stairs and fell."

"Tom has gone home, as should you," offered Bayard, smiling and leading her toward the steps and up to the lobby.

"I know, I'm sorry. My mother's sick and home by herself. I'm really stupid."

"No harm done. Let's go up." He guided her firmly, his hand under her elbow.

When they reached the top of the stairs, he flipped the switch and the basement went dark. "May I walk you to your car?"

Claire was shaking. "N-no, I'm all right now." He was giving her a look that turned her knees to jelly—she'd stared into those eyes mere minutes ago, only then he'd had just one. Claire probed the inside of her lip with the tip of her tongue, but found no injury. Her head was spinning, her brain trying to deny the real pain and terror she'd just lived through…or imagined she had. The lights in the lobby flickered. With difficulty, she tuned back into what Bayard was saying.

"…all the wiring should be replaced, or so I'm told by the city fire marshal. I suspect they'd like to condemn the place and just boot us all out, even though I own the building. It's highly valuable…on the historical register, you know. "

"It is?" Claire was surprised. She'd just assumed he rented the theater space, like the ballet company upstairs. "I had no idea. I've lived here all my life and didn't know it was that old." Claire was babbling, making small talk to get her mounting hysteria under control. "I live at home, with my mother, who has emphysema. She has social security and my dad's life insurance money, but it's pretty tight. I was going to go back to school, the Chemistry program at Emory, but had to put that on hold to pay the bills and take care of her." She clamped her jaws shut. What the hell was she telling him all this for?

He nodded, guiding her to the front door. "A dutiful daughter. Well, you take care driving home, Miss Porter."

"Right. I will." She hurried through the door and down the sidewalk, hesitating just long enough to take a quick look over her shoulder. Bayard stood with both feet planted evenly in front of the Janus entrance, hands buried in the pockets of his voluminous trousers, standing there as if he owned the very ground under the two-faced god. She gave him a quick nod and walked briskly away, feeling his steady gaze on the small of her back.

Turning the corner and heading to the parking lot, Claire felt herself coming unraveled. She desperately needed to talk to someone about what she'd just gone through, but she had no idea who that person could be. Adelaide was New Age-y but seemed a lightweight for the terrors Claire had just seen and felt. What she'd experienced wasn't possible in her known universe. Who would believe such a story when she didn't believe it herself?

CHAPTER 14

Monday morning

"Sir? Can you hear me?" Paul's voice rose over the babble of people surrounding the scene in the parking lot of a mid-town office complex. "Look at me, stay with me, sir."

Claire got an oxygen mask over the nose and mouth of the man strapped to the stretcher while Paul made certain he didn't fade away before they could get him into the ambulance. She tore open his dress shirt so Paul could stick heart-monitoring electrodes onto his chest. Feeling underneath the frame of the stretcher, she pulled out a compact screen and watched the data uploading. Heart attack or stroke, from the way his vitals were hopscotching.

"I don't know what happened," a woman behind them was saying. "He just collapsed beside his car. His name is Gary Reynolds...he's in the law office next to ours."

Paul caught the name as they prepared to move the stretcher. "Gary? Gary! Can you see my hand—how many fingers?" The man shakily raised his own three fingers. "Three. That's good. Okay, you're gonna be fine. Just stay focused on my voice..."

Claire never ceased to be impressed with the bubble of calm that seemed to surround Paul whenever he was interacting with a patient. No one doubted for a second that he had absolute control of the situation. If anybody could keep the guy alive till they got to the hospital, it was Paul.

They rolled the stretcher up into the back of the ambulance, Paul smoothly securing it in place and keeping one eye on the heart monitor readings. Claire prepared the I-V and inexplicably missed the vein. Blood ran down the patient's arm.

"Claire! Focus!" Paul was looking at her in disbelief.

She gulped, horrified. Her hands were shaking as the scarlet trail of Mr. Gary Reynold's blood stained his shirt and held her transfixed. "S-sorry. I—"

"Don't be sorry. Be competent." Paul's voice was firm, with an edge she hadn't heard him use before, especially not toward her. "I don't know what's going on with you, but put it in a box until we get Mr. Reynolds safely delivered—alive—to the hospital. Then you and I will have a talk. Got it?"

Claire nodded. Her cheeks flamed. Mortified, she cleaned the I-V site and tried again, focusing only on this one task in front of her. The needle went in perfectly and she taped it in place. Paul gave her one last searching look and climbed into the driver's seat. He hit the lights and the siren, and pulled out of the parking lot, accelerating into the four-lane highway traffic. He talked to the dispatcher, confirming the status of the patient and their approximate location. Paul's voice was matter of fact, urgent but controlled. Claire did as she was told and put the Janus Theatre with all its attendant weirdness in a virtual box with a locked lid. She was a professional, a good one, and no matter what kind of mental breakdown might be looming, it wasn't going to jeopardize the safety of this man who was relying on her to save his life.

"Don't worry, you're going to be all right. We're only a few minutes away from the hospital." She went into her patient-calming mantra, putting her hand over the man's wrist to check his pulse and give him a comforting touch. Oddly, it comforted her as well.

He said something, muffled by the oxygen mask. She leaned close. "What?"

His eyes fixed hers. "Am I going to die?"

"Absolutely not. You've had a little heart complication and it's stabilized now. Just try to relax. You'll be fine."

"My wife...call..."

"Don't worry, as soon as we get you situated at the hospital, everyone who needs to know will be contacted. Everything's under control."

The man squeezed her hand and tried to smile. His voice was very faint. "Thank you. You're an angel."

She could hear the gears grinding and ambulance engine under full throttle as Paul maneuvered around vehicles and through traffic lights, and finally he was slowing, and turning into the Atlanta Medical Center's emergency entrance. Her patient was still awake and coherent...he would make it. Claire let her breath out.

Paul parked and came around to the rear doors, helping her roll the stretcher out. Two emergency orderlies were waiting for them at the door. They whisked the stretcher through the entrance and into a holding room as Paul briefed one of the intake staff on the patient's condition and what medications and treatments had been administered during the trip to the hospital. Finally Gary Reynolds, Esq., lawyer and heart attack patient, was fully transferred out of their hands.

They walked in silence out to the ambulance and climbed into the cab. Claire bucked her seatbelt and stared out the window while Paul checked in with the dispatcher, relating the details of the handoff to the Medical Center staff and confirming they would be heading back to base in a few minutes. He signed off and turned to Claire.

"Talk to me." Paul's tone was less intimidating now.

Claire's throat tightened, her voice going squeaky. "I don't even know where to start."

Paul shifted in his seat, facing her more directly. "Try me. I've seen a lot of shit you wouldn't believe and lived to tell it to my discharge psychiatrist."

Claire tried again, but there was just no easy way to explain what had led up to her obsessive need to go down into the theater basement, much less the disconnect with reality that happened after she fell and hit her head. She rubbed the back of her skull and found the tender lump where her brains had met the basement floor. At least that was irrefutable evidence for part of the story.

"I knew the minute you came in this morning something was off," said Paul. "Not a word to anybody, not even 'how the hell are yah?'…just sitting and staring at the floor, which is not like you. What's got you so uptight you can't even get a simple I-V in straight?"

Claire shut her eyes and held her head, just in case it decided to explode. "Something happened last week."

Paul said nothing, apparently willing to wait for her to get it out.

"I did something very stupid and very dangerous. And something happened that I can't explain…and now it feels like I've lost my mind." There, that was it in a nutshell. Her sanity had come unglued.

"Maybe you should have a chat with the staff shrink when we get back."

"God, I really don't want to do that." Claire slumped in her seat. She might get put on medical leave or even lose her job if the psych decided she was unfit. She couldn't allow that to happen. "Paul, when you came back from Iraq, what were your PTSD symptoms? Did you…see things that weren't real but you were convinced they were happening at the time?"

"Did I hallucinate? Yeah, a few times. Mostly waking up from nightmares and seeing things that weren't there."

Claire tried to collect her thoughts. "How real was it? I mean, did you think you were touching and smelling things that were imaginary?"

Paul's face pulled into a frown. "This 'something' that happened to you sounds traumatic."

"Yeah, you could say that."

"If you were assaulted, you should've gone to the hospital, you know."

"No, it wasn't anything like that. I went meddling where I shouldn't have, and fell and got knocked out."

Paul shook his head. "You know concussion symptoms as well as I do. Blurred vision? Head still hurt?"

Claire touched the back of her head. "Just the lump where my head hit the floor. No lingering headaches or double images the day after. I didn't really black out. Well, I did, but I couldn't wake up. I mean, I was awake but in a hallucinated scene that seemed physical. The place was absolutely solid, and smelled, with people who physically interacted with me. I didn't know how to make the hallucination stop."

Paul's voice was even, nonjudgmental. "So how'd you get out of it?"

"Someone woke me up. I heard him calling my name, like he was far away, and then my eyes popped open and I was back in the real world. My real world. I don't know where that other world was. Well, I know it was England, sixteenth century, historically accurate, but not my reality. Oh shit, I sound like a crazy person."

"And the things that happened in that imaginary place…you can't process the experience. Can't shake it off."

"That's about it."

"Is that what happened when you froze during the call this morning? Some trigger flashed you back?"

Claire looked up, relieved this was Paul she was unloading this crap to and not somebody else. "Yes. That's exactly it. I can't get the experience out of my mind. Could a hallucinated state seem so real that you were convinced you'd been hit in the face and could feel the pain and taste the blood?" She looked down, embarrassed. Her hands were trembling again.

Paul reached out and took one of them in his big calloused fist. "Okay, here's the deal. I need a partner I can absolutely rely on, and in your present state you shouldn't be on call. Agreed?"

"Yes," Claire said in a small voice.

"What's it gonna take to get you past this? Just talking to me probably won't be enough. You need to go see the staff psych."

"I don't want to be medicated. A couple of Zolofts and I won't be able to function."

"There are meds, and there are meds. It doesn't have to be anything that turns you into a vegetable. The point is, if you slipped up with a routine procedure, what else could happen?"

"I can't lose my job."

Paul chewed his thumbnail for a minute. "Tell you what…you call in sick and take the day off. I won't report this morning's screw-up. See if sleep and a stress-free day puts things right. If not, promise me you'll get help. Why do you think we got the services of a shrink? This is the kind of work that drives people crazy because you can't just leave it at the office, and the longer you do this kind of work, the more susceptible you become. You should take advantage of having a professional on staff to talk to. " He gave her hand a gentle squeeze and let go. Settling back in the driver's seat, he cranked the ambulance.

"Thanks." Claire's voice was barely audible.

"Just do what I said." He pulled out into the flow of traffic. "'Cause if you don't, I'll be a hard-ass like you never saw before."

She nodded. "I promise."

* * * *

Claire turned the key in the lock and slipped inside. The house was cool. She checked the thermostat—67°—and cranked it up to 72. Normally she kept the house warmer at night, but she also hadn't expected her shift to run three hours late.

She went down the hall to her mother's room. Her mother was lying on her side, her back to Claire, wrapped in the comforter she used on the couch. "Mom? Everything okay?" No response. Claire's stomach clinched. "Mom?" She'd steeled herself countless times in her imagination for *the* moment, which could be now, but which she hoped with rising panic was not.

She clicked on the bedside lamp, its shaded glow barely illuminating the room. Claire touched her mother's wrinkled cheek. It was chilled. She pulled Gwen over onto her back and put her ear to her mother's thin lips. There was a ghost of breath. Maybe.

"Mom! Wake up!"

Gwen's eyelids fluttered, and Claire sank down on the bed beside her. It appeared now was not going to be that time.

"What?" Her mother's voice was faint, dream fogged, as if she'd come a long way back just to find out what her daughter was on about. Her eyes opened fully and she tried to sit up. "What's...the matter?"

"Nothing. I just had a hard time waking you."

"I heard you." There was a hint of peevishness in Gwen's soft voice.

Claire allowed herself to not obsess over how this might have been the perfect end to the unbelievably crap day she'd gone through. Losing her mother at the close of this shift would have been the end of the line, she knew that much.

"What time is it?" Her mother rubbed at her eyes.

"Seven-thirty. I was going to make supper...what do you want?"

Her mother shook her head. "I don't need anything. Just knowing you're home..." The sentence remained unfinished.

Claire got up. "Well, I'll check on you in a bit. Maybe you might want to watch TV or something."

Her mother gave her hand a squeeze, the one Paul had engulfed in his massive paw. "Maybe."

Claire went down the hall to her own bedroom and changed into her shapeless old sweats. Comfort clothes. She went back into the living room, took a quick look at the mail she'd pulled from the box by the front door—snail mail spam and a nasty looking bill with an address window—and went to the kitchen. She got pump 'n rye marble bread out of the fridge along with sharp cheddar slices, spicy brown mustard, and a stick of butter. Heating an iron skillet, she melted chunks of butter, swiped mustard on the bread, stacked it with cheese, and watched it sizzle in the pan. Comfort food. She flipped the sandwich over at just the right level of toastiness and sagged against the counter. Who was she kidding? These comforts were all surface tricks, disassociation, going through the motions and pretending everything was normal when she knew effing well it wasn't.

She plunked the grilled cheese onto a plate and took it to the table near the patio doors. Insulated drapes were pulled over the glass, protection against the cold. Claire scarfed the sandwich down in a few bites and then went looking for something sweet to balance it out. Nothing but a nearly empty jar of Nutella, which she smeared on a couple of vanilla wafers. It was almost acceptable, as desserts went. Close to chocolate but not quite.

Licking her fingers, she went back to her room and sat on the edge of the bed, staring at the floor. This had once been her safe space, her one place where everything was the way she wanted it and regardless of what went on in the world outside, here she was happy. The smallish room was filled with the oversized crème and gold trimmed French Provincial bedroom set her parents had given her the Christmas before she'd entered middle school—wide gray-white dresser and mirror against the wall that held her tiny closet, double bed with scrollwork headboard and footboard lodged against the wall opposite the dresser, three-shelf nightstand beside the door. She'd picked it all out herself from a display set up in the furniture store where they'd gone looking for an upgrade to the rollaway bed and second-hand chest of drawers from their old apartment. An extravagant choice at the time, she understood it now as a deliberate attempt to step outside her narrow notions of self image, of what she thought she was allowed and what she could be. The room had been her fantasy escape pod all through middle and high school. These days, functional modern suited her tastes better.

The large pieces left little room for anything else beyond a small modular desk under the single window. She'd spent a lot of time studying at that desk, for whatever good it had done her. The folding white-painted door to her closet was open and a jumbled mess of shoes, socks, medical scrubs, backpacks, clothes destined for Goodwill, and empty shoeboxes filled the shallow space. Not too many clothes on hangers. She'd always preferred jeans to dresses.

Claire wrapped her arms around her ribs and shut her eyes. It felt like everything that had anchored her to a meaningful reality was being relentlessly stripped away. Her dad was gone and with him the means to pay for any further schooling she might have fantasized about. Jackie would be gone soon, and probably her mother in the not too distant future. Her job was in peril, and even the stupid theater gig she'd joined for recreation had turned sour. In fact, it had turned upside-down stark raving crazy. Claire shivered. Maybe she had a fever coming on. Just her luck to catch a virus when she needed to be on game.

Paul had told her to rest and get some stress-free sleep. She couldn't help but laugh, sleep being the one thing she most wanted to avoid, no matter how exhausting her day had been. Sleep brought dreams of that terrifying presence she'd touched in the Janus basement. The resident ghost? She sure as hell hoped not.

She didn't believe in the supernatural the way Addie did, but she did believe people could go insane and delusional—total barking mad. It occurred to her that all her attempts to repress the black void of depression and its break with reality had shunted that lava plume of craziness up a side fissure. The blowout had let her obsessions over *Dr. Faustus* and everything connected to it morph into a full-blown psychotic episode. Claire began to shake uncontrollably. She considered adjusting the thermostat again, just to get her hands and feet warm.

The only shred of comfort in all this was knowing that Paul had experienced the dream state/waking delusion syndrome and somehow moved past it. She knew that PTSD dreams played the same traumatic event over and over like a broken record because the brain wasn't able to process the threatening memories—it would just keep cycling through them, again and again, until you cracked up completely or found some way to abort the cycle. In her case, the nightmare she'd been locked in before coming on duty this morning was the same one that played in her slumbering mind every night since she'd hit her head in the Janus basement.

There was one particular detail of that dream that had transfixed her with the I-V in hand over poor Mr. Reynolds. Before the alarm went off that morning she'd been dreaming of the ghostly woman wrapped in her gray windswept shroud, staring at Claire with those dead-fish eyes. And she'd seen herself walk into her mother's room with a pillow and place it firmly down over the sleeping face. It hadn't taken much pressure, and just a couple of minutes...almost too easy. Then she'd hooked up an I-V that drained all her mother's blood into an airtight bag. Part of her sleeping mind was screaming in revulsion while the rest of it felt daring, even exhilarated, to be doing something off-the-charts terrifying and forbidden. She'd startled awake, covered in sweat with tears leaking from the corners of her eyes. But worse, the spectral woman had been in her room, at the foot of her bed, hovering about three feet off the floor with her seaweed hair strung out in a swirling wind that Claire neither heard nor felt. But the fingers-on-chalkboard shriek that came out of the creature's mouth had sent Claire diving under the covers with her pillow over her head, shaking so violently she could barely breathe.

She hid, paralyzed, under the quilt until her muscles ached from the strain, waiting for cold hands to rip out her spine or worse, but when she finally dared to look, the terrible manifestation was gone. She lay crouched and awake, barely breathing, until gray daylight began to fill the room.

CHAPTER 15

Bayard sat on a folding chair in the center of the basement, arms crossed over his chest, facing the alcove at the bottom of the stairs. The stainless steel thermos he used to hold blood rested on the floor beside his foot. He'd been careful not to make contact with the stone during this morning's libation, as he had no wish to repeat his encounter with Mistress Ó Braonáin. He remembered her name quite well. In fact, he remembered the night on which he'd first been shown to her as if it had happened this week.

The year was 1589. Three years before that, he'd been a scholarship student at Corpus Christi College, Cambridge, about to graduate at age twenty-two with his M.A. However, certain naysayers had tried to prevent his matriculation and void his scholarship. Bayard remembered with perfect clarity a conversation he'd overheard in a quiet cloister. The College administrator's querulous voice and that of the bishop were unmistakable.

"The man is impious, a known atheist, a wastrel, a blasphemer, and moreover 'tis said he doth consort with both men and women."

"But my Lord Bishop, his scholarship is unquestioned—"

"He is a danger to this College and the Church itself."

"'Tis most likely idle boasting, my Lord, just a student's merriment—"

"Art thou defending the troublemaker?"

"Nay, my Lord, but..."

Bayard had listened to them talk of tossing him out of the university altogether in spite of his obvious intellect and creative genius. But then, someone from the Queen's Privy Council had intervened, and a certain very famous gentleman, the Queen's counselor and advisor in all things scientific and arcane, Dr. John Dee, had interceded on his behalf. Shortly afterwards, the objections and obvious calumny had been waved aside and his degree duly granted. Bayard smiled a wicked little smile, remembering how his liturgical benefactors had expected him to repay them by taking Holy Orders, when instead he'd bid them farewell and made straight for London, copies of his plays under his arm.

The following year, a production of his first serious drama, *Tamburlaine the Great, Part One*, was mounted at The Rose, a small theater in south London, and met with thunderous acclaim—demands for more from the talented pen of Kit "the Fox" Marlowe poured in. He'd considered his playwriting career well and truly launched, yet all the while he continued to be tagged as a wit and a wag, a hothead who'd say anything with a few tankards in him, just to draw a rise out of his audience. Idiots all. Irony and subtlety were unknown to them. He'd been quite willing to thrash his defamers to a bloody pulp in the street, but he preferred sparring with words, his best weapon. He relished a spirited debate among friends whose knowledge and intelligence matched his own, ignoring the dimwitted knaves who presumed him to be all one thing or all another without understanding his intellectual complexity. Bayard frowned. He suffered no fools, not then and not now. Especially not now. Which went some way toward explaining his brief dalliance with Morris, with whom he was in complete agreement concerning the moronic and the ignorant.

And which brought him round to Claire Porter, who'd done a very foolish thing that he could not explain. When she'd joined the company, she'd seemed to be extremely level-headed, dependable, predictable, what have you...all those things that made for an excellent crew member, right there on task when someone's lines got dropped or a prop couldn't be found. She was reserved, even-tempered, and of a humanitarian disposition, although he'd begun to get annoyed at her sudden interest in the welfare of the unfortunate Danny. But what in the name of all the gods had she been doing lying unconscious at the foot of the stairs in the basement? That was a dilemma his superior powers of deduction could not answer and his inner guidance could not suss out. She told him she'd been looking for Tom, which was plausible enough, but such a simple explanation wasn't sitting well. So here he was, tasting the room with his not-quite-human senses (a faint whiff of the charnel house permeated the air when the banshee hovered near the veil between their words) and plotting how to trick the creature into revealing what was really afoot...because something certainly was. He hadn't lived in thrall to the cornerstone for nearly four centuries not to recognize that something was different, the balance shifted. The witch had never attacked him openly like that, and he wondered what had made her so bold.

He shifted his butt on the chair and thought back to the invitation that had come in the winter of that year when his career was just taking off. The language of the letter was formal, even academic. A scholar's tone that had immediately piqued his interest and hooked his curiosity—as he now understood was its intention. That single sheet of vellum had launched his life on a trajectory he couldn't have imagined then in his most lurid opium dreams, and even now, at times, the fact of his non-life seemed impossible, yet inescapable.

"To Mr. Christopher Marlow, a briefe and graciouslie sent request and invitation," Dee had written in careful, elegant penmanship. He alluded briefly his recent trip to Poland, "my last voyage beyond ye Seas, was duly undertaken by her Maiesties good favour and licence," during which he had been entertained by certain members of the nobility, not the least of whom was Emperor Rudolf II who received him at Prague Castle. He mentioned having met numerous influential scholars and thinkers whose writings on matters spiritual and arcane— "thinges invisible, thinges transitorie, & momentarie, thinges mortall"—far surpassed that of anything he'd read before arriving on the Continent. He skirted around the notion of being Her Majesty's eyes and ears abroad, and finally arrived at the kernel of the invitation: Marlowe's name had been put forward by both Sir Philip Sydney and the right honorable Secretary of the Queene's Privy Council, Sir Francis Walsingham. In short, Marlow had guessed, reading between the lines, it was a recruitment letter: an offer of patronage of his theater endeavors in return for a little spywork on the side, something a clever fellow like himself "should fynde no great inconvenience."

The letter had promised a "humble repast in ye company of learned gentlemen," with the promise of a showing of what remained of the fabled library known to many of the London *literati* and that still held untold rare volumes in spite of the thievery inflicted upon it. The letter concluded, "Very speedily written, this twelfth even, and twelfth day, in my poore Cottage, at Mortlake: *Anno. 1589. Your humble servaunt, John Dee.*"

Bayard still had the very letter somewhere among his personal papers. While the offer of becoming a spy in Her Majesty's service appealed to his sense of adventure, his strongest incentive to honor the invitation had been to see Dee's famed library. He'd hoped the rumors of a break-in and plundering while the entire household was abroad hadn't been as dire as reported. He remembered feeling intense loathing (as he did now) for knaves who held theoretical discourse of the thinking mind to be of little value and the books chronicling such thought worth even less, but it had then occurred to him that someone who knew the value of the books had probably taken and sold them to a collector much like Dee himself. In fact, it was highly likely many of the missing books would resurface years hence in someone else's rare collection. Bayard smiled, seated on his metal folding chair in his theater basement in the twenty-first century, knowing now that this was exactly how things had turned out. You could even look it up on Wikipedia and find out where some of those missing Latin and Greek tomes had landed. Four-hundred-year-old hindsight had its perks.

He'd sent a response back to Dee almost immediately, accepting the invitation. Remembering the letter sent his thoughts arrowing back to the day when life as he'd experienced it had stopped forever. He could see it now, Threadneedle Street, set amidst a twisted maze of alleyways and crowded cobble-paved roads defining the London neighborhood where he rented rooms at the top of a five-storey timbered building—his landlord's tapestry shop on the ground floor and living quarters rising two rooms per level above it. He'd stood at the window of his sitting room, surveying the hustle of life flowing through the narrow street below. The sun was still well above the line of trees and church spires across the river, but heading westward. He turned away.

It was time to set out. His stomach tightened with anticipation—one didn't visit the Mage of Mortlake without some trepidation, even on a formal invitation. The man might be the Queen's official astrologer and counselor, and she might even stop her palfrey at his front gate on her way to Richmond Palace, but villagers living within shouting distance of Mortlake House on the Thames kept their distance and averted their eyes as the infamous philosopher took himself across the street to St.

Mary Magdalene's Church for prayers. Other acquaintances spoke of his kindness, generosity, even piety...but the fear of sorcery clung to the man's flowing scholar's robes like invisible smoke.

Marlowe shrugged into his jerkin and tied it shut over his least-mended doublet. He pulled his heaviest woolen cloak out of the chest at the foot of his bed. Despite the pallid light filtering through clouds, the day felt raw with the promise of rain or possibly sleet on the wind. The horse he'd hired to carry him to Dee's home in Mortlake was a fine beast that had cost him a purse of silver, but he had no intention of arriving on foot, looking dusty and road-weary. Likewise, his dislike of being on water (due mostly to his inability to swim, but also in part to the drowning death of an acquaintance near this time last year) prevented him from walking down to the nearest quay and shouting "Oars!" to hire a boat to make the eight-mile journey downriver beyond the city walls.

In addition to his cloak, he donned a new woolen cap with a hawk's feather fitted rakishly into the band, and as a precaution against highwaymen, tucked a wheellock pistol into the waistband of his breeches. A short dagger hidden in a secret pocket, and he pronounced himself ready. Latching the door to his rooms, he took himself down the steep narrow staircase to the ground floor and out onto the street. Walking briskly, avoiding the usual detritus of horse dung and chamber-pot tossings fouling the town's roadways, he reached the stables of his hostler friend, a fellow who'd been the stable-marshal for an aged viscount on an estate near Tewkesbury before the old man's death.

These days, stablemaster Kent Castorbridge kept a small mews of his own near the Bridge over the Thames, mostly hiring out carthorses for tradesmen and palfreys for riders. In addition, he stabled a courser and a destrier he'd brought with him from the old lord's estate. The warhorse was a magnificent animal that could have been sold for enough gold to set the stables up in fine style, but for sentimental reasons, as he'd explained to Marlowe, he was unwilling to part with it. The courser, as powerful as the destrier but lighter and more agile, he hired out to riders with skill enough to handle it properly. Marlowe was that sort of man.

"Mind ye keep a tight hand on the reins w' this one," Kent told him as he slid into the saddle. "He likes to run."

Marlow reached back and ran his hand over the horse's powerful hindquarters. He'd admired the well-muscled chest and strong arched neck of the beast immediately upon entering the stable. "Likewise do I." He grinned at the stablemaster. The horse danced sideways, impatient to be off.

"He taketh a liking to thee, 'tis clear." Pocketing his payment, Kent waved them off.

Marlowe guided the horse out of the stableyard, heading toward High Road that ran parallel to the Thames. On a mount like this, he was likely to arrive at Mortlake House somewhat sooner than he'd anticipated. Kent had given him directions to the village, although they weren't really needed. Anyone with two wits to rub together knew how to find it—on horseback, you could head south and westward through the Southwark district where the Rose and Swan theaters and at least two bear-baiting arenas were located and keep going along the main road till you reached Mortlake, where you'd look for the three-storey stone house in a cluster of smaller dwellings that constituted the village, or you could put yourself in the hands of a ferryman who'd take you downriver to the small quay adjacent to the alchemist's property.

Marlowe sat the horse with his knees holding it tightly and negotiated the crowded streets of the city around London Bridge, avoiding an overturned wagon and a pile of smashed wine barrels and narrowly missing collision with a carriage bearing some lord's crest. Along the bankside of the road, teeming river commerce bustled about among quays on both sides of the waterway. The scent of the river was both fair and foul, with the foul lessening the further he traveled away from the town center.

He passed without incident through Southwark with its army of cutpurses, trollops, and knaves loitering out front of its taverns and brothels. Once he was well beyond the city walls, he gave the courser its head and let it gallop some distance before reining it in. It did them both good.

The sun had just begun to dip below the trees when he spotted the house long before his horse trotted up to the iron gate. Tethered to the fence was the tallest horse he'd ever laid eyes on—a dappled grey with smoky mane and tail, a magnificent Andalusian, if he was not mistaken. Under the Iberian saddle he made note of the dark red saddle blanket trimmed with tiny gold tassels. In front of the towering gray sat a sleek black carriage with a Royal crest on its door, harnessed to a handsome bay. The coachman sat on the bench with a heavy rug around his knees, clearly resigned to waiting till his employer's business should be concluded.

The house was situated between two others facing the river, with a small courtyard in front, a windowless stone building at the side used for the deity knew what, a large informal tree-lined garden behind, bare now, that nearly abutted the walled cemetery grounds of St. Mary Magdelene's Church. Across the narrow track that served as the "high river road" it was a mere couple of yards down to the riverbank where the aforementioned stone quay for tying up small boats thrust itself a dozen strides out into the water. The property of Mortlake House was clearly of better means than the dwellings around it, but it wasn't what anyone would call a manor or an estate. A gentleman's house, but fairly modest.

As Marlowe sat his horse thinking these thoughts, a young lad of no more than nine or ten, shivering in a thin doublet and wool jerkin, came around the side of the house.

"Be ye Master Marlow, then?" he asked in a squeaky voice, through teeth chattering with the cold.

Marlowe made to dismount. "Aye, and who might ye be?"

"Arthur Dee, your worship," said the boy, taking the reins of his horse. "My father bids thee go in where 'tis warm. I'm to take the horses down to the stable out of the weather." He pointed toward a fairly new stable beyond the second house, its stalls packed with hay. "And to thee, sir," he said to the coachman, "he doth bid me say thou'rt welcome to come round to the kitchen and have a cup of warmed cider."

The coachman nodded and climbed down somewhat stiffly from the bench seat, and made to lead the bay off toward the stable. Marlowe turned his back to the boy, pulled the pistol out of his breeches and stowed it in a bag affixed to the saddle. Now that he'd arrived safely at his destination, there was no need to alarm the household with a display of weaponry.

At that moment the heavy oak door of the house swung open. On the threshold stood a tall begowned figure who could only be the famous—or infamous, depending on one's opinion of astrologers and sorcerers—Doctor John Dee. He made an imposing figure framed in the doorway, thin of face with a salt and pepper beard that flowed down his breast but was meticulously trimmed to a point. He wore a heavy scholar's gown of some dark material over his woolen jerkin, breeches, and stockings.

Marlowe was normally not intimidated by any man—and often in fact enjoyed exercising the force of his own considerable charisma—but for one instant he was speechless. Only for an instant, however. He moved forward quickly to greet his host.

"Christopher Marlow, at your service, m'lord counselor."

Dee bowed slightly from the shoulders and his long arm swept gracefully toward the warmly lit parlor beyond the door. "Master Marlowe. Enter and be welcome." His manners were elegant, reserved, and somewhat effete, an effect Marlowe supposed was the result of his years spent in foreign courts.

Dee led him through the parlor and into the main hall. Marlowe silently blessed the warmth radiating from a massive fieldstone fireplace blazing at the far end of the high-ceiling room. Two other men stood near, enjoying its red glow. The floor of the hall was set with well-fitted flagstones, a surprising discovery when he'd expected to find bare wood or mats made of rushes, which was typical of most country houses.

An ample young woman with straw-colored hair escaping from under her linen cap came out of the cavernous kitchen, accompanied by two ruddy-faced girls somewhat younger than the boy who'd met him at the gate.

"My wife Jane," said Dee, "and two of my daughters, Frances and Margaret."

They curtsied as if he were royalty, although Goodwife Dee gave him a steady gaze that let him know who really managed this domestic scene. He had no doubt that she was a wench who knew her own mind and kept a tidy household. Mistress Dee collected his cloak and folded it neatly before placing it on a chest beside two others.

Dee turned to the guests in front of the fire. "My Lord Sir Francis Walsingham, Secretary of the Queen's Privy Council." Marlowe met the man's eyes and gave him a short bow, which was returned with a genial nod of the head.

Of medium height, the Secretary was dressed in somber black wool from head to foot with a lace-trimmed white collar. His features were equally devoid of humor—small suspicious deep-set eyes, tiny thin-lipped mouth partially hidden by a tightly trimmed dark goatee in a rat's face. Marlow held his tongue as the man looked him up and down, and nodded again with a half-smile. He was a dangerous man to know, people said, especially if you were on the wrong side, which included Spaniards and anyone opposing the Protestant Reformation.

Dee introduced the other dinner guest as Magister Coronzon of Wittenberg, a university lecturer and dealer in rare books engaged by Dee to track down the "volumes stol'n from me during my absence when my family and I were abroad." The man was the most elegantly clad and groomed of the four. His breeches and jacket were of dark claret velvet brocaded in thin silver and gold thread that shown like stars from one angle but looked flat ruddy black from another. Marlowe blinked several times to see if the effect was just a trick of the light, although he could not be sure. The man's features, however, were even more unsettling. From one angle the sharp planes of his face seemed lined and world-weary, but from another the firelight lit him up with the exquisite beauty of youth. His pale hair was tied back at his nape with a velvet ribbon in a somewhat old-fashioned style. Marlowe had to force himself not to stare.

"Shall we sup first, then deal with weightier matters anon?" Dee stretched out his long-fingered hand toward a ponderous oak table laden with food. Four high-backed chairs, two to a side, awaited. It was clear that Mistress Dee had outdone herself, considering the high-ranking guests. River-caught mackerel and perch baked with plums and apricots were served beside mussels, oysters, and crabs piled on platters. A large basket of hard-crusted white bread sat beside a pot of wildflower honey. Pewter tankards of ale and cider marked each place. Marlowe salivated, having eaten only a hunk of cheese before setting out.

Dinner conversation ranged from the chance of snow to the cost of a perfectly matched pair of horses, to the writings of John Calvin and the perils of sea travel. Gradually the feast disappeared as their talk lingered over the intrigues of Court and Marlowe's latest triumph at The Rose. Quickly Mistress Dee and an older daughter cleared away the repast and put in its place a porcelain compote filled with walnuts, hazelnuts, and candied dried fruits. The delicious aroma of sliced gingerbread spiced with cloves and cinnamon and crusted with anise seeds filled the room.

Sated at last, the men retired upstairs to the famous library, which occupied the entire second floor. Marlowe had to stop himself from gawking, as all four walls, from the floor to the heavy-timbered ceiling, were covered in shelving containing priceless books from every corner of the world. A long mahogany table took up most of the space in the center of the room. It was covered with opened books and scattered sheaves of parchment bearing notes, calculations, sketches, and blocks of writing in a flowing, looping hand. Clearly this was a workroom, used for study and invention, not a museum.

Magister Coronzon crossed the room in long strides to stand at the tall window with its lead glass panes set in intricate tracery. It occurred to Marlow that although the house might seem ordinary to the likes of Lord Walsingham and his palace cronies, there was evidence throughout this ordinary house of money spent. He imagined Dee had patrons capable of thanking him in expensive ways. Coronzon turned his back to the room, seemingly not interested in the discussion of spies and intrigue.

Walsingham, however, made it clear where his motives lay. Marlowe listened intently to his description of how Her Gracious Majesty Elizabeth I "could make use of the talents of a man such as yourself, who is known to many and can go places where perhaps others cannot." He further explained how plots against the Queen's life were fomented by enemies abroad and at home, and how the network of spies he'd established was the front-line defense against these plots. Would Marlowe consider joining their ranks?

"My lord Secretary, 'twould be an honor," he'd answered, wondering what he'd gotten himself into. He couldn't very well refuse an offer that came from Court, but he wasn't entirely convinced it would turn out to his benefit. He well knew from his many contacts that spies, once compromised or no longer needed, tended to meet a swift and secretive end.

Walsingham offered his hand to grip. "We'll speak more of this anon. For now, 'tis enough that you've agreed. I bid you farewell, then. The Heavens grant us success in all our endeavors."

"Shall I accompany your Grace downstairs?" Dee asked him.

"Nay, sir, I require but a kiss of thy lovely wife and I am on my way." Dee gave him a withering smile. Watching the subtle sparring between these two masters of intrigue and deception, Marlowe wondered if, for once, he might possibly be out of his depth. In spite of protestations, Dee followed the minister down the stairs, leaving Marlowe alone with the tall stranger from Wittenberg.

"I sense a hesitancy," the man said, looking over his shoulder at Marlowe. "Playing at spies not to your liking?"

Marlowe startled. Again, Coronzon's strange accent caught him up. At times during the evening he'd sounded like a proper Englishman, even addressing Dee in the familiar with his *thees* and *thous*, but at other times syntax and figures of speech entirely foreign peppered his discourse. It wasn't German, or French, or even Italian because Marlowe knew those languages. It had a Latinate punch to it, but he wasn't sure. In fact, everything about Coronzon was slippery, shifting, hard to pin down. It was most unnerving.

"The theater's more to my liking," he said, feeling strangely detached from his words, as if he were a lurking presence high up in the gallery looking down on a play in progress. Heat flamed his cheeks. Marlowe stilled the urge to open his jacket and unlace his jerkin at the neck, even though the room was chilly.

Coronzon watched him with a lazy, half-lidded gaze. Marlowe's mind was suddenly filled with the fleeting image of a stalking reptile. The silver threads gleamed on the man's jacket as he turned his back to the window and faced the eight-branched candelabra alight on the book table. "My own interest is in observing man's hidden drives and desires. Such a complicated species." The words were delivered barely above a whisper, yet Marlowe heard him perfectly well.

Unbelievably, Christopher Marlowe—the great London wit and master of words—had no comeback…his brain seemed to have come unhinged from his vocal cords. He could only stare at the sharp planes of Coronzon's face, etched in firelight.

"So much want and need, yet so much repression." Coronzon's voice and breath brushed his cheek below the ear, yet the man stood several feet away. Marlowe staggered a step backward and swallowed hard. Inexplicably, surreptitiously, he was certain the Magister had begun to seduce him without even touching him. How this could be he was at a loss to explain, but his deepest, most hidden secrets suddenly seemed opened and laid out on the table with all the books and documents, on display for any who could read the secret appetites of his heart.

Coronzon reached inside his coat. "Care for a smoke?"

"Nay…I…failed to bring a pipe with me." He'd only recently taken up the practice made popular by Sir Walter Raleigh and his privateering friends from the New World colonies.

Coronzon smiled and licked his top lip. Marlowe's heart balked for a beat or two—was that tongue forked? He rubbed at his eyes. Surely not. The Wittenberg scholar or book dealer or whatever he was removed from an inner pocket a delicate pipe with a slender stem of four or five inches attached to a small round bowl. It was already filled with a pinch of tobacco that wafted the scent of cherry blossoms into the room. The man produced a thin straw from the same pocket, held it to a candle flame and as soon as it took light, applied it to the leaf in the pipe bowl. He inhaled deeply and allowed the smoke to escape slowly through his nostrils. He handed the pipe to Marlowe.

Without a word, he took hold of the pipe by the bowl. It was smooth and silky to the touch, ivory, yellowed with age. He also realized the bowl was carved with the gamboling figures of nymphs and satyrs—he could feel them under his fingertips. He inhaled and tasted the sharp, sweet aroma all the way down to the bottom of his lungs. He was certain that nothing had ever tasted as blissful or produced as satisfying a sensation in his body and mind in the mere quarter century he'd been alive. He moved to return the pipe, but Coronzon raised his hand.

"Nay, my good playwright, have another taste. It's the best leaf available. I've carried it here straight from the highland fields of Peru."

Marlowe inhaled again. How could he not? At that moment, a rumbling under his feet and the growing din of iron-shod wheels on cobblestone gave him a start. From the increasing avalanche of noise, he was convinced a monstrously huge coach or wagon must be passing outside. Gripped by an irrational fear, he strained to see though the leaded panes to the rutted dirt track that passed through the village but all was total darkness, neither starlight nor torchlight on the river, nor falling snow in the moonlight. It was as if he were looking out the window with his eyes pinched shut. He staggered back from the sill, heart pounding in his breast. The ivory pipe slipped from his fingers but somehow ended up in the grasp of Magister Coronzon before it hit the floor.

Coronzon stowed the pipe in its hidden pocket and smiled cordially, as if he'd heard nothing unusual. "Did you know our learned Dr. Dee has an alchemical laboratory?"

Marlowe swallowed. "I-I did not."

Coronzon nodded sagely. "Aye, 'tis a wonder. What he does in there is part of the reason men fear him for a sorcerer."

Marlowe struggled to get his brains unscrambled. Had the pipeweed been laced with something? "He seems a fair gentleman to me. I...see no reason to fear him."

Coronzon laughed a most melodious laugh that insinuated itself around the room, caressed the candle flames, and stroked the heavy timbers of the ceiling before settling itself in Marlowe's thick russet hair. Or so it seemed. He shook his head as if to wake from a dream.

"I believe my Lord Walsingham has departed. Come below, sir, and have a final cup with the Professor and myself. We have something to show you that I think you will find fascinating." Coronzon crossed nimbly from window to doorway almost before Marlowe could register that he had moved at all. Struck dumb, he followed the tall, slender figure out of the library and down to the main room where Dee waited beside the great fireplace.

Coronzon nodded without speaking, and Dee pulled on his heavy cloak and handed Marlowe's to him. The three of them exited the front door and went out into the night.

Kit Bayard rose to his feet. He'd wasted too much time dawdling around with ghosts of the past when those in the present demanded immediate attention. He stretched to his full height, letting the kinks unwind from his spine. To mere mortals, he cut a smart figure in a black turtleneck, khaki cargo pants which he loved for the many pockets, and Moroccan leather boots with a slight heel. To the minions of Death, however, he must seem a withered, pallid shade who refused to cross over. This pending afterlife, for want of a better term, had its attractions, but lately it wasn't following the agreed-upon rules as he understood them.

"I don't know what you're playing at," he said aloud, "but I am still master of the *buachloch* and don't either of you forget it. You cannot remake the terms of the bargain." At least he didn't think so.

The image of Dee and his black-caped companion ignited in his brain. What had they told him, those two, when his ownership of the stone was sealed? He tried to remember the exact words.

"Have a care not to touch anything," Dee admonished him as they made their way around tables packed tight with beakers, retorts, cauldrons, vials, and grinding stones. He followed as bidden, Dee's tall gangly figure ahead of him, Magister Coronzon's presence behind him like a warm breath on the back of his neck although the man was several feet away. They'd entered the mysterious building in the side yard with a raw wind at their backs, but once inside with the heavy iron-hinged door latched shut, the air was still with no hint of the escalating storm. In the pitch dark, Dee had struck flint with practiced accuracy, which caught a piece of charcloth and produced a tiny flame. From it he lit a fat beeswax candle ready beside the door. He held it aloft and details of the room leapt into view.

At the back of the laboratory, on one of its windowless stone walls hung a drawing nearly as tall as a man. Marlowe stared at the lone symbol inscribed there—it wasn't an astrological sign or a foreign letter like a Hebrew *aleph*. Black ink on parchment, it took the shape of a circle with a smaller circle inside like a single eye, a crescent on top like horns and a vertical line descending from the bigger circle to represent perhaps a body with a shorter line midway across it where arms might be depicted. The vertical line terminated in an inverted crescent, somewhat suggestive of legs. It bore the vague suggestion of a humanoid figure (a horned Cyclops came to his mind), but in truth, it looked like nothing he'd seen before.

Dee followed his gaze. "'Tis a glyph given to me in divine meditation. Thus you see an angelic expression of the ineffable unity of all Creation. I have used it as guidance in my philosophical and mathematical studies."

Again, Marlowe could think of nothing to say. The man was obviously deadly serious, but it was clear that his mind operated on planes not normally frequented by ordinary people. Dee seemed to sense his confusion. "A difficult concept to grasp, of course. Some years ago when I was much younger I penned an exhaustive interpretation of it. *Monas Hieroglyphica,* 'tis not likely you've read it."

"The Hieroglyphic Monad," offered the Magister, crowding from behind in the tight squeeze between a heavy, long worktable in the room's center and deep shelves containing laboratory glassware and corked vessels filled with who knew what. If Marlowe had decided to retreat and leave these two to their own dark devices, he could not have done so without a physical struggle. He stood, trembling, caught between the two taller men, grim in their black cloaks.

"You'd something to show me—was it this?" He nodded toward the glyph, hating the fact that his usually sonorous actor's voice had gone tremulous.

"Nay," answered Dee. "What I have for you rests there." He led them to a small round table hidden in the shadows of a corner. On the table rested a leather bag closed at the top by a thick drawstring. It seemed innocuous, a simple leather bag containing...something round. Marlowe could not stop the imperceptible trembling that had gripped his frame.

"Magister, if it please thee..." Dee stepped to the side of the table. "Thou hast the better skill to describe what is within," he said, indicating the bag.

Marlowe felt sweat slick under his armpits, despite the cold. It was vaguely disturbing how Dee spoke formally to himself and Walsingham, but slipped into the informal mode of address when conversing with Coronzon. They were much more than mere acquaintances, that much he kenned.

Marlowe jumped as Coronzon laid a hand on his shoulder, but then his muscles relaxed, the shudders flowing out of him like the trickle of spring water over a rill. "What we wish to show you was made by the two of us, using the blended skills of sorcery and alchemy. It has served Dr. Dee well these many years, but now we feel that to achieve its full potential, it would better serve a lusty younger man of the quickest wit and possessed of a hotblooded taste for life and adventure." He paused, as if to let that much sink in. "Would you not say, my good playwright, that this is a most fitting description of yourself?"

Marlowe rubbed at his eyes, trying to clear the clouds in his head. But yes, he did feel a surge of potency at Coronzon's recognition of his charisma and intellect. It was gratifying to find company who could recognize a man's worth for what it was. "Aye," he said, looking from Dee's long serious face to the closed bag. Coronzon he could feel at his back, but not see. "I believe the description is apt."

"Perfect! I can think of no better candidate for her ladyship." Coronzon squeezed Marlowe's shoulder ever so slightly and let go.

"Behold." Dee untied the knot and spread open the mouth of the bag. He pushed it down around the sides of what appeared to be an ordinary chunk of weathered granite.

Marlowe leaned in closer. "'Tis but a rock."

Coronzon's lilting laughter again. "Only to the uninitiated does it appear so. Look again."

Upon closer scrutiny Marlowe saw in the flickering candlelight that indeed the roundish surface was incised with whorls and spirals, punctuated at intervals with diagonal slashes. A clear image of the sun, with uneven rays extending from a perfect circle, appeared near the top. Although certainly no expert in antiquities, he knew enough to recognize the stone as something ancient, akin perhaps to the monument at Stonehenge, which he had in fact visited.

"What you see is a kerbstone from a passage tomb in the Boyne Valley of the Irish isle." Dee pointed to the solar disc. "Sun worshippers, holding in reverence the elemental powers of Creation. Do you know what that portends?"

Marlowe took a breath. "Earth magick...the strongest kind."

Coronzon clapped him on the back. "Did I not say, my esteemed doctor, that Master Marlowe was the perfect choice?"

"Is't enchanted, then?" Marlowe felt as if he could hear it singing right at the edge of hearing.

Dee pulled the bag away so that the stone sat unfettered on the round table. "'Tis not the rock itself, but what is within that holds the power."

"Power that may be yours," added Coronzon softly at his ear, "if you choose."

They stood, shoulder to shoulder, in silence as Marlowe stared at the stone, its barely felt siren's song a tickle in his ear. "What lies inside?"

Dee ran thin fingers over his beard. "By my troth, 'tis a *bain-sídhe*."

Marlowe fell a step back. "God's death..." Words failed him, something growing alarmingly common the longer he kept company with these two.

"Yes, my illustrious wordsmith," purred the scholar from Wittenberg, if that was indeed his real profession, "we have trapped a banshee within this ancient burial stone. Moreover, the witch who called her for us resides there as well."

Marlowe took another step away from the baleful stone. "But...to what end was it made?"

"The power over life and death." Coronzon's pale eyes caught the firelight. "More specifically, the one who claims ownership over the stone literally holds his own death at bay, for an eternity if he so chooses."

Marlowe wiped his brow. "And which of you is its master?"

Dee bowed imperceptibly. "That honor is mine."

Struggling to work it out, Marlowe fought with his muddled thoughts. "But why give't up? I fail to see—"

"I was an older man when the *buachloch* was made. I have not aged greatly since that day, but it takes all my strength to retain that *status quo*. A man more robust in nature and personal ambition could profit beyond measure from it."

"The binding spell that holds the *bain-sídhe* requires that she, as the Herald of Death, cannot call the Black Coach for you until you wish it. Further, she must ensure your life force continues to thrive. If, for instance, a poetaster such as yourself were to embed the stone in the foundations of a theater, all your endeavors there would likewise prosper."

Marlowe's imagination began to take flight. His ambitions to become the greatest writer of his age could perhaps be realized with certainty. He tried to think it through. Looking back to Dee, he asked, "Can your body be killed while you possess the object?"

Dee shuffled his feet. "In a manner of speaking. This body can be damaged, even to the point of death, but gradually it will revert to the state it inhabited when ownership was sealed. For expediency, naturally, if this seeming death were witnessed by ordinary men, one would need to take on a new identity once the body recovered...to prevent the Church from burning it to ashes as a manifestation of the Devil."

Coronzon cleared his throat. "Part of the bargain of ownership is that the banshee must protect the life of the owner, especially where discovery is concerned."

Dee added, "If, mayhap, the soul's earthly vessel is destroyed, as by burning, not even her ladyship can prevent the Black Coach from coming to collect its due."

Coronzon breathed in his ear. "But a careful man might live indefinitely, thriving on the bounties of an extended life. You have all the time in the world in which to accomplish your most cherished ambitions."

Again silence descended as Marlowe contemplated the stone. Could he truly wield control over such a talisman? He knew himself to be a willful personality with a strong sense of identity and arrogant confidence in his mental agility—tonight's escapade excepted—but he was no mage. He felt there must be details Dee and his companion were not disclosing, perhaps a lot of details, but his growing desire to have the stone was pushing his sense of caution to the side. It also occurred to him that if his spywork for the Crown were to turn deadly, here was a means to save his life.

"How does one take possession of the *bain-sídhe*?" he heard himself ask.

Coronzon stepped forward. "A simple blood seal. 'Tis quickly done, and the stone becomes yours."

Marlowe licked his dry lips. "How, exactly?"

Dee pushed back his voluminous sleeves and bent toward the stone. "Observe." He pressed both palms down over its surface, and appeared to be communing with the entity he claimed was ensorcelled inside. Then he released the stone and stood to his full height. In the flickering shadows, he resembled nothing so much as a carrion crow. He gestured toward the stone. "Touch and feel her presence."

Marlowe reached out tentatively with his left hand and rested it palm down on the cool surface. He felt the spirals under his fingertips and then something else—a tingling sensation that raised the hairs on his arm. He could almost make out the voice now, a keening *Dies Irae* such as one might hear at a Mass for the

Dead. He raised his eyes and found Coronzon's riveted to him. "That's right," the soft voice whispered, "you hear her, do you not?"

Marlowe nodded.

"If you agree to take ownership and make the seal, she will appear to you in your mind, as your servant."

Marlowe's hands were shaking, but there was nothing he could do about it. "Verily, must I shed blood to claim the stone as mine?"

"The *bain-sídhe* is nourished and bound to you by blood. This you must do if you are to bind her to your will."

Marlowe cast his eyes back toward the carved stone that continued to tingle under his fingers. "H-how much blood?"

Dee reaching into his robe. "A small amount." He opened his hand and a slim dagger with a handle of inlaid mother-of-pearl lay across his palm. "An ensorcelled athame, which also belongs to the owner of the stone."

Marlowe's breath hissed. That blade looked sharp.

Coronzon said, "Do you wish to become owner of the *buachloch* and master of the *bain-sídhe*, who will be bound by spellcraft to preserve your life?"

"Y-yes."

"Done." Swifter than thought, Dee plunged the dagger into the top of his hand, driving it through meat and bone into the very rock itself.

Marlowe howled from pain and shock as small bones splintered, blood vessels ruptured, skin shredded. His body shook as if with palsy as he stared at his hand, pinned to the stone. The athame was embedded to its hilt, dark red blood pooling and spilling over the rock and tabletop. His knees buckled, but Coronzon swiftly caught him with an arm tight around his waist. A cacophony of screams, voices old and very young, roared in his ears and he felt consciousness slipping away as pain beyond endurance flared up his arm and over his body. He was barely cognizant of Coronzon grabbing his free hand and pressing it onto the stone awash in his blood. The stone turned red-hot and seared the flesh from his fingers as they made contact.

Smoke rose from the granite surface and slowly coalesced into a shape, a woman in a shroud, at first with luminous sea-gray eyes and silver seaweed hair, but then dissolving to rot and finally revealing a death's head with a few scraps of hair and flesh clinging to its whitened surface. The ravening mouth, from which came the unbearable shriek that he'd imagined only a moment before as faint singing, rushed toward him, gaping black as a starless night.

Marlowe screamed and screamed till his throat was raw, but the Magister's grip around him was iron. And in a blink, his soul fled his body.

He hovered above the table with the glass retorts and crucibles, watching two tall men inflicting bloody torture on a shorter man, for what reason he couldn't immediately fathom. At that moment a presence materialized beside him—a young man of perhaps nineteen or twenty with golden hair and eyes the color of the midsummer sky. The youth smiled at him with full, rose-tinted lips. The features were otherworldly, but familiar. Coronzon.

In his disconnected state, he knew it was a glamour, but welcomed the artifice anyway. How not? The youth was beautiful almost to the point that Marlowe could not bear to look at him. *Come with me,* the shining figure said, holding out its shapely hand. Marlowe's shade took hold, and instantly he was astride the back of an enormous dragon, its scales like armor plate beneath his thighs, sweeping over unfamiliar lands far below. The youth's body melded itself against Marlowe's back, arms around him in a warm embrace that belied the freezing cold of the dragon's flight. *See what we two can do?* said the voice beside his ear. *Say to me now...what is your will?*

Marlowe leaned backward into the caressing arms and gave himself over to the swoop and glide of the dragon's muscular wings. He said without thought, "I am yours."

The vision popped like a soap bubble, and his soul slammed back into his body, still held on its feet by the unyielding arm of Magister Coronzon. But now, oddly, he felt nothing as he studied his bloody hands gripping the stone. The elegant demon who was now his pledged companion took hold of Marlow's right hand and wrapped it around the hilt of the embedded dagger. "Pull it out and the bargain is sealed."

Marlowe gripped the pearl handle and looked up at Dee, who had retreated further into the shadows of the laboratory. Without a word, he tightened his flayed fingers around the hilt and withdrew the athame as if pulling it from butter. In shock he stared as the stone soaked up his blood like water over a diver's sponge, and slowly, inexorably, his hands began to heal. Flesh rebuilt itself, bones realigned and made themselves whole, veins knit themselves together. He watched in fascination as the pearl-handled dagger fit itself perfectly to the palm of his open, unscathed hand.

"How now, sirrah," Coronzon said in a tone that could only be described as gleeful. "How does it feel to be immortal?"

Immortal indeed. Kit Bayard ground his teeth. Had he been duped into taking ownership of the stone? Most certainly. But he had to face the fact that his inflated ego and overweening bravado had allowed it to happen. Although he'd asked Dee why he was willing to relinquish immortality so readily, he'd not gotten a straight answer. He could see now how artfully the two had steered his questioning away from that critical point and toward the wonders that awaited him if he took possession. Yes, he'd been a fool, an overreaching coxcomb greedy for power over his own destiny, not unlike his poor protagonist of this week's production. Was his fate eventually then to follow that of his doomed Faustus? Bayard clenched his fists. Had four hundred years spent wresting life from Death's pall been a wasted effort? He recalled with revulsion his discourse with Dee's shade here in this very spot. The answers to his questions were obvious to anyone with eyes to see.

In a fury, more at himself than anything else, he grabbed the metal thermos, turned on his boot heel, and thudded up the stairs to the lobby, slamming the basement door behind him.

CHAPTER 16

Thursday, 3:00 P.M.

*"Qui non intelli...*something or other." Tom startled at Nanette's voice, close to his shoulder. "My Latin's pretty rusty."

He closed the store's only copy of Dr. John Dee's *The Hieroglyphic Monad.* "*Qui non intelligit, aut taceat, aut discat.* Who understands not, should either be silent or learn."

"Testy old buzzard, wasn't he?" Nanette laughed. The Rookery did a brisk trade in the writings of John Dee—translated, edited, paraphrased, anthologized, riffed on, and rarely, an unabridged scanned reproduction of an original. "You're a fan of Dr. Dee?"

He slid the book back into its slot on the shelf. "Not a fan, just curious. I think he was brilliant in some ways—mathematics and his work on maps and navigation. But I also think he went off the deep end with all the Enochian stuff."

"So you don't buy the angelic dialogues bit?"

Tom smirked. "He wasn't talking to angels, I can assure you." He gathered up a handful of books that needed shelving. Funny how used bookstores tended to be like libraries. People thumbed through books and then left them lying wherever was convenient.

"Maybe he was hitting ye old absinthe bottle too much."

Tom smiled at Nanette in her Addams family makeup and hair. He was going to miss her. "I guess I may as well tell you. This is probably my last day on the job."

Her eyes went wide and liquid. "But why? I thought you were happy here. I'd love to pay you more if I could."

He was a little surprised. She seemed genuinely upset, more than just losing an employee. He'd tried to avoid getting too close to people, but sometimes they managed to get past his defenses anyway.

"It's not about money. I have some family business to take care of. I really enjoy working here. Believe me, I'd stay if I could."

"Well, family comes first, of course. I'm sure your parents must miss you. Do they live near Atlanta?"

Tom studied the books in his hand. "No. I never met my father. Don't even know his name. No siblings, either."

"Oh. So it's just you and your mom—" He gave her the answer before she could ask.

"My mother's been dead for awhile. Murdered, actually." He was careful to show a neutral expression.

Nanette's hand clapped over her mouth. "God, I'm sorry. None of my business! I never should have asked." Her cheeks were bright red.

He smiled indulgently. "It's all right. I knew the person who did it, recognized him from a picture."

"Wow." She was staring at him. "Did they catch the guy?"

Tom shuffled his boots and stuffed his free hand down into his jeans pocket. "Nope. I tracked him for a couple of years, mostly across Europe. When I lost him, I just bummed around, which is how I picked up German and a smattering of French. Did a lot of poking into museums and libraries. Didn't catch up with him until right before he died of natural causes."

Nanette was transfixed. "That's an incredible story."

"Yeah. I've been on my own for a long time."

"No wonder you seem so, how should I say this, old-soulish, even though you're obviously pretty young." She continued to stare at his face. He wondered what was going through her mind.

"Well, I wish you'd stick around. You're one of the best bookstore assistants we've ever had. You practically manage the occult section by yourself. What could I do to bribe you to stay?"

Tom shrugged and tried to arrange his face into a less than dour expression. "Dunno, probably nothing."

Nanette gave him a wan smile. "Well, if you ever come back, your job's waiting for you." She turned toward her office, then stopped. "What about *Dr. Faustus*? Doesn't it open this weekend? Are you leaving them, too? The hubs and I were going to try to get tickets."

Tom shifted his weight. "I'll be there. The director has something I want, so I'll stick around long enough to get it from him."

Nanette stepped up and gave him a quick kiss on the cheek. "You take care." He nodded and felt an unwanted pang in his chest as she walked away.

He headed across the store toward the fiction stacks. Why had he opened up like that? He had no business telling her what his plans were. He needed to focus. Maybe it was just the simple, gut-level knowing that if things played out as he anticipated tomorrow, nothing he said or did today would make a hill of beans worth of difference anyway.

* * * *

Tom goosed the Harley as soon as he was out on Highway 285 heading south away from the city—traffic thinned considerably once he got off the beltway. With few cars ahead of him, he pushed the bike wide open, feeling the acceleration rumbling under his boots. He leaned forward, cutting down on the wind drag, the trees along the highway flying by in a blur. He had two hours before he needed to present himself at the Janus Theatre, ready to dress rehearse the role of the ill-fated scholar of Wittenberg. For that matter, his own ill-fated life could be seen as a dress rehearsal for what was coming. He would be sorely disappointed if his expectations did not play out as he hoped.

But that was unlikely. All his inner guidance and heightened sensing told him what he sought was here, in this city and in the possession of this man. Kit Bayard. Tom had no doubt as to who this self-important and overbearing person really was. But he had to be extremely careful not to punch the PLAY button too soon, so to speak. He would just end up getting himself destroyed without taking care of business, and that would be unforgivable. Oddly, he felt no fear for his safety here on the highway as his monster machine hummed its song of raw existential power; he leaned with it into every bend of the road, trusting it completely. He and the bike were one and existed within a cone of here-and-now time that nothing else could touch.

The bike's speedometer inched toward 90, with the road ahead all clear. For the next few miles his mind was empty of everything but the engine's growl and the visceral sense of speed. One last adrenaline rush in his physical body before…

His mind wandered.

"'Tis a wonder indeed. Thou hast not aged a day." The old man's rasping, dying voice so long ago had made his blood run cold. Even now he could see every detail in his mind's eye…a sweltering pestilence-ridden summer in 1609, the iron-gated courtyard choked with weeds, the angry barking of a cur chained to the fence, broken flagstones leading up to the heavy front door. A shrew of a woman, middle-aged and life-weary, had opened it to him on his fifth knock. He'd doubted his guidance at that moment and had been prepared to turn away, but she'd let him in.

The dark-timbered main hall was bare of furniture save a single ornately carved high-backed chair beside a great stone fireplace against the far wall. He followed the mistress of the house, the man's daughter as it turned out, up two narrow flights of stairs. He saw two rooms at the top of the landing. She nodded him toward the one with the open door.

"My father lies abed yonder."

He'd taken a step forward, then stopped in the doorway, blood thudding in his ears at the glimpse of the white-bearded figure sunken into the bedclothes. The room was hot, and smelt of sweat, urine, and death. He took a step back.

The daughter laid a soft hand on his arm. "Nay, 'tis not the plague. A wasting disease, the doctors say."

"Aye, Mistress," he'd answered. "I'll take naught but a moment t'say farewell." He'd told her some story about being the son of one her father's acquaintances from the old days, before astrology and alchemy had fallen into disfavor under the Protestant King James I.

She flashed him a hint of a smile, which surprisingly lit up her otherwise very plain and careworn face.

"What is thy name?" he'd asked, out of courtesy.

"Katherine, an't please thee, sir." She'd smiled openly then, her fingers resting lightly on the sleeve of his coarse linen shirt. He read many things in that smile—not the least of which was raw sexual need. He disengaged his arm and went in to face her father.

He'd stood by the old man's bed for silent moments, just watching the stuttering breath that wracked the frail body. At last he spoke. "Merry meet, my lord."

The old man's eyes had popped open and he'd stared in disbelief. "How now? A-art thou become an angel?"

Tom remembered his bitter laughter at this. "Nay, my good sir, thou and thy companion hath made certain that joy would be denied me. And my mother."

The dying man had wheezed and coughed and finally got control of himself. "I see it now...thou'rt tied to the stone," he'd whispered, his amazement naked as the truth that filled his watery gaze. "I ne'er would've thought..."

Tom roared around a curve and another dip of the highway, playing the scene out again in his mind, for maybe the millionth time.

"Verily, thou'rt the walking dead, e'en like unto the master of the *buachloch* himself." Dee's skeletal hand had reached out and taken hold of him, as if he still could not believe the evidence in front of him. His rheumy eyes blinked in disbelief.

"How can this evil be undone?" Tom had demanded.

The bedchamber had grown frigid as a winter's night, the daylight dimmed as if a storm cloud had passed over the sun. And then with shaking fingers, the Queen's astrologer had pulled him close to those gray sunken cheeks and told him everything.

Tom's attention jerked back to the road. Not far ahead, a car was pulling onto the highway from a side road. A long, shiny, black car with dark-tinted windows and chrome trim around the doors…a hearse.

An earthquake rumbling began to play counterpoint to thundering, galloping hooves—he could feel his teeth rattling in his head. He throttled back and burned the brakes but the hearse was too close. Tom shut his eyes and braced for the crash…which did not come. The bike was coasting, slowing down with the empty road stretched out for miles. Yet the roaring clatter of iron-shot wheels over cobbled streets filled his ears as a bone-jarring rumble pulsed up through the frame of the Harley. The sensation continued in full force until the bike rolled to a stop onto the shoulder of the highway and he killed the engine. Suddenly all was silent. Tom wondered for a moment if he'd gone deaf while blood pounded in his ears. Two ordinary cars drove past while he sat astride the Harley in shock, breath coming in short gasps as his heart pounded in overdrive.

Finally, reluctantly, he brought the bike to life again and turned around, heading back the way he'd come. Yes, he was now quite certain that once those words in the play, potent with spellcraft, were spoken in the right context, some serious shit was going to hit the fan.

CHAPTER
17

Thursday, 10:30 P.M.

Claire was so tired she felt jetlagged. Not that she'd ever actually been jetlagged, but she had a sense of what it must be like. Foggy-headed and heavy limbed, with a feeling that you were moving in slow motion or trying to swim against a current. She'd pulled a very long day at work, starting with a 6:45 A.M. traffic crash and moving non-stop to an attempted suicide, a drive-by shooting, a near-fatal heart attack, and a baby delivered in the backseat of an SUV in traffic. She'd been ultra-focused and single-minded, so Paul would have nothing to complain about.

Now, with the *Faustus* dress rehearsal just completed, she slouched in one of the theater seats, boneless, like a jellyfish. Bayard sat on the edge of the stage, waiting for the cast to get their makeup off and costumes hung up, so they could gather one last time for performance notes. Tomorrow it was do or die, but tonight he could still make tweaks in the production. He looked alert enough, but she felt drained and wondered if the others were feeling it, too.

There was no doubt tonight's performance was somehow subdued. Everyone had been letter perfect and all the effects worked exactly on cue, but there was a sense of going through the motions, as if people were sidetracked by their own thoughts and concerns. She remembered, too, something Jackie had said about dress rehearsals…that performers tended to hold back a little in final dress for fear of giving too much and then not being able to do as well on the actual opening night. She'd thought that was just stage entertainment folklore, but now it seemed to make sense.

"Could I have your attention, please? Is everyone here?" Bayard's voice cut through the low-level buzz of voices as the troupe waited for notes. Stragglers were still coming in, but he ignored them. "All right, then. You know what I'm going to say. Although perfect in many respects, tonight's rehearsal was what I would call tepid. Mr. Brennan, would you agree?" He turned his attention to Tom, seated on the front row between Addie and Ruben. Tom merely cocked his head and declined to answer. Bayard looked at Addie. "Ms. Murphy?"

"I think we're all just a little tired. It'll be fine tomorrow when the adrenaline gets flowing, don't you think?"

Bayard shifted his gaze out to the rest of the company. Claire felt fleeting eye contact from him, but quickly studied the script in her hands and avoided being called on.

"We have a stellar cast, a top-notch production crew, and possibly the best play ever written. So, what I want tomorrow on opening night is everything you have, no holding back. I want fire and brimstone! Nothing less." His voice boomed at the back of the theater and echoed in the rafters. "I know that everyone here is capable of delivering such a performance, and believe me, no one is looking forward to seeing it more than I."

He wasn't angry, Claire was pretty sure. This was the coach's pep talk, trying to pump them up to make damn certain nobody dragged their butt through the show tomorrow. As if that were likely to happen. She knew how much everyone involved in the play was anticipating its opening—once they got going tomorrow night, everything would be fine. But tonight the whole scene just felt very low key. The calm before the storm, she supposed. If she hadn't been so incredibly dog-tired, she might have cared a bit more.

Bayard stood up. "Go home, go to bed early, get a good night's sleep. Curtain goes up at eight, so I want everyone here and accounted for by six. That is all." With a wave of his hand, he dismissed them.

Claire pushed herself to her feet and gathered her belongings. She shuffled down the row and into the aisle to wait for Addie by the back doors. Morris joined her.

"M'lady Claire, were we really that bad tonight?" He looked serious, but she felt there must be a hint of sarcasm in there somewhere.

"I didn't think so. Nobody missed a single cue. Not even Lucifer."

Morris laughed in a short bark. "The Lord of Hell should certainly be able to get his entrances sorted out, although having him show up onstage unexpectedly does keep one on one's toes."

Addie plodded up the aisle, with Tom not far behind her. "What's so funny? I can't believe Morris is actually laughing."

"I don't know about you, but I need a drink before going home and hopping into bed like a good little thespian. Anyone else?" Morris put on his best Mephisto leer.

Tom shrugged. "Why not?"

Claire sighed. "Okay, but not for long. I've never been accused of being a thespian, but I'm dead on my feet and really do need to go to bed."

"One round only, I promise," Morris said, leading the way.

They headed outside. The weather had faired and although the air was crisp, Claire welcomed it. It helped her stay awake. Tom straddled the Harley and cranked it to life, then sat with it idling in throaty chugs underneath him. He turned to Addie. "Want a ride?"

"Oh god, you mean it? Can I?"

"Sure, why not? I don't have an extra helmet, though."

Addie was already unwinding the scarf from her neck, wrapping it over her hair and tying it under her chin. "Doesn't matter. Good thing I wore jeans tonight." She slipped onto the seat behind him and wrapped her arms tightly around his waist.

"See you there," he said, pulling the visor down on his helmet. The Harley growled and sprang onto the road.

Morris looked at Claire and shrugged. "Need a ride?"

She swallowed a yawn. "No thanks, I'll drive myself."

Doyle's Tavern was crowded for a Thursday night. They sat at a table near the front window, yellow streetlight shining in. After about ten minutes of waiting, Tom said, "Just tell me what you want and I'll go put in the order at the bar."

"Guinness," said Morris.

Addie took another quick look at the beverages menu. "Samuel Adams."

"Got it. Claire?" Tom shoved his chair back and stood.

She looked up and caught something in his gray eyes that telegraphed...what? He'd never paid her the slightest bit of attention before. She blinked and looked again, but the moment was gone. "I don't care, anything light." She watched him thread his way through the tightly packed tables and throng near the bar. He was actually attractive, in a rough sort of way. Some girl ought to snatch him up.

She turned back to find Addie giving her a knowing look. "Nice butt, yeah?"

"Butts all look alike."

Addie crossed her arms over her chest. "No, Claire, they do not. You definitely need a drink, or three."

Morris was smiling his usual snarky smile and giving Tom a guarded look. Claire slumped in her chair—they could think what they wanted. He wasn't her type, if indeed anyone was.

Tom returned with a mug of his favorite stout in hand and resumed his seat at the table. "Order's in, but it may take a few minutes. Apologies for getting a head start." He took a long swallow from the mug.

"Why's it so crowded, I wonder?" Addie craned her neck to look down the room.

"Doyle says it's a wake, or the remnants of it. Those who'd had enough of the party came here."

Morris laughed. "A good Irish pub, indeed."

"Tom's got an Irish tattoo, don't you?" Addie touched his arm.

Morris leaned his elbows on the table. "Yeah, what is that design? Ruben seemed impressed."

Tom sighed and leaned back in his chair. "I got it years ago, traveling."

Claire's interest was piqued. "Can I see?"

Tom gave her what she now thought of as his patented "why not" look, and pushed up the sleeve of his sweatshirt. "It's a four-cornered knot," he said, index finger tracing the point where the thorned vines converged.

"Hey, I know what that is…that's a shield knot. Very important in Celtic folklore and *sidhe* magick," Addie said. "The shield knot is protection against evil forces. The practitioner uses it to call on the gods from the four corners of the world, or the elements like earth, wind, water, and fire." Addie looked at Tom. "It's a pagan protection charm."

"I thought he was a Buddhist," said Morris.

Tom pulled his sleeve down. "Buddhism's an attitude, not a religion. And the shield knot design was suggested to me by someone I had no choice but to trust."

Morris's lips pouted and then smirked. "Did it work—have you been protected from evil spirits?"

Tom's eyes narrowed. "Who's to say?"

Claire listened without joining in. She normally had no deep opinion on things religious and/or supernatural, but this revelation of Tom's was skewing all to hell her notion of who she'd thought he was. What did he think he needed a protection charm for, and more to the point, why would he put faith in such a thing to begin with? Of the four of them, Addie was the only one likely to believe in such stuff. Claire cut her eyes toward Tom again. Surely he was putting them on, although she wouldn't mind having a protection charm herself right now if it would banish her nightmares. She pushed those thoughts away as a waiter arrived with their ales and stouts. Tom had ordered her something in an amber-colored bottle with the name Finnegan's on the label.

"I don't want us to lose touch with each other after the play's done," Addie was saying. "I think we've created something really great together, and...I just want to stay in touch."

"Adelaide has a point," Morris said. "I will admit I went into this play with some reservations, but once you joined the cast," he said, nodding toward Tom, "that sort of upped the ante. I do like a challenge."

"I'd like us all to stay friends, too." Claire hoped she didn't sound too needy.

Tom sat with his hands clasped in front of him on the table. "A toast, then."

"Great idea!" Addie was all smiles.

Tom rose and spoke in an Irish accent so spot on he could have passed for a native. The pub fell silent as the dozen or so lads from the wake stopped to listen.

"Of all the money e'er I had,
I spent it in good company.
And all the harm I e'er have done,
Alas! 'Twas all to none but me.

And all I've done for want of wit
To mem'ry now I can't recall.
So fill to me the partin' glass,
Good night and joy be with you all."

He put the half-consumed mug of stout to his mouth and drained it dry.

"Here, here," said Morris and took a long pull from his bottle.

"Cheers!" Addie did likewise. The members of the wake hoisted their mugs and drank.

Claire felt numb. There was no joy in Tom's expression. Unless she was grossly mistaken, his toast had sounded like he was telling them all goodbye, not simply good night. Reluctantly, she tasted the ale Tom had selected for her. It was lightly sweet with a butterscotch undertaste. "Salute."

Tom sat down and the chatter of voices rose again, but Claire recognized the old familiar shroud of despair wrapping itself around her shoulders, settling in, shutting everything down. The others laughed and talked, but their voices slipped through her consciousness with no meaning attached. She hoped she could get home without driving into the headlights of a semi.

It was past midnight when Claire finally pulled into the bungalow's driveway. She'd driven home slowly, paying excruciating attention to the yellow lines on the six-lane parkway as if she were landing a 747 at Hartsfield. Once inside, she checked on her mother and found her asleep in bed. The idea of making some tea, something soothing like chamomile, was appealing, but instead she buttoned up her coat and went back outside. The night was clear and cold, the stars all pinpricks of ice. Unable to face the idea of getting in bed and trying to fall asleep, she started walking.

She automatically headed northeast, toward the houses a block over. As a kid, she would have gone out her back gate, run down a narrow dirt alley, cut through a neighbor's yard, and been at Jackie's house in under five minutes, but this time she took the long way around, coming to the end of her own block and following the sidewalk over to the next row of small, cozy houses drowsing under ponderous oaks older than the city itself.

She didn't expect anyone to be awake at Jackie's house this late, and had no intention of stopping there if the lights happened to be on. It was just the comfort of seeing the house, feeling its proximity ripe with memory that she craved. That helpless sense of time fast-forwarding, slipping away even as you tried to nail it down, was a visceral ache in her gut. People at school and then at work always said things like, "You're still young" or "You have your whole life ahead of you," which made her want to vomit. Physically. It wasn't so much the idea of the years stretching out in front of her with no end in sight that did it to her…it was the sense that it meant nothing. A speck on the eyelash of the deity, which she didn't believe in anyway. In the long run, what was the point of everything you went though? She couldn't see it.

She wandered down the block, feeling the cold air on her face. The Suttons' house was up ahead. She hardly saw Jackie anymore, but still the knowledge that within another week or so she would be gone for good was an emptiness Claire didn't know how she was going to face. She knew she had an oversized problem dealing with change, but change involving this kind of loss was like a pit opening up in front of her. A shrink would have a field day with her, she was sure, which was probably why she'd resisted getting that kind of so-called "help" for so long. Paul seemed to have benefitted from it, but she simply could not see herself in the psych's office, stretched out on a couch, stripping away all her defenses and blathering about her innermost terrors to a stranger. Not happening. She'd rather step in front of a truck.

The Suttons' house was dark when she reached it, everyone tucked in their beds like they were supposed to be. She stood in front of it, thinking of Jackie and all the time they'd spent growing up together. Time to move on. She allowed the misery of the situation to fully sink in, and then headed home.

Reaching her own yard by the alley, Claire came in at the back gate. She found the tire swing in the yard and settled herself into it. She was tired to the bone. Somehow she'd managed to pull her shit together at work on the surface, so there were no more mistakes for Paul to bitch about. But she was barely hanging on. It would be fairly easy to self-medicate, since Paul did the driving while she rode in the back with whoever they'd picked up. Also too easy to get caught, and she knew it would happen eventually. The drugs were available and tempting, but she wasn't that far gone.

Her thoughts wandered as she pushed off the ground and held onto the tire. How many times had she sat in this swing as a kid, wondering where it would all end. Even then, as a first-grader, she'd had those feelings of helplessness in the face of a future she couldn't see. Even that young, she'd done a lot of what she did now—attempting to ease her fear that she was going insane by doing things that carried surface meaning, things that promised fleeting, manufactured moments of what those around her considered fun or important or exciting.

She remembered a selfish outburst as an adolescent when she'd clung to the swing screaming and wailing with tears because her parents wouldn't take her to the beach on a sunny Sunday afternoon. She now understood that tantrum better. What it had really been about was a crushing sense of emptiness, of lost opportunity that had consumed her when the afternoon could not be spent in a fun physical activity that kept the scary thoughts of losing her grip at bay. Life had seemed irreparably damaged on that long-ago afternoon, when the possibility of something potentially meaningful had failed to materialize. Like so much that came after.

Claire closed her eyes and savored the cold as it brushed over her face while the swing slowed its pendulum rush, back and forth, slower and slower...and suddenly the air was so frigid it took her breath away. Her eyes flew open just in time to realize the specter from her nightmares was right in front of her. The thing was transparent, so that she could see the outline of the house and back patio through it, yet defined enough to have shape and movement. She fell out of the swing and cowered like a trapped rabbit on the damp ground. This was it—she'd finally snapped. Claire curled into a tight ball, her head tucked down, as if that could possibly protect her from the terrifying shroud-draped creature that hovered above her.

Images began to take shape in her mind, eyelid movies impossible to interpret. She saw a rocky hillside, wind-scraped and pummeled with rain. A corpse lay at the entrance to a tomb, a bloody rock nearby. She saw herself coming out of the storm. She stooped to pick up the stone, stepped over the bodies (now there seemed to be several), and staggered down the slope with the heavy treasure in her arms. The scene abruptly shifted to the basement of the Janus Theatre, where she sat in the center of the floor, cradling the blood-soaked stone in her lap while flames ate the shadows and cobwebs but left her untouched. Claire whimpered in terror, knowing that her rational mind was truly past repair and all that was left was to be locked up in a straight jacket somewhere, medicated for the rest of her life in a fog of paranoia.

Gradually the freezing sensation abated, and she dared to open her eyes. No apparition. She lifted her head, and then sat up. She was shaking, her teeth clattering loud enough to be alarming. She was alone, but utterly unhinged. How long she sat in the dew-covered grass beside the tire swing was anyone's guess, but when she finally got to her feet, the sky was more gray than black. She stumbled into the house and fell onto her bed in her coat and shoes and knew nothing until the sun was well risen.

* * * *

Red, and frozen black. These were the colors the witch tasted most. Sometimes she smelled white, but the sensation was fleeting. Colors and senses as she once remembered them were a continuous gestalt of consciousness, formless yet discrete. Sometimes she even remembered her name. She should be dead, but wasn't. And there was another here with her, also trapped, a thing that had never been human, unlike herself.

On occasion, the elemental was a frenzied, raging beast lashing out, inchoate, in all directions, mindlessly clawing to get out. When that happened, it shredded her etheric body without mercy, or possibly even without cognizance, so that each time her soul, or what was left of it, felt more dispersed, less viable than before.

At other times, the banshee folded itself into a frigid black space of coiled baleful cunning, scheming the way a trapped animal would, trying to find an opening in the walls of its prison. When it wanted to communicate with its human captor, it slid into her mind and used her voice. This was nothing she could control—it was beyond her powers to keep it out, not that she particularly wanted to. It provided her some entertainment to torment Master Marlowe when the opportunity presented itself. The crushing of his bones had been particularly tasty.

Lately she'd noticed the banshee probing the mind of a female presence that it sensed was vulnerable, ever since the woman had touched the stone while it was wet. An accident, she assumed, because who would willingly open themselves up to a brush with the essence of a *bain-sídhe*? She'd felt the young woman's spirit—frustrated, easily dispirited, yet oddly strong in some ways having to do with the care of other humans—as it fled past her, sucked into the vortex where the stone had first been transferred to Master Marlowe's keeping. He'd somehow managed to pull her out again, although her tenuous connection to the elemental remained like a scent that couldn't be scrubbed off. But whatever the creature hoped to gain from this effort seemed futile, a plan hatched in mindless desperation. The witch had other options.

The elemental enjoyed no conception of time—it simply was—but the witch remained aware of the passage of years from the taste and impressions of the blood of the victims with which the stone was bathed. She could also feel the march of time and the shift of centuries through her connection to the stone's masters, first the hated sorcerer John Dee and after him the rash and sometimes foolish playwright Christopher Marlowe, and through them occasionally others within their sphere of influence. And exactly twenty-one days ago, she'd been shocked to her core by a brief spike of energy, a long-forgotten essence, a soul lost and recovered and lost again. She'd quested out for it immediately after that first blinding flash, and tasted it in the auric field surrounding her so-called master. And little by little, against all odds, she'd begun to hope.

CHAPTER 18

Friday – Opening Night

"Where's the patron seating?" A white-haired, overdressed woman leaving a heavy floral perfume trail took one of the elaborately designed programs Claire held in a box.

"First four rows." Claire tried not to breathe too deeply. "They're marked off, just sit past the red ribbons."

The theater was filling up. Claire counted the rows that still had empty seats and there weren't many. Standing at the back where the double doors were propped open, she and a couple of volunteers were handing out programs. Bayard had ordered 550 printed, which was fifty more than the exact number of seats, but it seemed to her they should have done more. If they ended up with a full house, there wouldn't be many left as souvenirs of the show, considering some people had asked for two. The price break wasn't significant unless you ordered at least a thousand, and the promotions budget hadn't allowed the company to spend that much money unless they were willing to scrimp somewhere else. That's what Morris had told her, knowing as he did all about the cost of getting things printed. She'd already stashed away a copy for her mother, who'd asked for one because Claire's name was listed among the crew.

She'd dressed in her one good outfit, a gray velveteen pantsuit that had already earned her a number of compliments. With her hair pulled up and a piece of her mother's jewelry, an 18k gold brooch of a butterfly, on her lapel, she felt as much in costume as anyone in the cast.

She doled the programs out without paying much attention to the stream of people filling the auditorium until a young man stopped in front of her and opened his palm for a program. He was tall and so incredibly good looking she thought he must be a model or an actor. Golden blonde curls framed his chiseled cheekbones and caressed the collar of his perfectly fitted tux. She caught her breath at his incredibly blue eyes as he whispered "thank you" in a voice that in any other circumstance would have sounded overwhelmingly seductive. His fingers lightly brushed hers as she gave him the program. So cold. He should have worn gloves to the play. She watched him maneuver with feline-hipped grace around the people still lingering in the aisle chatting. Beautiful men had never given her much heart flutter, but she would've made an exception for that one. Was he a celebrity? She'd have to ask Addie after the show if they had any famous guests on the patron's list.

Claire felt butterflies in her stomach, in a good way. The whole air of opening night was tense with anticipation, something she'd never experienced. Sure, she'd been to a couple of plays and live concerts, but never from the other side of the aisle, as a member of the group putting on the show. The audience buzz was lively, especially because of the way Bayard had directed the stage setup. The curtains were wide open with Faustus' study fully revealed under a single spotlight while the rest of the stage was in shadow. Dressing the set was being done in front of the audience, as if they were watching through a window into the room. Two stagehands dressed as pages ambled across the stage, carrying Faustus' ornate chair and placing it just so in front of the desk. Then another in a scholar's robe came out of the wings with the tall desk candle and placed it carefully beside the books and papers. Although she'd seen this bit practiced any number of times, Claire watched all the stage business from the audience's perspective now, feeling excitement build as the set came together.

The house lights dimmed, which was Ruben's cue that Act One was only minutes away. The opening notes of Bach's ominous Passacaglia and Fugue in C minor recorded on some massive sixteenth-century pipe organ in Amsterdam came through the theater speakers, and Claire shivered. She loved this part of the preshow, especially the way the opening theme built slowly, relentlessly, first as single notes and then gradually layering counter melodies under the first one, and finally driving the whole thing through the pedals in the bass into a massive crescendo of polyphony. It was the perfect setup for the emotional underpinnings of the play.

Claire put the box of programs on a chair by the door and slipped down the aisle to the side door that allowed access backstage. She found her place in the wings, opened the script, and took a deep breath. The lights went down and Act One got underway.

Bayard emerged from the wings and stepped to the footlights to deliver the Prologue.

Claire found herself holding her breath. He looked amazing. In full period costume, he looked every inch an actor from the Rose or the Swan. From his rakish cap with a long feather to his midnight blue quilted doublet and breeches, down to his silk hose and leather handmade shoes, he was exactly what she imagined a sixteenth-century player would have looked like. She wondered where he'd had the costume made and how much it must have cost.

"...we now perform the tale of Faustus' fortunes, good or bad..."

His British accent was impeccable, his timing and delivery nuanced. Claire shook her head. The man was good.

"...On waxen wings he did extend his reach too far, and melting, heavens conspired his overthrow..."

After he'd wow'd the audience with his perfect delivery and strode offstage, the bar was set. Act One proceeded in high gear. Faustus declared his intentions to seek unholy knowledge, and cemented his blood pact with Lucifer's lieutenant Mephistopheles. Claire's stomach clenched as they went through the stage business of the knife and writing the pledge in blood, but all went smoothly. Tom seemed in total control of the action, playing off Morris with fierce concentration.

"*Consummatum est,*" said Tom. "Receive this scroll, a deed of gift, of body and soul." He rolled up the parchment and handed it to his Mephisto. Morris took the scroll with a slight bow and a wicked leer at the audience. As the act drew to a close, they had the audience in the palms of their hands. Tom was so good at this, Claire wondered if he'd been sandbagging all this time and really did have acting credentials he'd neglected to mention.

By the time intermission rolled around at the end of Act Three, Claire found she was mostly watching the play as a rapt spectator, being swept up in its intricacies and the inevitable downward slide of the brilliant but flawed main character toward his doom. Audience applause so far confirmed what she was seeing: Tom and Morris were riveting. The secondary actors were giving stellar performances as well, maybe in response to the energy flowing between the two principals. She slipped into the green room during intermission, unable to calmly sit on her stool and wait for the action to start up again.

The green room was crowded, but Addie spotted her as soon as she stepped through the door. "Hey, it's Claire. Don't you look beautiful!" Claire thought Addie, costumed in the voluptuous one-shouldered silk gown of Alexander the Great's paramour, her auburn hair done up with strands of pearls like a Greek goddess, was pretty much a knockout herself.

"As if." Claire smiled, self-conscious at suddenly being the center of attention.

Alexander the Great, a drama major from the university, hulking next to the coffee machine in his short cape, fighting kilt, and little else, gave a low wolf whistle and winked.

"Stop, you guys." Her cheeks flushed. She felt embarrassed, but oddly pleased.

"Well, it's true. Who knew there was a princess under those medical scrubs?" Addie was grinning.

Claire gave her a look. "I promise this is the last time you'll see me in this outfit." Looking around the room, she did a quick head count to see who else from Act Four was ready and accounted for. The German Emperor Charles sat on the long sofa with Frederick and Martino, two members of his court. He was laughing at something the Persian King Darius, sprawled in an overstuffed chair to his right, had just told him. Darius and Alexander, along with Addie, were part of the mime commanded by Faustus to enthrall the German sovereign. Morris, tall and inscrutable in his devil's makeup, was texting on his cell phone beside the water cooler. Finally, she spotted Tom.

He'd taken the folding chair in the corner, which set him somewhat apart from the others. He sat with his scholar's robe pulled up off the floor, revealing his jeans and boots. The costume mistress had decided not to put him in a wig, and instead had made a period-accurate academician's cap that covered his head and tied under the chin, although he'd left the strings undone, which seemed to fit Faustus' rash personality. Far from rash, though, Tom seemed lost in thought, staring off across the room. Claire started to go speak to him, and then held back. He didn't look all that approachable at the moment.

The lights blinked twice.

"That's it—places, everybody," said Addie, gathering up the hem of her dress and heading for the door. Claire held it open as the actors filed out and down the narrow corridor to the backstage area. Tom was last out. He gave her a tight smile.

It was unsettling. "Everything okay?"

"It's all good," he said, and gave her hand a quick squeeze. Before she had time to register how out of character that was for him, at least as far as she knew him, he'd disappeared into the darkened hallway.

Still mulling this over, Claire took her station as Act Four got underway. She sensed Bayard's presence behind her. She whispered to him, "It's really good so far, isn't it?"

He smiled grandly. "Beyond expectations. I'm very pleased."

Well, as long as the impresario was happy, she refused to let Tom's distant mood dampen her spirits. She was having a good time, the best in weeks. As long as Tom got his lines right, she didn't care what was up with him. Except the sensation of that quick squeeze of his rough hand lingered in the back of her mind.

The cast romped through Act Four, which was mainly comic relief with Faustus playing unholy tricks on courtiers and foiling their plot to take him out. The mood lightened for a bit, the audience laughed aloud at all the right places, and then everyone settled in for the climactic Act Five, where Faustus' Wittenberg colleagues beg him to repent his ways and ask for divine mercy. He repudiates them, remorseful and yet resigned to his fate. Claire realized she was holding her breath again as Faustus, in the solitude of his study, hears the clock tower bell begin to toll the hours, forcing him to acknowledge the fact that his time is running out and shortly Lucifer's lieutenant will come to claim him.

The Good Angel glided out of the wings and stood behind his chair, reaching toward him, palms up in supplication. The bell tolled again.

"Ah, Faustus, if thou hadst given ear to me, e'en now Heaven's bliss might still be yours…"

From the opposite wings, brushing past Claire and Bayard, Addie now garbed in red as the Evil Angel went to Tom and crouched at his knees. More bell sound effects.

"But instead you gave ear to me, and now must taste what Hell will give thee."

Defeated, the Good Angel withdrew. Addie stood up and spread her arms wide, as Ruben slipped a red filter over the spotlight.

"Now, Faustus, stare with thine eyes in horror at what lies before thee…" The bell tolled for the eleventh time. "And so I leave thee, till 'tis time…" She made her exit, and Tom got up from his chair to approach the footlights and speak his lament for his lost salvation, which was actually a two-and-a-half-page soliloquy that to Claire seemed the most daunting of anybody's lines in the play. She watched the script closely as he began, although she was sure he wouldn't forget anything. He hadn't so far and tonight he was definitely on a roll.

"…*O lente, lente, currite noctis equi,* slowly, slowly run, ye horses of night…" The twelfth bell clanged. Thunder boomed through the speakers and lightning danced over the stage.

"…If only this cursed soul could be changed into drops of rain and fall into the ocean, and ne'er be found…"

Tom stared into the audience as if peering into the very pit of Hell. Morris entered upstage, at first a darker shadow against the backdrop and then stalking slowly forward, his retinue of devils and minions, including the Evil Angel, hanging back behind him, which was a little odd, Claire thought, because they'd practiced this entrance with everyone clustered tightly around him.

Tom turned to them and his body language telegraphed both fear and confrontation.

"Adders and serpents, let me breathe awhile." He faced the audience again. "Ugly hell, gape not, come not, Lucifer!" But Morris's red-caped frame came out of the shadows and into the spotlight to stand beside him. Tom turned once more and looked him in the eyes.

There was a beat of silence, and then another. Claire's stomach flipped. Their timing was off, something wasn't right.

Tom's voice took on a harsher tone. "Art thou indeed Mephistopheles?"

Morris waited a beat and then answered. "One name among many."

Claire frowned—that wasn't in the script. What the hell were they doing? And there was something wrong with Morris' voice. Was the sound guy playing with the effects? She'd heard that peculiar inflection before somewhere—it iced her blood and filled her mind with black despair. And then she knew with certainty where, and when. With a catch in her breath, she cut her eyes to Bayard. Even in the dim light his face was bloodless, his expression a mask of stark terror.

She leaned in and whispered to him, her voice unsteady. "T-they're not following the script. What's happening?"

He looked at her for a blank second or two, as if empty air had spoken to him, then fixed his gaze back on the two figures center stage.

An acrid, sulfurous tang invaded the theater and rode the air circulating the room. A red haze lit the stage as the proscenium curtains began to smoke.

"Well, Tom," said the voice that wasn't Morris. "We meet again."

"Nay, demon, my name is Orin Ó Braonáin and I am come to free my mother."

Wicked laughter filled the theater, bouncing off the walls and reverberating across the rows of the packed house.

Fire blossomed along the open rafters over the stage, and the smoke alarm erupted for a few shrill bleats before the flames ate the wiring and silenced it. People began to panic and scream as the auditorium filled with smoke.

Claire's mind was spinning. Orin? Who the hell? The script in her lap fell to the floor as she slid off the stool. She stared speechless at the stage, engulfed in fire, then turned to Bayard, but there was no one. She looked back onstage just in time to see Tom push against his adversary and break into a run, heading straight toward her, his scholar's robe billowing behind him.

"Tom! What...?" But he ran past her like a hound after the fox, oblivious to his surroundings. In total confusion, she looked back where Morris has been standing, only now he was a crumpled form swathed in a voluminous cape lying near the footlights. Fire roared over the stage and across the ceiling of the theater. The audience was transformed into a shrieking mob, panicked beyond all reason, shoving and knocking others down to get out into the lobby.

Claire's emergency training kicked in and she ran to Morris. She shook him and felt for a pulse. His arm was cold, but gradually he began to wake up.

"Claire?" he looked her uncomprehendingly, then took in the inferno that was the stage.

"Get up! We have to get out of here!" She was pulling on his sleeve, dragging him toward the wings.

Morris staggered to his feet. "B-Bayard..."

Claire grabbed him by the arm and tugged. "Forget him! We have to get out!"

Morris seemed to wake suddenly, as if a light had been turned back on in a dark room. "Holy fuck, the building's going to burn to the ground—it's all century-old heart pine." Morris grabbed her hand and they felt their way through the dark backstage to the dressing room hallway. "C'mon, we can get to the lobby this way." They were both coughing and broke into a run as the narrow corridor filled with cast members and crew who'd been backstage.

Claire felt panic rising in her chest as smoke blinded her eyes and filled her lungs. She clung to Morris in the press of bodies pushing toward the red EXIT sign ahead. There was a momentary bottleneck as he wrestled with the door and then they all spilled, choking, into the smoke-filled lobby.

The lobby was utter chaos. Five-hundred theatergoers had shed their sophisticated civility as easily as their raincoats, shoving and screaming and stepping on or over those who fell under the blind panic of the herd. The single front door was barely wide enough for two or three at a time to escape.

Morris, his Mephisto cape torn off and his makeup streaked, dragged Claire through the crowd toward the door, but then a sudden surge from the side pulled them apart.

"Claire!" She heard him over the din, but another voice called to her more clearly, inside her head. It came from the basement. She fought her way across the lobby, falling, losing the dress shoes she'd only worn once, scrabbling to her feet again, and then running down the basement stairs into the dark.

CHAPTER 19

Friday, Opening Night

Bayard leapt down the basement stairs in the dark, heedless of his footing. He'd recognized that arctic, echo-chamber voice coming out of Morris's mouth and needed to get his hands on the cornerstone as fast as possible. Confronting the banshee, or the witch, with all his will could not wait. He knew betrayal when he tasted it, and this might even qualify as a full-fledged mutiny. As much as he'd railed against the way he'd been tricked into taking possession of the stone, and just as often complained to himself about the things he was forced to do to maintain his suspended life, these were nothing compared to the presence that had just revealed itself on the Janus Theatre stage. The probability that the real Mephisto had come to collect him, body and soul, trumped everything.

He knelt in front of the alcove at the bottom of the stairs but was tackled by a body coming full-tilt down the steps after him. His breath nearly knocked out, he grappled with the fury that was Orin Ó Braonáin.

"You'll not have her!" the boy shouted and landed the hard heel of his motorcycle boot in Bayard's face. Lights exploded in his head.

"Whoreson!" Bayard shook his head and scrambled on his knees for the stone. Orin pulled him back, but Bayard was quicker. The athame, concealed in the secret pocket of his sleeve slid easily into his palm. He sliced blindly without thinking and connected with Orin's forearm, severing the big veins and tendons just above the wrist. Orin let go for precious seconds as blood spurted over them both.

The light came on at the base of the staircase and a woman's scream tore through the basement. Bayard jerked his eyes away from his attacker for a second and saw Claire pressed against the wall, her eyes wide with shock and disbelief. He cursed under his breath, forcing his attention back to what needed to be done. He grabbed Orin's bloody arm, bathing both their hands in the steady red stream.

"I name thee my sacrifice," Bayard shouted as the first red drops hit the stone. *"Ecce signum!* As master of the *buachloch* I command—" A spiral of mist rose from the cornerstone, coalescing into the shrouded form of the Irish witch. Quick as thought her spectral arms speared Bayard's body through the abdomen to grab hold of her son Orin struggling behind him. The floor was slick as the wound across his arm bled out. Pinioned, Bayard spasmed in horror as he felt the banshee squeeze through the witch's arms and outstretched fingertips. It sprang free with an ear-splitting shriek. A loud crack like controlled thunder shook the Janus Theatre to its foundations. The cement pillars began to crumble, wiring fried and shorted out, and the Black Coach began to materialize through the walls, impossibly huge within the confines of the basement. The witch gripped her son with all her strength as Bayard struggled to see behind him.

The Black Coach, drawn by beasts that resembled dragons more than horses in spite of their wild tangled manes and tails, partially materialized into the basement space. Its driver, the headless *dullahan*, rode high in the coach-master's seat, cracking a whip fashioned from the bones of a human spine. It held its severed head aloft by the hair, its bright black eyes like those of a raven scanning the assemblage. The head gave off a faint luminescence like a will o' the wisp. Bayard felt the subsonic rumbling of the coach's arrival in his bones, punctuated by the thumping crash of walls and ceiling timbers falling in the fire above. A smoky stench invaded the air and combined with a deeper scent of the grave that surrounded the carriage. Under his feet he sensed the grinding of the earth's very bones against each other, spawning earthquakes Hell knew where.

Death's carriage loomed over his head. Hewed of ebony that seemed to have been aged underwater, covered as it was in wormholes and barnacles, the coach bore door hinges and undercarriage axles of red bronze, and the giant wheels, taller than a man, were shod in black iron that struck sparks wherever it touched the floor. The black silk curtains over its door windows billowed like tattered sails in the vortex of energy that was pulling it into the earth plane. The carriage resembled nothing so much as the magnificent wreckage of a great ship. Its dragon-steeds clawed at the air, shrieks rending their foam-flecked mouths. Bayard took in the sight, knowing it could well be the last thing he would see in this life.

Then, in an eyeblink, everything went still, freeze-framed into utter silence.

Bayard saw the tall figure step out of the gloom, his elegant black tuxedo now claret red. Golden hair framed his head like an infernal halo, the individual strands lifted as if by static electricity. Sparks from his summer-blue eyes revealed the hellfire banked within. "How convenient, all the players in one scene together." His voice stilled the tumult of the fire raging upstairs and the terrifying wail of Death's Herald as she celebrated her release.

He turned his gaze to Claire, frozen in mid-scream. "Lady Claire, the ultimate bystander. As much as I'd like to include you in our little charade, you sadly have no part in this morality play. You've lived your life in a safe little shell where nothing *outré* ever happens and there's no compelling reason to believe in things you can't explain. Stand out of the way, where you belong, and observe." Claire staggered backward as if pushed and fell against the basement wall like a pile of sticks.

The prince of devils then turned his attention to Orin. "You, however, are a different case. Unlike poor Claire, who cannot get invited to the party, you have crashed its merriment in your own unique way." He stepped closer, so that Bayard could not mistake the baleful gleam in his eyes. As he stretched out his graceful hand, all the hairs on Bayard's body stood alive with the energy crackling off the demon's alabaster skin. If there were such a thing as a force field, he was feeling it now.

The demon reached around Bayard to Orin and laughed softly. "Oh, I would so love to present this one to my Master. I would, indeed. But that unpleasant image inked on your skin and infused with spellcraft from my old partner in crime prevents me from taking you." Bayard felt Orin's defiance flowing through them even though his lips were frozen shut.

Mephistopheles stepped behind Bayard, and although he could not see him grasp the Irish witch, he felt her venom as her limbs remained speared through his own body.

"We come now to Radha Ó Braonáin, a wicked witch if ever there was one." Mephistopheles chuckled. "I can hardly absolve you of your many sins, even if I wanted to. And I don't, of course. I claimed you as mine long before you raised the spell that called the *bain-sídhe*. Shall I be merciful and give you the death you crave, alongside your dutiful son? Alas, I am afraid that was not in the mission statement I received from the One I serve. So sorry, but you'll be coming along with me and Master Marlowe."

Bayard trembled at the sound of his name in the beautiful man's mouth. The sensations that played along his paralyzed nerves were an unfathomable combination of ecstasy and pure horror. So, it was as he'd feared…he would not be spared.

Mephistopheles turned to Claire again. "Don't look so terrified. You won't die. Not here, anyway. That little gold pin from your sainted mother is quite distasteful to my driver and I'm afraid he won't let you in the carriage. Don't understand? Google it." His grin was so bright Bayard had to shut his eyes— it was like looking into the fiery heart of a star going nova.

Mephistopheles damped down his powers to a tolerable level and addressed Orin. "You should be happy. You accomplished part of your mission. Your mother will be set free…she just won't be allowed to accompany you into the afterlife. Sure you won't come along with us? My Master would accept you in a heartbeat, if you had one." Bayard felt waves of silent fury beating against his back.

The demon from Hades laughed softly. "No? Well, my loss, I suppose. I hadn't factored you into the bargain from the start. But it all works out in the end, eh?" He stepped up to the coach and snapped his fingers. Instantly, all bonds of silence and movement were loosed.

With hands still affixed to the cornerstone, Bayard looked up and saw the banshee hovering above him in her fully humanized form. He saw her first as a beautiful Irish maid with glossy black hair and a rosy flush over her cheeks, but instead of the emerald eyes one would expect to find on a fair colleen, hers were red—pupil, iris, the entire eyeball. Her fair features then slid into the decaying flesh of a rotting corpse. She leaned her head back and shrieked twice more. Three deaths in all.

From the *dullahan's* head came a chilling voice with a thick Irish brogue, like the sound of screeing wind over the moors: "Orrrin Ó Brrraonáin."

Bayard felt, but could not see, the flesh suit worn by the witch's son quiver and fade until its presence was gone. Craning his neck with great effort, he saw the source of the summoning voice. The *dullahan* cracked its bone whip with a dry, clacking snap and again held up its glowing head. It called out the witch's name, *r*'s tumbling out like rocks in a landslide. "Rrrradha Ó Brrraonáin." The door of the coach flew open and her essence was sucked into its black maw, leaving a raw wound gaping in Bayard's midsection as she passed through. He stared down at the hole where his heart should have been. It did not bleed.

Once more, the *dullahan* lifted its head. The brazen voice called out a third name. "Chrrristopher Marrrlowe." In the space of a thought, he found himself inside the coach, seated beside the Shining One. The essence of the witch as a young girl of no more than fifteen cowered naked on the horsehair seat opposite them, whimpering. Marlow was shocked at her guise, but then realized this must have been the age at which her sorcery had turned wicked. Had she sealed her infernal fate while dancing skyclad?

The demon beside him pointed at her. "Stop that sound. I've no tolerance for weepers." Her lips sealed tightly shut, of her free will or the demon's command Marlowe could not tell.

He understood he must be dead, but inside the coach, facing the cowering figure of Radha Ó Braonáin, he felt every bit as corporal as ever he had. He smelled the musty confines of the carriage, felt the hard upholstered seat beneath his legs. He was still clothed…and looking down realized he wore not the fancy outfit of the play's Chorus but the very clothes he'd had on the night his soul had been taken.

Three names had been called, yet there were but two newly dead in the carriage.

Marlowe dared to find his voice. "Where is Tom? Is he not dead as well?"

The Right Hand of Satan smiled, showing perfect white, sharp teeth. "Quite dead. But the shield knot made from ink infused with the bloodspell of a certain Dr. Dee and his dutiful daughter forbade me from claiming him. He'd died once already in any case, and his path elsewhere was already set. Still, I might have beguiled him with a bit of glamour into making a last-minute bargain had the charm not protected him."

Marlowe dared yet another question. "What's become of the *buachloch?*"

The demon's musical laughter floated around the confines of the coach, lifting the stringy dark hair of the young witch and caressing Marlowe's cheek. "*Das macht nichts.* It has served its purpose."

Mephistopheles slipped his hand around Marlowe's thigh and gripped it tightly. Marlowe felt the blood in his veins turn to ice. He cut a sidelong look at his companion. "It's s-said the Devil has a b-barbed shaft." He couldn't stop himself from shaking.

The fires blazed up in Mephistopheles' summer-blue eyes. "Perhaps you'll find out." He leaned toward the carriage window and called up to the *dullahan.* "Come, let's be off!"

Claire woke as from a nightmare, head splitting and ears ringing. The coach was exiting its basement enclosure. She could feel the pressure dropping as her ears popped. Tasting blood, she touched her fingers to her face—she was bleeding from the nose as if she'd been punched. As the coach withdrew from the earthly plane, she felt like a fish in a tank watching a cat pulling its paws out of the water. Less and less of it was visible. And then with a shudder, she was alone in the basement.

Dazed, she couldn't get the terrifying face and voice of the beautiful young man...or whatever he was...out of her head. When he'd faced her directly his camouflage was perfectly in place, but when he faced away and turned his attention to Bayard or Tom, she'd glimpsed the skull and bones beneath his pale transparent skin. But what chilled her most was that she now knew him to be the one who'd captivated her attention before the play began. She'd actually spoken to, and been fleetingly touched by, a supernatural creature of some kind. It was he, she now assumed, who'd created the destruction raging upstairs. Claire began to shiver.

Screaming voices pulled her back to immediate danger as smoke rolled down the narrow stairs in thick pillows of black and gray, red-hot flames from the engulfed lobby at its heels. The building groaned around her as a section of the ceiling gave way, right over the spot where the cornerstone was lodged.

Gasping and coughing, Claire reeled to her feet and sprinted headlong for the back door, jumping across splits in the tiles as the floor bucked and cracked underneath her feet. A sinkhole opened behind her and nearby pillars gave way, falling into its void. She flung herself at the back door, pulling the handle and struggling to push it open. For a heartstopping moment it resisted her, then gave way, spilling her face down into the alley behind the theater. Barefoot, her gray suit torn at the knees, hair in her face, she stumbled blindly down the alley away from the theater and the roar of the fire.

She made it out into the street, hacking through smoke-scalded lungs, just in time to see flames shooting out the top windows of the building as glass exploded and rained down on the people below. It was too much to take in. Claire felt like she couldn't get her breath. The two-storey Janus was an inferno, engulfed from its foundations to the attic in sheets of flame. People could die in fires like this. Her mind reeled, remembering that some people had already died in it.

The fire blazed out of control, so hot it seemed the firefighters and their pitiful streams of water could do little to stop it. The streets around the burning wreck were filled with terrified patrons, gawkers, police, fire trucks, and emergency vehicles jammed together, their wheels up on the sidewalks.

On all sides, panicked theatergoers who'd made it to safety huddled in the streets or were stretched out being tended to by paramedics. Of Bayard or Tom there was no sign. Among the ambulances pulling in and spilling their crews into the melee, Claire spotted Paul. She searched the faces in the crowd and saw Addie and Morris among a throng out in the middle of the street half a block down. Addie slid to the ground in a crouch, her legs giving out. She sobbed loudly, her face streaked with tears and soot. Claire simply stood where she was, overwhelmed. Her mind was shutting down as she watched the beautiful orange lights rippling up and down the sides of building, swirling in gusts as the night air fanned the flames. It was like watching the Aurora, only more concentrated. And hotter.

At the edge of the crowd, the shade that had once been Christopher Marlowe watched impassively as frantic humans scrambled around the scene like ants, trying to make order out of the carefully orchestrated chaos. His writer's mind appreciated the contradiction in terms.

"A most satisfactory fire," said the honey-smooth voice of his equally ephemeral companion.

"Aye, it is that," he agreed, becoming more detached by the second. They stood silently, two shadows at the periphery of the action. "It was a good play as well. My best."

The other laughed, a musical sound in counterpoint to the harsh human voices that shouted and screamed over the wailing of sirens.

"I can show you a better conflagration, if you like. A friend of mine, one Nero by name, set a little town alight some years ago. Would you like to see it, as it happened?"

"You can do that? Yes, I would. Perhaps I might write about it."

The other draped his arm around the shoulders of his shorter companion and drew him away from the scene of destruction, chuckling. "Be assured, I shall be your perfect companion."

* * * *

Claire did not remember driving home. She sat in her Honda, in the carport, trying to find the motivation to open the door and get out. She'd finally connected with Paul at the fire and offered her services, but he'd taken one look at her slightly manic, disheveled appearance and ordered her home. So here she sat.

She had no coping mechanism for what had happened. None at all. The fire itself was bad enough, but knowing what had caused it—that was so far out of her realm of comprehension she feared she might need a heavy dose of duloxetine from the men in white coats. Otherwise she was going to start screaming until she was too hoarse to make a sound.

At least she'd verified that Addie and Morris were safe. She wondered if the rest of the cast and crew were all right. Concentrating on the individual people she knew and whether they'd survived brought her slowly round to the real world, and real people, pushing phantoms of the night for the time being into the far reaches of her brain. Later, she knew, she'd have to deal with that stuff, but not now. She took a deep breath and got out of the car.

Safely inside, she padded barefoot to her mother's bedroom and poked her head in the doorway. Asleep. That was good; it meant she didn't have to answer the inevitable question of "How did it go tonight?" She might not ever be able to answer that question.

Numb, she made herself go through the motions a normal person would do after surviving a crisis. She peeled off her clothes and shook out her hair. Removing her mother's gold pin, she rolled up the ruined gray suit and stuffed it in the trash. Then she got in the shower and stood under the hot water much too long, having a hard time finding the motivation to turn off the water and get out. But eventually she dried off and dressed in her comfort clothes: baggy sweatshirt and loose jeans, thick socks on her feet.

There was no way she was going to bed, so she wandered into the kitchen and put on water for tea. Closing her mind off from the hell that had erupted in the theater basement, she focused her thoughts on the play, trying to pinpoint the moment where things had turned weird. The fourth act had been fine, so obviously it was somewhere in the final act. She replayed the last few scenes in her mind. Tom had delivered his important soliloquy perfectly until...the image of Morris's entrance with his minions swam into her brain. There. They'd hung back, as he'd trod, heavy footed, downstage toward Tom. Orin. Whoever. It was pretty clear to her now that the creature who'd cheekily played with her before the show had taken possession of Morris at that point. And what had Tom's next line been? "Art thou indeed Mephistopheles?" And Bayard had known, too, at that same moment.

The kettle shrilled, and her heart slugged against her chest for shocked seconds. Claire let her breath out and poured water over the bag of green tea with lemon. For most of her life, from adolescence onward, Claire had not believed in a god or the devil or salvation or heaven, or even the possibility of an afterlife, but this evening her denying senses had been witness to things she could not explain. Wasn't that what the beautiful demon had accused, that she'd sealed herself in a shell that kept away the Dark and the Inexplicable? It was bound to rupture, that kind of rigid hold on one's psyche. So what now? Was she certifiable?

She took her cup of tea and went to check on her mother again. She slipped into the bedroom quietly and sat down on the edge of the bed.

"Mom? I'm home, sorry I was a little late." Her mother gave no sign if she heard. "Mom?"

Claire put down the cup and touched her mother's uncovered shoulder. Cold, and still. She knew what dead flesh felt like, especially when it had been in that state for hours. Her mother had likely died shortly after she'd arrived at the theater. An unspeakable sadness filled her mind and heart. She was now officially alone. Sitting on the edge of the bed, she wished her mother a silent farewell. Then she went to her room, pulled her cell phone out of her purse, opened her contacts list, and called Paul.

CHAPTER 20

Three weeks later

It was raining. Not a hard rain, but a light drizzle that wet the leaves of the shrubbery outside Dr. Patel's office. The glistening branches half-covered the room's only window, affording a limited view of the parking lot outside. Claire's mind was drifting, watching the drops falling on individual leaves.

"Claire, are you with me?" Dr. Patel's voice was gentle, but insistent.

Claire tuned back in. She'd been coming to the company therapist twice a week since the death of her mother on the night when the black hole of her worst fears had opened up and swallowed any sense of normalcy she'd ever owned. These days she was someone else, not the Claire who had naively taken a volunteer job as part of the stage crew for an acting company. Not the Claire who'd lost the only person she'd maybe really loved to another woman, and certainly not the Claire who'd seen time freeze in its tracks while the Right Hand of Satan had come for the lives of people she thought she knew but obviously hadn't. No, not that Claire. This new one got up and went to work and duly attended therapy sessions and tried not to think too hard about what the next day, or even the next hour, would bring. This new Claire was finding her way in the world, determined to cling to it as best she could.

"I'm sorry," she said, shifting her focus back to the young woman in the business suit who sat comfortably in the cushioned chair opposite her. How could someone be that relaxed while on the job? Claire wanted her secret. "I was just watching the rain." She liked Dr. Siri Patel, who didn't look like she could be more than five or six years older than herself. They'd established an easy, non-confrontational relationship, and Claire wondered now why she'd been so dead-set against coming for help in the first place. Paul was right, she should have done it earlier. So far, their discussions remained mostly superficial, at least from Claire's point of view, but that was all right. There were parts of her psyche damaged beyond repair, but she had vowed to herself that in order to have this new Claire who functioned in the real world and went shopping and paid her bills on time, those unthinkable moments seared into her brain by flaming blue eyes would never be allowed to see the light of day in this safe little office tucked into the administrative building. She would allow Dr. Patel to probe anything else she felt was useful, but access to that one segment of old Claire's experience was locked away out of reach. She'd claimed at first that she couldn't remember clearly what happened the night of the fire, and after a few weeks that assertion was becoming more truth and less deception. But there were two people with whom she was willing to talk about the Janus fire. When she'd felt ready, she'd finally called them up.

"Would you mind if we stopped a little early this afternoon?" Claire checked her watch.

"Is there somewhere you need to go?" Dr. Patel was curious, as always.

"You suggested I try to get out more, so I'm meeting some friends for a drink at a pub…a law assistant and a journalist. They make good conversation."

"That sounds positive. Are these new friends?" Dr. Patel was making notes.

Claire wondered how to answer that. In the grand scheme of things, compared to Jackie, for instance, these were definitely new friends. But when you considered she'd known Adelaide and

Morris for nearly half a year, maybe their friendship wasn't that new. "Not so much," she answered. "I haven't seen them in awhile, and I'm looking forward to getting back in touch."

Siri Patel smiled brightly. "That's good. I'd like to hear how it goes when we meet next week."

Claire nodded. She had a knot in the pit of in her stomach at the thought of what she needed to ask Morris, but she couldn't move on until she'd made the effort.

The Janus Theatre was gutted, the site cordoned off with a hastily installed chain-link fence. Claire took in the charred pile of what had once been a city landmark. It looked bombed out, the way the roof and floors had disintegrated and fallen into the basement—all charred timbers and melted glass. A chunk of the two-faced god's marble profile poked up through the rubble and drifts of ash. Whether it was the smiling face or the tragic one she couldn't tell.

Given the all-consuming ferocity of the inferno and the complete destruction of the building, it was agreed by all who'd witnessed it, and the city cleanup crew who'd erected the chain-link safety fence around the ruins, that it was indeed miraculous so few people lost their lives. News reports mentioned that of the more than five hundred people who'd been in the theater that night, a goodly number suffered minor injuries or fire-related damage such as smoke inhalation as they'd fought to exit the building. Of the half dozen who perished in the blaze, one was so badly burned his body could only be identified by the tattoos on one arm. Crossed swords, it had seemed.

Three others were identified by dental records, and two simply could not be found, but were assumed to have been in the basement when the building collapsed into itself, creating a crater similar to an explosion. Excavations with backhoe and shovel turned up nothing with the tantalizing exception of a single charred motorcycle boot. Of Kit Bayard, impresario and owner of the doomed Janus Theatre, according to the news reports, there was no trace at all, not even the slightest fragment of bone. Attempts to locate next of kin were equally fruitless, as were efforts to find relatives of the missing actor Tom Brennan, the presumed owner of the boot. Brennan's employer at The Rookery bookstore supplied information from his personnel folder that included a driver's license number, which turned out to have been issued to a false identity. As far as any official records could prove, the person known to a small circle of acquaintances as Tom Brennan did not exist. Claire thought of that final toast in Doyle's pub and wished she could cry, but there were no tears for what she felt. She was cold inside.

"Claire! What're you doing here?" Footsteps crunched on the sidewalk behind her. Addie's voice.

Claire turned. "Same as you, I guess. Just wanted a last look."

"There aren't any presences. They're all gone, even Kit and Tom." Her eyes got watery. "Especially Tom, or whoever he was. He'll always be Tom to me."

The desolation in her face was so overwhelming that Claire reached out, in spite of her normal anti-hug tendencies, and pulled Addie close.

"I know." There was no way to explain what she knew, but just saying the words carried its own comfort.

Addie sobbed into her shoulder. "It's horrible. No remains, no next of kin...no closure. He should at least have a funeral or a memorial or something." Her shoulders heaved as she wept. Claire had thought those same things, but kept them at a distance for fear they would derail her fragile recovery. She let Addie mourn for them both.

"Morris'll think we stood him up. Want to go now?" Claire released Addie and gave her a pat on the shoulder. It was strange, holding and comforting someone other than her mother. Oddly, Claire felt better.

Addie wiped her face and blew her nose into a Kleenex. "Yeah, let's go. I feel like it's important, for Tom's sake and ours."

Claire nodded. "I'll see you there." She started walking toward her car and thought how curious it was that neither of them seemed as distraught over the similar vanishing of Kit Bayard. Claire's thoughts surrounding Bayard were viscerally disturbing and connected to things she'd agreed to herself were dangerous ground as far as rebuilding her mental health went. And the less her shrink knew of screaming banshees and bloody stones the better.

Claire parked on the side street across from Doyle's Tavern and saw Addie standing in front of the pub, waiting for her. She hurried across the street and followed Addie through the door, feeling vaguely unmoored. It wasn't that they were out of place here—it was a cozy spot she might have hung out in by herself if she'd found it on her own. But it was so imprinted with her memory of Tom that it felt strange to be coming here without him.

Morris sat alone in the round booth where they'd all first gathered that night after rehearsal so long ago…weeks, months? Time seemed to have dilated in her memory. Morris' nose was buried in a copy of the newspaper he published, savoring his own work, Claire supposed. Her chest felt constricted, tight with unvoiced emotion, but she kept a lid on the sensation. This was therapy, this meeting…closure and moving on. Paul had assured her that facing her fears might be hard, but in the long run it was a good thing.

Morris looked up as they approached, his expression somber. Something around the eyes, a pinched look, made his gaunt face a study in shades of conflict. Claire remembered when that sharp hawk-nosed profile had been the height of intimidation for her. But not now. They'd all experienced too much.

"I was thinking you might not show," he said, folding the newspaper and laying it aside.

"We owe it to Tom." With a huge sigh, Addie heaved herself into the booth across from Morris. Claire slid in beside her. They were an odd threesome, unlikely friends, united by loss.

George the bartender appeared tableside almost before they were seated and settled in. "Is it true? Was that our Tom in the list of people who died in the theater fire up on Highland?"

Our Tom. Claire flinched. She nodded, not meeting his eyes.

"A stout in his honor, on my bill," said Morris.

Claire gave him a look. Who would've thought Morris capable of such a gesture. Maybe they'd all gone through some changes.

They placed their orders and then sat silent, as if reluctant to acknowledge the evidence of the empty seat beside Morris.

"I just wish I had something to remember him by." Addie sniffed and wiped at the corner of her eye.

"I have something." Morris reached inside his briefcase and handed her a small hardback book. It looked used—well-used, in fact, with frayed cloth binding and battered dark green cover. "It was the only thing of his left in the garage apartment he rented."

Claire was surprised. "You went there?" She could have sworn Morris looked embarrassed, a first as far as she knew.

He shrugged. "I just wondered if there was anything left behind that would explain who he was. His landlord let me in, told me his few clothes had been given to the Salvation Army. There was nothing but that," he said, indicating the book.

Addie opened the cover and Claire could see the Rookery Bookstore stamp on the title page. The page itself appeared to be a facsimile of a much older document, printed in London for The Camden Society, 1852. The full title of the book took up most of the page: *The Private Diary of Dr. John Dee, and the Catalogue of his Library of Manuscripts, from the Original Manuscripts in the Ashmolean Museum at Oxford, and Trinity College Library, Cambridge.*

A chewing gum wrapper used as a bookmark stuck out about a third of the way into the volume. Addie turned to the entry and placed the book flat on the table so they could all see. There were penciled notes in the margins; whether they were Tom's, who was to say? One passage had been highlighted with yellow marker. Addie read aloud:

But Coronzon (for so is the name of that mighty devil), envying man's felicity, began to assail man and so prevailed...man became accursed in the sight of God, and so lost both the garden of Felicity and the judgement of his understanding, but not utterly the favour of God. But he was driven forth (as scriptures record) unto the earth which was covered with brambles. ...Coronzon is the name of that very Serpent of Genesis, also synonymous with the rebellious angel Samael, well-known in Jewish midrashic and kabbalistic writings.

She looked up. "I don't get it. Why would Tom be reading this?"

Morris sipped his ale. "Research for his part in the play, most likely. Actually, I could've used it myself. Mephistopheles was a great character to play, especially the way Marlowe wrote him." A shadow clouded his expression.

Claire lowered her voice. It was now or never. "I have to ask you...what really happened onstage between you and Tom? You went off the script and just...made stuff up. And then you fainted. Why?"

Morris' black eyes held hers for several seconds before he spoke. "I don't think I have an answer for you, Claire. At least, not one that's suitable, not to me or to you. Or possibly even you." He looked at Addie, holding Tom's book pressed to her chest.

They waited, and he eventually continued.

"That whole last act was supercharged. Everyone played their parts to the hilt, and at some point it stopped...being a play."

Claire barely dared to breathe. "What do you mean?"

Morris swirled the amber liquid in his glass. "The stage, the audience, the lights...it all just faded, and I felt like I *was* Mephistopheles and that man confronting me really was Faustus. We said things to each other that I can't remember now but I know they were above and beyond the tiny world of the play. The play seemed insignificant at that point. Then it all went black." His voice trailed off and he sat for a moment, staring into his glass.

"I *knew* something was wrong," Addie said. "When we entered from the wings behind you, you felt...scary...and then Drew whispered to me that you guys were ad-libbing, although I couldn't imagine why. And then you did that funny thing with your voice, like it was some special sound effects illusion."

Morris looked up. "Like I said, there was no theater. It was just me and him, and then he suddenly didn't look like Tom in costume."

Claire's mouth went dry as she relived the moment with him.

"For just a second or two, he seemed thinner, paler, with black hair to his shoulders. Then I felt...empty, and the lights went out. I didn't come to until Claire started shaking me. I didn't even realize the place was on fire until you were dragging me offstage." He was looking at her with an expression she found impossible to read.

They fell silent. Finally Addie said, "Something supernatural happened. We all know it. It was that ghost in the basement, don't you think?"

Since they were in a confessional mood, Claire thought about telling what she'd really seen in the basement before she'd bolted for the back exit—how she discovered the resident "ghost" was actually a banshee, how she'd seen the Black Coach of Death driven by the terrifying *dullahan* of Irish legend, and how she could even think those thoughts without going insane. The confession sat there on the tip of her tongue, waiting to be shared. She opened her mouth, and shut it. Finally she said, "We've all been through hell, on some level."

Addie looked troubled. "I wonder whatever happened to Danny."

"I'm pretty sure he's dead." Claire tried not to sound like one of those CSI cops on TV, but it was hard. "I thought about filing a missing persons report on him but finally just decided not to get involved any further."

"You think Bayard killed him, don't you?" Morris asked, without a trace of sarcasm.

Claire was careful with her answer. "I think he had something to do with Danny's sudden disappearance. Maybe let him bleed to death or some stupid thing like that, and then hid the body. It's just a gut feeling. I don't have any proof. Maybe someday

Danny's bones will be excavated from the theater basement, but I doubt it."

They sat, drinks in hand, wrapped in their own thoughts. A full glass of stout sweated a wet circle on the table in front of the empty seat.

Finally Addie broke the silence. "Who owns the property, anyway?"

"Kit Bayard," said Morris. "He bought it when he first came to Atlanta. Bragged to me that he paid cash for it. There's no next of kin that can be tracked down, or I would have found it when I researched him for the story I wrote up for the paper. Maybe the city will take it over."

"The Preservation Society might get involved," Addie said. "They had some investment in it, I think. Too bad about the building, it was a landmark." She turned to Claire. "So sorry to hear about your mother. Are you going to stick around?"

Claire shook her head. "I don't think so. I'm going to put the house up for sale. It's in an old, stable neighborhood, and well-preserved Craftsman houses like it don't go on the market that often, or so I'm told."

"Well, I'll be sorry to see you leave. Where do you want to go?"

Claire looked out the window at the rain coming down and allowed herself to smile. "Someplace warm and dry."

"Egypt. Go sign up for a tour of the Pyramids in the desert." Morris was smirking, the first sign that afternoon of his old personality. "I have friends at a travel bureau who could get you a good rate."

"Now there's a thought," said Addie. "Maybe I'll go with you. I don't have anything to hold me here." Her wide eyes were very green.

"Except a good job," Claire reminded her. Yet the idea was somehow appealing as she turned it around in her mind and looked at it from all sides. A trip abroad. It could happen. When the house was sold, she'd have money. Her bills would be paid, and she didn't have anyone who needed looking after except herself.

"I'll pay my way. I'm great fun on a trip, and I love to travel. " Addie was bright-eyed.

Claire studied Morris and Addie, the wheels in her brain turning. Then she reached across the table and picked up the honorary stout. Mimicking that shrug of Tom's she would miss forever, she took a swallow and really smiled for the first time in weeks. "Sure. Why not?"

~ finis ~

www.ingramcontent.com/pod-product-compliance
Lightning Source LLC
Chambersburg PA
CBHW050738180626
46814CB00002B/815